EARTHWORLD

The Doctor Who *50th Anniversary Collection*

EarthWorld

Jacqueline Rayner

BOOKS

3 5 7 9 10 8 6 4

First published in 2001 by BBC Worldwide Ltd.
This edition published in 2013 by BBC Books, an imprint of Ebury Publishing.
A Random House Group Company

Doctor Who is a BBC Wales production for BBC One.
Executive producers: Steven Moffat and Caroline Skinner

The Random House Group Limited Reg. No. 954009
Addresses for companies within the Random House Group can be found at
www.randomhouse.co.uk

A CIP catalogue record for this book is available from the British Library.

ISBN 978 1 849 90520 6

Editorial director: Albert DePetrillo
Editorial manager: Nicholas Payne
Series consultant: Justin Richards
Project editor: Steve Tribe
Cover design: Two Associates © Woodlands Books Ltd, 2012
Production: Alex Goddard

To buy books by your favourite authors and register for offers,
visit www.randomhouse.co.uk

The Random House Group Limited supports The Forest Stewardship
Council® (FSC®), the leading international forest-certification organisation.
Our books carrying the FSC label are printed on FSC®-certified paper.
FSC is the only forest-certification scheme supported by the leading
environmental organisations, including Greenpeace. Our
paper procurement policy can be found at
www.randomhouse.co.uk/environment

MIX
Paper from
responsible sources
FSC
www.fsc.org   FSC® C016897

Printed and bound in Great Britain by Clays Ltd, St Ives plc

INTRODUCTION

I suspect many people have a 'time travel' list, the things they'd do if they suddenly had access to a time machine. Mine includes the standard things about seeing lost loved ones again, rescuing will-be-extinct animals, maybe a quick whirl round Ancient Rome, and of course going back to 1965–1966 and recording all of Season Three of *Doctor Who*. Now, however, I would add 'rewriting *EarthWorld* before it's published'.

Don't worry, this introduction isn't going to be a thousand words of tedious self-analysis. It's pretty much inevitable that an author is going to look back at something they wrote more than a dozen years ago – in this case, actually the first book they ever wrote – and cringe at elements of plot and prose. I can't change it, so all I can do is hope that you enjoy it, whatever shortcomings I may see in it now. Anyway, if I criticise the book but you go on to like it, I'm essentially criticising your tastes, which would be awfully rude of me. And if you dislike it, you don't need me to point out the problems. So instead of a detailed look at *EarthWorld* (and to save my sanity as reading through my own junior works is doing my head in) I shall take you via a wibbly-wobbly flashback to *Doctor Who* in the last days of the twentieth century…

Considering the globally important and multi-managed brand *Doctor Who* is today, it's odd to look back to the late 1990s, when the entire operation was controlled from one desk in BBC Worldwide. *Doctor Who* didn't even have its own office, just a tiny corner of the Children's Books department, and it was from there that the amazing Steve Cole coordinated fiction, non-fiction, audio, video and anything else that came along in a practically superhuman feat. I had the enormous good fortune to become his (part-time) assistant in 1998, although probably didn't succeed in taking much of the burden off his shoulders as he had to teach me the ropes on top of everything else.

Eventually Steve moved on, and the powers-that-be realised he had been doing the jobs of about 27 people, so shared out the work among vast hordes of staff in many different departments. Guardianship of the books passed off-site to the lovely Justin Richards, and after a bit of to-ing and fro-ing I became project editor for the Eighth Doctor range. (Justin was the creative force, planning and recommending commissions to the commissioning editor, I did the nuts-and-bolts day-to-day stuff like sending manuscripts off to proofreaders and keeping track of Fitz's girlfriends.) Between them, Steve and Justin came up with the plan of destroying Gallifrey before sending the Doctor off in a new direction. I mean, how mad is that? You'd never catch TV *Doctor Who* destroying Gallifrey, never in a million... oh. Er, yeah. Right.

So Gallifrey was destroyed, and an amnesiac Eighth Doctor started a hundred years stuck on Earth in

Justin's *The Burning*. When his century was up and his memory was sort-of back, the Doctor reunited with old companion Fitz, a Sixties layabout of German descent, and took on board smart young British Asian professional Anji Kapoor. Colin Brake, an experienced soap writer, was brought in to shape Anji and introduce her to the range, and then Justin asked if I'd like to send the TARDIS crew out into space once more. Woo! It wasn't my first professional writing credit, but it was my first *Doctor Who* book, so I said yes please very quickly and ran away giggling to myself.

Off I went, read a load of books about British Asian culture (research which failed to appear in the book in any way whatsoever) and started plotting. I think it was Justin's idea to launch us off into time and space by echoing the end of *An Unearthly Child* with the TARDIS landing in a prehistoric landscape and a caveman approaching. That took us to Earth – or at least somewhere that looked like Earth – but we'd just spent a century on Earth, so… yes, marvel at the breadth of my imagination, I decided to bridge the gap between the stuck-on-Earth era and the new travelling-in-space era by creating, er, Earth in space. Ta da! Seriously, whether rightly or wrongly, I felt that being confronted with things she sort of knew but which were just *wrong* would be more of a culture shock for Anji than a completely alien world.

I'm endlessly fascinated with the exploration of identity, and caught up with that is a fascination with androids of the *Blade Runner* indistinguishable-from-humans type, which led to Michael Crichton's

Westworld, which led, fairly obviously and directly, to *EarthWorld* (and I suspect I am the only person in the entire universe who actually sticks the capital in the middle à la *EastEnders* and *SpongeBob*). All it needed was some homicidal triplets, one or two dinosaurs (because everyone loves dinosaurs. Oh all right, because *I* love dinosaurs), the obligatory Hartnell reference (which seems to be the bit most people remember!), and there we were.

Writing a book turned out to be a lot easier than I thought it would be, right up until the point where I discovered quite how many words you have to fill it with. Now, a dozen years later and about 20 novels further on, I still know the Wordcount Dread. (When I was working at BBC Worldwide, authors would submit manuscripts that were tens of thousands of words over length and I would boggle in disbelief. How can that even happen?) I like to think I 'write short' as a favour to the readers, really. If you like the book, think of it as compact, concentrated essence of *EarthWorld*. If you don't, the dreadful experience is over sooner. You see, we were caring folks at BBC Books. Your enjoyment was our utmost concern. Let's just hope this brief foray into the world of the Eighth Doctor is still at least a bit enjoyable today.

Jacqueline Rayner
August 2012

My original dedication thanked my Mum, Dad and sister Helen, Justin Richards, Gary Russell and Simon Axon, and Mark Wright (who kindly loaned his initials to Anji's firm), and I am still just as grateful to them now as I was then – with a little bit more appreciation added on top for all for the support, friendship and care they have given in the years since.

CHAPTER ONE
THE FLUFFY FROG
IN THE SKY

A rocky plain – barren and dull. Nothing but grey, as far as the eye could see.

And then a flash of blue. And another. And the blue was there, solid, part of the landscape, as though it had always been.

The watcher felt no surprise. But he moved closer to the strange, tall box, anyway.

Fitz kept shutting his eyes, clicking his heels together, yelling 'There's no place like home', and opening his eyes again with a big happy-sounding sigh.

This was one of the more irritating things he'd been doing since they'd stepped into this amazing magic wardrobe the Doctor called his TARDIS, ranking just above the endless tales about how they used to fly round the universe in a stroppy redhead. Anji *so* wasn't going to go there.

And Fitz seemed completely unconcerned that they were not, as the Doctor had promised, back in Soho – at least, not if the image on the closed-circuit-TV thingy was to be trusted. The Doctor seemed unperturbed, too, blithely swanning off deeper into the TARDIS to 'fetch something', despite having quite obviously and definitely broken his promise to take Anji home

1

– but then he'd also promised her he wouldn't let her boyfriend Dave die (don't think about that).

'Sand and rock,' she muttered. 'There's no sand in Soho, and even less rock.'

'Rock music?' said Fitz. She ignored him. 'Like I said, we might be in Soho. Just – not the Soho of your day. Or that could be alien sand,' he continued cheerfully. 'We might not even be on Earth at all.'

The inner door opened, and the Doctor swept through the console room, pulled a large red lever on the way, and was out of the still-opening TARDIS doors in a dash of bottle-green. 'I'm just going to collect some samples,' his voice filtered back. 'Find out where we are!'

'Can he do that?' Anji asked. 'Find out what planet we're on by looking at bits of rock?'

'The Doctor,' Fitz said, 'can do anything.' But she noticed he had his fingers crossed. 'Come on, let's see what it's like out there.'

'Let me just get my jacket,' said Anji. Fitz gave her a look. Well, it was all right for him, he was wearing his overcoat. Who knew what alien weather was going to be like? She nipped back to what she was alarmed to realise she was already thinking of as 'her' room, and picked up the blazer she'd left lying on the bed. *Her* bed. She glanced round the room. Lucky she liked minimalism. Lucky she didn't have any sort of phobia about circles.

Fitz was still waiting for her when she got back to the console room, and they both followed the Doctor's path through the doors. To Anji's surprise it was pleasantly warm outside – just right, in fact, even though there was a bit of a breeze. The sky was almost clear – there was only one biggish cloud, which looked, to her still rather dazed mind, like a giant fluffy white frog – and the sun was nearing its apex. The sun was – just possibly – perhaps, maybe the tiniest fraction smaller than she was used to. But it might not be. She'd never spent a great deal of time solar-gazing, because of the scare stories about losing one's vision and also because... well, what on Earth would have been the point? So... it could be somewhere other than twentieth-century Earth, or it could just be her memory playing tricks, trying to persuade her she was seeing something unusual.

She took a deep breath. It certainly smelled like Earth. Although – and this was odd – for some reason she couldn't quite put her finger on, it reminded her of London more than any wide open space, which wasn't quite right. But it wasn't London (obviously), because there were no people, no noise, not even a pigeon.

Just a big blue box. She shook her head, her mind still rebelling at the idea of this museum piece being a space-time machine. Or perhaps it was her sense of style objecting to a space-time machine looking like a museum piece. Really, the TARDIS, seen from the outside, looked absolutely ridiculous. A 1960s British (British? Or just English? Goodness knows) police box, from the days before police radios or mobile phones. Interesting thought. Did the advent of mobile phones help catch more criminals, or help more criminals evade capture? Would her mobile phone work in space (or wherever)? Presumably not. But what if she were in the future? Phone networks might still be around. Might as well try it. Just to see.

Anji opened her bag and fished for the slim black phone. No network. Surprise surprise. So they were in the past – or on an alien planet – or, just possibly, in Wales.

Fitz wandered over. 'Ah, a mobile phone,' he said, in the manner of someone being particularly clever. 'I used one of those once, you know.'

'I'm impressed,' said Anji, deciding to save the demonstration of her Psion organiser for another day. 'Look, do you know where we are yet? And while I'm on the subject, why exactly does this ultra-fantastic alien space and time ship look like that? Isn't it a bit embarrassing?'

'The Doctor,' said Fitz, 'is supremely self-confident, and unconcerned with superficial appearances.'

She sighed, irritated. 'That doesn't explain anything. Well, it probably does explain some things, but not what I was asking.'

Fitz glanced over to where the Doctor was kneeling on the ground, happily scooping up earth into a small plastic tube. 'Because he –' gesturing over there – 'once landed it on Earth back in my time – but before my time, if you get me – and the gizmo that used to make it change so it looked like something people wouldn't notice, got stuck. Like, it should be a rock or something now. But he likes it like this.'

Anji looked at the guy who 'likes it like this'. She had the distinct impression that he was pretending

4

not to be listening to Fitz. Trying not to let Fitz know that this was all news to him, too. Maybe wondering exactly why he liked his spaceship looking like a mid-twentieth-century relic. A bit worrying. She shivered.

'What is it?'

'Nothing,' she answered, automatically. Then reconsidered. There was something else... 'I think we're being watched.'

'That,' Fitz informed her, 'is because you're not used to being out of your own time frame. It's a perfectly natural phenomenon.' Patronising git.

Anji considered it was to her great credit that she didn't say, 'I told you so' when the caveman appeared.

After you've seen aliens kill your boyfriend and been in a spaceship that's bigger on the inside than the outside, bumping into something that you've at least seen in books/movies/ancient American cartoons isn't as scary as all that.

It looked somewhat cartoonlike, too. Exaggerated jaw and forehead, hunched back and muscles and a lot of hair, and – unbelievably – dressed in what appeared to be leopard-skin rags. It was glaring at them, but making no move to approach. Apart from the leopard skin – and its willingness to keep at a distance – it reminded Anji irresistibly of an ex-boyfriend: Tom, the one who was, um, one, two, three before Dave.

Don't think about Dave.

The Doctor had leapt up off the ground and darted back to Anji and Fitz. 'Don't make any sudden moves,' he said, ridiculously. 'It's probably far more scared of us.'

'I'm not scared at all,' Anji informed him. 'It's not threatening us.'

The Doctor frowned, and told her that it was perfectly reasonable, even sensible, to be scared of things until you knew exactly what was going on. Boy, was he so obviously a proponent of 'do what I say, not what I do'.

The caveman began to move cautiously towards them, grunting inquisitively. Anji stood her ground, turning to Fitz and the Doctor to see what they were making of this. None of it seemed real to her.

Fitz raised an eyebrow and smiled smugly. 'Just leave this to me. One look at this –' he took a lighter from his jacket pocket – 'and he'll be worshipping us as gods.' Then the stupid prat flicked up the flame and started walking towards the caveman – was that PC? Caveperson? Evolutionally challenged, perhaps? – going 'ug ug ug ug ug ug ug' for goodness' sake. Anji raised her eyes heavenwards.

And then kept them there. Hang on a minute! No, it was her imagination. It had to be her imagination. But… there was the giant fluffy frog in the sky. In exactly the same place. Surely it was imagination, coincidence, whatever? Because whatever weirdo world this was, and however light the breeze, surely the clouds had to move…?

Her attention was ripped back to earth as the caveman suddenly screamed – it sounded like a shrieking chimpanzee. But it didn't sound like fear, more like… oh, help! It started charging towards them. The idiot (meaning Fitz) had obviously enraged the creature.

6

'*Aaargh!*' yelled Fitz, and dropped the lighter.

'Run!' cried the Doctor.

They ran. To Anji's horrified realisation they were running away from the TARDIS. She breathlessly commented on this, once again admiring her own restraint.

Fitz tapped his nose as he ran. 'If we'd gone (*gasp*) back to the TARDIS (*gasp*), the Doctor'd never know (*gasp*) where we were (*big gasp*). And that's not (*gasp*) how it works.'

'But we know where we are! This is obviously prehistoric Earth!' Anji was having enough problems trying to keep up with the Doctor and Fitz, who were both much taller than she was and weren't wearing heels.

The Doctor slowed down momentarily to take her hand, and motioned for Fitz to do the same on her other side. Between them, they dragged Anji on, making her feel like a piece of meat. The Doctor spoke for the first time. Anji had the feeling that he'd been too busy taking everything in himself up till now to comment on it to them. 'Not necessarily,' he said (Anji had almost forgotten what they were talking about – and was sickened to note, as she panted away, that the Doctor was not even the slightest bit winded by their speed), 'it could be parallel evolution on another planet.'

'Or a parallel (*gasp*) Earth,' added Fitz, who still seemed to be on his 'I know more about space-time travel than you do' kick. 'That can happen. If it were night-time, the Doctor could tell exactly where we are just by looking at the stars.'

The Doctor shot Fitz an amazed glance.

'It's not night-time, though,' Anji said. The Doctor looked relieved. 'And I think there's something wrong with the sk– What the hell's that?'

With a horrific screeching noise, an enormous leathery creature glided down from a rocky outcrop. Bigger than an eagle – than two eagles – and with the ugliest long pointed mouth thing – not exactly a beak, and with hundreds of tiny, pointed *teeth*…

'It's a pterodactyl,' said the Doctor helpfully.

'I know that! But they weren't around with cavemen!' Anji said, trying to concentrate on keeping her footing and not pulling all three of them over. Without turning round she could hear the grunts that told her the caveman was still behind them, not distracted by the huge flying reptile.

'So it *could* be a parallel Earth, then!' The Doctor sounded quite excited.

'And are giant dinosaur bird things less ferocious on parallel Earths in general? Is it likely to attack us?'

'No idea!' He still sounded as if he was having a great time. 'But just in case, keep runni- *Oof!*'

'*Oof!*' echoed Anji and Fitz, unable to separate in time. All three sprawled on the ground.

'What was that?' yelled Fitz, obviously forgetting that he knew everything.

Anji clambered off Fitz, whose expression was alternating between fear and 'hey, there's a woman on top of me', and narrowed her eyes, peering ahead. Sand. Rock. Thin air. For the life of her, she couldn't see what they'd banged into.

The Doctor put a hand tentatively forward. The air around it shimmered, like a heat haze. 'Energy barrier,' he announced.

'Here comes the caveman!' Fitz shouted. 'And he's got a club from somewhere! Use your sonic screwdriver, Doctor!'

'What for?'

'To disable the barrier!'

'How?'

'*Aaaaargh*! I don't know!' Fitz seemed a bit stressed. 'You're the genius!'

The Doctor had brought his screwdriver thing out of his pocket and was staring at it.

The caveman was slow and lumbering – they could probably dodge it for a while – but unless they got back to the TARDIS there was nowhere really to hide. The pterodactyl was swooping around – interestingly, avoiding the barrier. The caveman had stopped, too, but lurked menacingly a short distance away. Perhaps they could sense the barrier. But the Doctor, Fitz and Anji couldn't. And if they kept bumping into invisible barriers, and the caveman and the flying dinosaur got over their wariness... The Doctor had to get them through it.

'I've seen you use the sonic screwdriver before,' Anji said, trying to sound encouraging. 'You just seemed to know what to do without thinking about it!'

'Yes!' the Doctor beamed. 'Good point! If I don't think about trying to use it and concentrate on something else instead – that pterodactyl, for example. It's not actually a dinosaur *or* a bird, did you know that? And, interestingly, no one's worked out how they managed to take off from ground level. I wonder if it'll land so we can find out? Also –' he was pointing the sonic screwdriver at the barrier, but looking at Anji – 'they probably ate fish and carrion, so we should be in no danger.'

'Oh? Really?' said Anji, remaining unconvinced as she watched the reptile swooping around. She made encouraging noises as the Doctor waved the sonic screwdriver around behind his back.

'And they could have a wingspan of fifteen or so metres. This one's just a baby,' the Doctor continued. Anji wondered if she was supposed to be grateful for that.

Fitz gave a sudden whoop. 'That's it!' he cried. There was a swirling, shimmering hole appearing in front of them, a sort of air-whirlpool, pale blue and the size of a dinner plate – a car tyre – a car door. Incredible. Fitz was on his feet and through it in an instant; it looked like he'd walked into a cloud. 'Fitz!' Anji called, alarmed – did he always jump into things without thinking first?

There was a whistle of astonishment from the other side of the barrier, and then she heard Fitz's voice. 'I'm OK!' he was saying. 'Come on!' A hand appeared through the swirling blue and made beckoning gestures at them.

Anji turned to congratulate the Doctor. 'You did it!' she said.

'I did!' he beamed, looking fondly down on the sonic screwdriver. 'Now, let's join Fitz before Mr Neanderthal catches up with us.' He spun round to face the hole he'd created. 'Fitz! We're coming through now!'

The hand made a thumbs-up sign and retreated. 'Hurry up!' Fitz's voice drifted back. 'You won't believe what's through here, it's – *Aaaaargh*!'

And that was all. Anji jumped instinctively towards the cry, but the Doctor was at the barrier first – just as the hole zipped into nothingness.

'Don't worry!' the Doctor cried, brandishing the sonic screwdriver again. 'If I can just distract myself for a few more minutes and you run around a bit and confuse the caveman and the pterosaur just in case… Don't worry, Fitz, we're coming!'

But as Anji turned from the barrier she saw that the caveman and the pterodactyl had gone. And she didn't think she and the Doctor were going to be joining Fitz, wherever he was, any time soon. In front of her there was a… a… she was ashamed to admit that the only term her mind was coming up with was Scary Robot! Scary Robot! With Gun!

'D-Doctor,' she said, backing off as far as she dared with an invisible barrier behind her threatening to knock her to the ground.

'Just a moment,' he said, not turning.

The scary robot took a clunking step closer. It was so tall and now so close that Anji had to angle her head back to look at its blank, golden face. 'Doctor!' she said again.

He turned then. 'Ah. Good distraction, Anji,' he said.

'Unauthorised presence in this zone,' said the scary robot. Its voice was deep and masculine, and surprisingly human. 'Unauthorised breach of zone barrier. You will come with me.'

It gestured with its gun – Futuristic Space Gun, Anji's mind said – and repeated, 'You will come with me.'

'Doctor?' said Anji, nervously.

'Oh, we'd better go with it,' the Doctor said with a sigh. 'These sorts of things get angry and start shooting if you don't do what they say. By the way, I've decided that we're probably not on a parallel Earth after all.'

Anji said nothing. As they were led off at gunpoint by the golden robot, the Doctor turned to her and whispered, 'You know, wherever we are, I'm glad we came. I'm starting to feel really at home.'

To: cybertron@xprof.net
From: anji kapoor@MWFutures.co.uk
Date: 14/2/01 11:03
Subject: Tyrranoriffic!

Dear Dave

I'm on another planet in what's apparently the far future. You'd like it here. There are robots that look a bit like the Terminator, but in gold. I travelled in a police box that's bigger on the inside than the outside, with a wild-eyed amnesiac and a man who's about five years older than me but was born before my parents were. But you met them, of course. Though you didn't know then what they were. I wish I'd never met them. I wish I didn't know what they were. I wish I were back in London C2lst, with you. I wonder if I can go back in time and stop us meeting them? Would that work? You'd know, you watch that sort of rubbish. Rubbish IMO, of course. Let's not get into that row now.

Incidentally, you know that time we went to the Natural History Museum when they had that display of moving dinosaurs? They didn't seem that scary, did they? Wrong! Dinosaurs = terrifying.

Oh, and I've just been arrested.

Love
Anji xxx

Send now/send later: send later

It had been a long walk to the edge of the prehistoric landscape. The Doctor had taken her hand, at the start, no doubt to reassure her, but now there was no sense of urgency she'd instinctively shaken it off. She'd felt guilty afterwards, although the Doctor didn't seem to have minded. Then after a while, when the realities of this horrific situation began to really sink in, Anji wished she'd held on to him tight. She couldn't summon up the courage to initiate the contact herself, though. What might he think?

Anji hadn't spotted the TARDIS on their way across the plain, though she had caught sight of a few more cavemen in the distance, and, terrifyingly, what looked like an allosaur. None of them had come anywhere near the two travellers or their guard, however, or even seemed to notice them. Perhaps they were used to scary robots. Or perhaps they'd been trained to stay away from them, or were wary somehow, just as the pterodactyl and the caveman had seemed to want to avoid the energy barrier. The Doctor had tried to escape a few times, yelling 'Look! Over there!' to the scary robot, or sticking out a foot to trip it up (the Doctor had limped for a while after that), but none of it had worked. On one bizarre occasion he'd shouted, 'Anji! Quick! Number seventeen!' and had then looked utterly confused. She hadn't asked him what he meant. She was too busy being scared. What was this thing going to do with them? Where was it taking them? And, as a general addition to that, where were they anyway?

The TARDIS could travel anywhere – *anywhere* – in space and time. They could therefore be… anywhere. Anywhere at all. At any time. She hadn't really had a chance to think about that up till now. It had all seemed so unreal, still, while they were actually in the TARDIS; she'd still been shell-shocked over her boyfriend's death (a bit inside her gave an ironic laugh: how was this for a distraction from the grieving process?), and the bits of her mind that were available for getting a grip on her new situation were taken up with trying to ignore the increasingly irritating Fitz, who was not someone she'd have chosen to travel around the universe with. Then she felt guilty about having felt that because Fitz, for all she knew, could be dead now. For a few moments, in the far distant past that was her time in the TARDIS, she'd wondered how they'd cope living together, just the three of them. She'd been in shared student houses with people she'd not got on with, but there'd always been the option of escape: to college, bars, other friends' houses. Now she couldn't very well stay in her room with a good book while the others went out exploring the universe, could she. Could she? Perhaps she'd suggest that next time. If there was a next time. You go and face the scary robots and dinosaurs, Fitz, I just want to finish *Sense and Sensibility*. Better be boring than die. She didn't want to die.

She was travelling with the guy with the time machine, and she knew because Dave had been into that sort of stuff that that made her one of the main characters. Fitz, too – so no more worrying about him, either. Name near the top of the credits, tied up and gloated at by villains but never killed by them; you knew you were always going to make it to the end of the story, except that one time in a hundred thousand, where even so, you only ever, *ever* died in a grand heroic tragic blaze of final-episode glory, and this wasn't one, so she shouldn't be this scared. But would anyone else realise this? Would the real universe play by those fictional rules? Should she get a T-shirt printed with I'M A MAIN CHARACTER, DON'T KILL ME? Would that help?

And then she'd thought (as she kept doing, however much she tried to stop it) of Dave. Dave, whose life's ambition had been to be a main character and yet who, even at the end, hadn't managed to progress beyond 'incidental'. He hadn't even made it to 'guest star, one story only'. Let's face it, he hadn't stood a chance. Anji had shot a discreet sideways glance at the Doctor at that point. He must have seen a lot of deaths. After a while it must really do your head in. Perhaps that was why he'd lost his memory. Couldn't cope with it any more. She shivered. Distraction…

Her feet. No time for grief, concentrate on the pain of each step, try to count the blisters you know have developed already, just think about one step after another after another…

And then she decided that right here and now she'd almost prefer to use grief to distract herself from the pain of her feet.

Need a different distraction.

Anywhere in time and space.

Was that likely to be true?

She'd travelled in space with the Doctor – excluding the possibility that the whole thing was a drug-induced fantasy, the space travel bit at least had definitely happened. But – well, they'd just gone up to your bog-standard bit of space near Earth. Perhaps the TARDIS could just shoot off into orbit really, really quickly, or she'd suffered some strange time dilation effect from the speed. (Ha! – velocity, not drugs.)

Again, discounting phantasms or figments of the imagination, however they were formed, she knew that aliens existed. After all, she'd not only met some, she'd pretty much killed a whole race of them (slight exaggeration for dramatic effect).

Aliens existed, and they had wanted to invade Earth. Therefore they didn't come from Earth. Therefore there were inhabited planets other than Earth (so far making sense – well, logic, possibly not sense).

Technology therefore existed that was capable of transporting people from one inhabited world to another. So… it was *possible* that she was on another planet.

However, just how far was parallel evolution likely? Would there be dinosaurs on another planet that looked just like those out of picture books? Would there be such stereotypical cavemen? And, if dinosaurs and cavemen had survived, how had the civilisation reached the level that enabled it to build energy barriers, holographic skies (that was what the Doctor had guessed when she pointed out her frog) and robots with guns?

Probable conclusion… they hadn't. Somehow, this was a fake. If the technology existed to build spaceships like the ones she'd seen, then it existed to build robots and guns, and, oh, to clone Neanderthals, that sort of thing. After all, they were talking about cloning dodos back home, and they'd already done some extinct cow or something. And that was just what the public were told about. So there was no reason at all to suppose she was on an alien planet in the far future (or distant past). The Doctor's ship may just have zapped back to another bit of Earth, say a developmental complex in America. Maybe she was in Area 51!

And then she thought of how Dave would react if he found out that Area 51 was actually a prehistoric theme park, which took her mind into those places she didn't want to go again, and she forgot about trying to rationalise things away.

*

In the end, they'd come to a part of the rocky plain that looked just like the rest of the rocky plain, but there the golden robot had finally stopped. Anji resisted the huge temptation to take her shoes off and air her blisters, because she knew that she'd never be able to put them back on again and presumably there was still more walking ahead of them. There was an electronic hum from the robot's head, and suddenly Anji could see the barrier just a couple of feet in front of them – nothing like before, with the sonic screwdriver: this was more like a sheet of rippling water that had suddenly become suspended somehow in the air. Rocky plain with added water feature. Tasteful. The robot had begun to move forward again, shepherding the Doctor and Anji in front of it. The Doctor had smiled encouragingly at her, and stepped through the watery wall without hesitation. Screwing up her courage – she didn't know what was on the other side, after all – Anji had followed.

It wasn't like she'd imagined. She'd expected to step straight through to the other side, but there didn't seem to be another side. It was – oh, she wasn't sure what it was like, sort of a cross between walking against the wind and forcing herself through a waterfall. The barrier pressed down on her, and she couldn't see anything but bright shimmering water stuff ahead. For an instant a dart of claustrophobia stabbed through her and she almost screamed. Then, as if sensing her panic, a hand came back through the translucence and unerringly found hers. A fraction of a second of further panic, and then she saw the distinctive blue gemstone ring on one of the fingers and recognised it as the Doctor's. Calmer, she let him lead her forward.

In the end, Anji had no idea how long it took them to walk through the barrier, though she suspected it was really only a few seconds, probably not much longer than it took her to get her breath back once she was out. But... out where? There was no rocky plain on the other side. Whatever Anji might have expected – not that she really had any clear ideas – she had at least thought that the plain would continue. That they'd seem to be on the same planet, in the same world, perhaps with a few DO NOT ENTER: TRESPASSERS WILL BE PROSECUTED signs stuck up. Instead they were somewhere else – no longer prehistoric, she could see a city in the distance – and when she turned to look behind her, the barrier had gone and the industrial landscape carried on as far as she could see. They were also surrounded by armed men. Human men. Was it Area 51? Or something worse? 'Have we... transmatted or something?' she had gasped at the Doctor, worried.

'No no no,' he had said. 'Remember Fitz? We're on the other side of the barrier – it's just that this barrier was quite a substantial one. Hello, there!'

The last had been said to the guards around them. She just *knew* they were guards. For a start they were in uniform – one-piece purple-and-silver outfits – and she knew uniformed men surrounding you with hard expressions and raised guns just *had* to be guards in the same way she knew that the beautiful female alien would definitely fall in love with Captain Kirk.

The guards had led the Doctor and Anji to a black-box-looking car thing, and the Doctor had kept smiling reassuringly at Anji, and she noticed with some surprise that she still had hold of his hand.

The Doctor had asked the guards where they were; who they (the guards) were; what planet they were on; whether they were being arrested for something and if so what; and where they were being taken. The guards had accused the Doctor and Anji of being terrorists, but wouldn't say what they were supposed to have been terrorising, or answer any of the Doctor's other questions. They just waved their guns and forced the two into the car. Two of the guards got in, too, and continued ignoring the Doctor's queries. The car started off, but the windows were blacked out so Anji had no idea where they were heading; she assumed the distant city. The Doctor (finally letting go of her hand) had tried to open one of the doors with his sonic screwdriver, but it hadn't worked. They'd sat more or less in silence for the whole journey. Anji had wanted to ask more questions, but wasn't sure if she was ready just yet for the answers. And anyway, she was just so relieved to be off her blistered feet that they could be taking her more or less anywhere and she wouldn't care.

Upon arrival, the guards had marched them out of the car, and Anji barely had time to see they were outside a large, dirty white building before they were bundled inside, herded down a few fairly grotty carpeted corridors (would anywhere but Earth have carpet?) and then – to her horror – the Doctor had been led one way, and she another.

'Doctor!' she'd called after him, totally anguished,

her only anchor in this sea of madness suddenly swept away, and he'd called back that everything would be all right, he'd see her soon.

But how did he know?

And now she was sitting in a bare white room, sitting on an uncomfortable plastic chair with a desk lamp pointed at her face – although it wasn't switched on, so she was able to see clearly the two purple-uniformed men pacing up and down in front of her, firing out questions. They kept saying she was a terrorist, and asking for details of her organisation, and looked incredulous when she tried denying it. They also kept telling her she was Anji, which confused her – she assumed they'd worked it out from the gold name necklace she was wearing, but every time she agreed with them they shouted at her some more.

But the shouting was actually a good thing. She'd been scared – pushed along, threatened with guns; she was close to tears. But unreasoned shouting – that she could deal with, because it was something she didn't take from anyone. In a strange way, it made her feel stronger, because, however scary they were, she'd always been told that bullies were cowards. She'd had to deal with bullies many, many times, and she knew she could do it. The more they shouted, the more she was able to stand up to them, and the further from breaking down she became.

'I'm not a terrorist. Do I look like a terrorist? Yes, all right, I don't know what a terrorist is supposed to look like. Balaclavas and camouflage jackets, I suppose, that sort of thing, but you can see that isn't me. No, I said balaclavas. They're a sort of... knitted head-covering thing. I suppose it should give me confidence to know that I'm in a civilisation that doesn't have them. They'd suit you, though.'

One of the men grabbed her necklace and tore it from her neck, breaking the fragile chain. Anji yelped, and the personal violation of taking something so precious from her made her really snap. She leapt to her feet (*Ouch!* Her feet!), pushing the chair back, and half shouted, half screamed, 'Give that back now!'

The guards had leapt to their feet too, and their guns were now pointing straight at her. She made an effort to calm down. Explain things rationally.

'It was a present from my boyfriend. The last present he ever gave me. It was for no more sinister purpose than to celebrate our anniversary. Our last ever anniversary. I would appreciate you giving it back.'

They didn't. They didn't seem to understand. Or care.

'I don't know what you think it signifies, but it's just my name. Anji It's my name. It was a custom where I come from to have necklaces with your name on.' They kept staring. Ridiculously, she explained further. 'Well, safety groups didn't advise it because they said that strange men could read your name and pretend they know you, but as I'm not six years old and can look after myself... Look, will you just give it back, please?'

The men wouldn't. They seemed to have got it into their heads that her necklace proved her to be a terrorist. She was getting very frustrated now.

'It's just a necklace! It's clearly not a terrorist badge. Look, where's the Doctor? He'll tell you you've got the wrong idea. The Doctor – the man who was with me? Tall white guy, brown curls, green coat? He's hardly forgettable. No, not "the other terrorist". Honestly, are you listening to me at all? It's quite ridiculous to say, "If you won't answer our questions…" I am quite clearly answering your questions to the very best of my ability, but they seem to bear no relation to reality! What you mean is that I won't give you the answers that you're after. Well, I can't. I don't know what you want me to say, and even if I did I wouldn't say it unless it were true. Now, would you please give me back my necklace?'

But they still wouldn't.

'Oh, this is ridiculous. Why on Earth is my necklace so important?'

The men gaped at her for a second. Then the questions started again, slightly quieter and with a puzzled edge. Anji was puzzled too.

'Yes, I said "Earth". Why? I'm beginning to figure that I'm not where I hoped I was. Yes, "Why on Earth." It's just an expression where I come from. It's not a big deal. Is it? Look, can I see the Doctor now?'

The men looked at each other. One of them nodded. At that, Anji's inner bravado collapsed almost immediately in a huge surge of relief. She tried not to show that as they led her out of the room, down the carpeted corridors, twisting and turning and finally reaching a solid metal door with a keypad lock, which they activated. But after the door had slammed, shutting her in a cell with the Doctor, she collapsed to the floor.

*

23

The Doctor's voice was saying 'Hello, Anji,' from somewhere above her, and Anji sat up, clasping her knees.

'Hi,' she said. 'Sorry about that.'

The Doctor smiled at her. 'I'm very glad you're all right.' He gestured behind him, and Anji realised they weren't alone.

'Everyone, this is Anji!'

Three teenage boys, probably about seventeen or eighteen, were sitting on one of the plastic bunks that lined the walls of the small, plain white room. The Doctor introduced them as Xernic, who gave her a shy wave, Zequathon, who grinned, and Beezee, who raised an eyebrow at her.

'They're all terrorists,' beamed the Doctor.

All three boys wore dull-green jumpsuit outfits, zipped up the front and covered in pockets. Xernic had red hair and was just the tiniest bit chubby, and was blushing slightly as she looked at him. Anji felt drawn to him instantly, and wanted to give him a hug. Zequathon she didn't want to hug; he was over six foot and looked a bit of a bruiser. He was a blond. And Beezee, the third boy, was dark-haired and skinny, and seemed rather shifty. But none of them looked like terrorists to her. Though, as she'd said to the guards, she didn't know what terrorists were supposed to look like. She'd seen photos of clean-cut white boys and middle-aged Asian men smiling out of newspapers under headlines about bombings and threats and executions; you couldn't tell by appearances.

'Those men kept shouting that I was a terrorist. They

wouldn't listen to me,' she said. 'And... it was very strange. They took my necklace. Not that it was valuable or anything, but... well, it was the last thing Dave gave me before – you know.' She was quiet for a moment. The Doctor nodded, showing her he understood.

After a minute, she gave him a half-smile, and brushed away the single tear that had escaped. 'Sorry,' she murmured.

He shook his head. 'No no no. Don't be. But I think I can explain about the necklace. Beezee –' he turned to the weasely-looking dark-haired boy – 'would you show Anji your badge, please.'

The boy called Beezee unzipped the top couple of inches of his jumpsuit, and pulled back his collar. There, on the inside, was a small round badge which read, ANJI. The other two boys followed suit, flashing their collars. They were both wearing identical badges.

'Meet your fan club!' the Doctor said, grinning.

This was bloody incredible. Fitz would have said unbelievable, if he hadn't already learned to believe six impossible things before breakfast (and another twenty before lunch). One second he was running about on alien sand and watching strange bird-dinosaur things wheeling in a strange sky, the next... well, the next he had jumped through a hole to Egypt. Still lots of sand piled around, and the odd strange bird thing too – ibises, were they? – but it was all yellow and sunny, and there were all these pyramids. So, either he'd just time-travelled without a TARDIS, or... or something else that he couldn't quite think of at the moment.

Like – Fitz yelled in shock – maybe he wasn't in Egypt at all, but Universal Horror Land. Because there was a huge great mummy walking down the street towards him, bandages dangling, arms stretched out towards Fitz, and maybe he'd be better off with the caveman and dinosaur after all, because at least they were *natural*, so he should go back with all speed... And, in a moment that definitely belonged in a horror film, Fitz turned back and found that the hole through the barrier had vanished. He couldn't even see where it had been, there seemed to be nothing but yellow sand until the horizon – but he put out a hand and drew it back sharply, as he felt the tingling of energy. No escape from the mummy that way: he was going to have to run but it was almost on top of him, arms out to strangle him as mummies did...

... but the mummy lumbered straight past without a sideways glance. Not that it had any eyes, but...

Oh God, there was another one over there. And another. Oh, and there was... a cat. That wasn't quite as scary. And a guy with a – jackal's head? Freak-show time! But no people.

How the hell was he going to get back to the Doctor now? And how was the Doctor going to get away from the flying dinosaur and the caveman now his escape route was shut off? But then Fitz decided that the Doctor was perfectly capable of dealing with such things – of course he was – and so Fitz might as well keep all his concern for himself.

Did he say there were no people? Well, no one except for that girl peering round that street-corner sarcophagus; a girl with heavy eye make-up who was wearing one of those Nefertiti headdress things, and looking straight at him.

'Um, hello,' called Fitz. The girl frowned, and came out from behind the coffin. She was only about thirteen or fourteen, but quite a looker anyway. And, um, slim but, well, um, reasonably developed. For her age. Or so it would seem from a casual glance.

'Are you lost?' she asked.

'Uh – yes,' said Fitz. 'Very.'

'Thought so. You look like you're from the twentieth century.'

Fitz gaped at her.

'Would you like me to take you back there?'

'You can do that?'

'Well, yes. Just don't tell anyone. Come on, this way.' She scurried off. Fitz, dodging cats and ibises and apparent embodiments of ancient gods and goddesses, followed her.

'ANJI.'

'Yes?'

'No no, not you, them. Apparently it stands for –'

'The Association for New Jupitan Independence,' supplied the blond boy. 'A collective of right-minded people who want to see New Jupiter go forward in its own identity, not kowtowing to ridiculous ancient ties.' He sounded as though he were quoting from something.

'There, you see!' said the Doctor, beaming at Anji. 'Well, I'm all for own identities.'

New Jupiter. 'I'm pretty sure there was only one Jupiter back where I come from,' Anji said. 'So this must be New Jupiter named after the first Jupiter, like New York or New Jersey. Which means... this is the future after all. Oh.'

'Well, a bit of it,' the Doctor said. 'There's actually rather a lot of it, you know. And tomorrow, it'll be part of the past.'

'I mean, it's my future,' said Anji 'If I were on Earth now, it would be later than AD 2001.'

One of the boys – Bee Gee? No, Beezee – spat on the ground. The Doctor tutted benevolently. 'That's rather unhygienic, you know.'

'You didn't mention you were Earth-lovers,' the boy sneered. 'That's what I call unhygienic.'

The Doctor gazed at him, frowning. 'What a strange insult,' he said. 'Were you just copying what I said? Although I suppose you could call loving the Earth unhygienic – the oceans are terribly polluted for a start, and I don't suppose anyone's washed the ozone layer recently –'

Anji raised her eyes to the ceiling.

'Shut up!' yelled Zequathon, the blond boy. 'Are you working for the President? Trying to find out our plans?'

The Doctor made an elaborate 'zipping' gesture across his mouth.

'If you refuse to tell us, that means yes,' said Beezee, coldly.

The Doctor raised his hands in the air, a pleading look in his eyes. Anji decided to intervene. 'I think he means,' she said, shaking her head (the Doctor knew how to be irritating), 'that he's shut up because you asked him to, and so can't answer any of your questions without un-shutting-up. Look, just tell him he can speak.'

'All right! Speak!' said Zequathon. 'Answer me!'

The Doctor unzipped his mouth. 'I don't know who the President is, and even if I did I doubt I'd be working for him. I didn't know about you until I was put in this cell, I didn't know you had any plans until you mentioned them, and unless you're going around blowing people up I'm probably on your side anyway. Now, could you imagine that I'm telling the truth and we really don't know what's going on – any of it – and tell us all about it? You don't have to talk about any of your plans,' he added kindly.

The boy paused for a second. He probably wasn't too bright, Anji thought. 'OK,' he said at length. 'You tell the tale, Timothy.'

Anji couldn't help laughing at the look of anger and consternation 'Timothy' shot him.

'Beezee!' Zequathon (or maybe that wasn't *his* real name) corrected himself hurriedly. 'I meant Beezee.'

'Beezee', with another angry look, started to tell the tale. 'Well, some of us got fed up with always being told how Earth was so much better than New Jupiter, so when the President started coming up with plans for this park thing, we –'

'Just a minute,' the Doctor interrupted. 'Could you go back a bit further than that? Who the President is, and so on?'

Beezee frowned, but obliged. 'The President's

descended from the leader of the first colony, way back years ago. John F Hoover, his name is.'

'What does the "F" stand for?' asked the Doctor. Showing he was taking an interest; gaining their sympathy. He was leaning slightly forward too, palms upright and open. Anji had done a seminar on body language in the workplace and knew what he was up to. Mind you – radical thought – maybe the Doctor *was* finding the story fascinating, and really did want them to open up to him, trust him, be his friends.

Whatever, the effort in appearing interested wasn't appreciated. Beezee gave the Doctor a 'you *are* dumb' look. 'What are you talking about? It's the Presidential F. It doesn't stand for anything.'

'Oh, I see,' said the Doctor, as if that made perfect sense. 'Please, carry on.'

Beezee shrugged. 'Well, he's just really into the whole Earth thing. Our ancestors came from Earth, therefore we're spiritually Earthmen. We're made to feel second class –'

'At least,' interrupted Zequathon.

'Mmm, more like tenth class,' added Xernic, the first time Anji had heard him speak, 'if there were only nine classes.'

'– because of us happening to be born a few hundred thousand light years away from our spiritual home. It's not as if he's even saying he's better than us, even though he's from one of the first families – that'd be more understandable – just that we're *all* inferior to some stupid faraway Earth types. Who care about us so much that they haven't lifted a finger to help "their" people here, now we've no money or trade.'

"Cept now Hoover's got this amazing plan to save us all with Earth's help,' said Zequathon.

'I was *coming* to that.' Beezee glared at him. 'Yeah, Earth'll do stuff when there's something in it for them.' He turned back to the Doctor. 'Hoover's got Earth Heritage to set up one of their theme parks here. You know, "imagine what it would have been like to live in Earth's Golden Times", all that stuff. Which I suppose is all well and good in that it'll bring in some cash. *But –*'

'And it's a big but,' put in Xernic.

'Just like Xernic's,' said Zequathon irrelevantly, earning himself a punch.

'*But*, it makes us yet another little profit-making enterprise for Earth Heritage, who are the biggest load of money-grubbing gold-diggers around; it makes everyone go "ooh, Earth is so great", and it completely ignores the fact that we do actually have some New Jupitan heritage of our own. But we can't have a theme park about that, oh no. We don't even have a poky little backstreet museum about *our* heritage.'

'And ANJI…?' asked Anji.

'We want to be independent from Earth. We can't rely on them for anything, so deferring to them in everything is just holding us back. Why should they get our taxes when they don't provide us with anything in return?'

('Ah, taxes,' muttered the Doctor in an aside to Anji.)

'The people of New Jupiter should be proud of their own planet, not forever spouting on about some distant ancestry.'

'And it's not just us who think that,' said Zequathon. 'There are even people in the government who support us.'

'Really?' said the Doctor. 'Who?'

'Why should we tell you?' snapped Beezee, at the very same moment that Xernic said, 'We don't actually know who, exactly.'

'*Anyway*,' continued Beezee, 'the fact is that we have support, and we're going to show the stupid "Earthmen" of New Jupiter that ANJI means business. The New Jupitans aren't going to let Earth leech off them for ever. We'll show 'em all!'

'When you get out of this cell, of course,' the Doctor reminded him kindly. 'And when is that exactly? When will they let you out?'

There was no answer. All three boys looked sheepishly at the ground, the ceiling, anywhere but at the Doctor, Anji or each other.

Anji began to have a bit of a sick feeling in her stomach.

The Doctor was leaning even further forward. 'Tell me,' he said. It was red-haired Xernic who answered, sounding nervous. 'Um. Well. They don't. Let us out, that is. This is the condemned cell. Didn't you know?'

Anji shut her eyes. She was a main character. They couldn't execute her just because they didn't like her jewellery. Could they?

To: cybertron@xprof.net
From: anji kapoor@MWFutures.co.uk
Date: 14/2/01 12:47

Subject: Teen Terrorists

Hi darling

Wow, what a morning. You'll never believe it, some aliens are going to execute me because I have the same name as a terrorist organisation consisting of three teenage boys. How's that for bad luck?! And ironically, the people who are going to kill me (led by a man named John F Hoover, believe it or not) revere Earth, and so they think that I must hate it. Hate Earth! The place where I want to be more than anywhere else in the entire universe!

Funny, the 'terrorist' kids have all given themselves different names to distance themselves from the culture they were brought up in. Did I ever tell you, when I first started school I tried to pretend my name was Angela, so I'd fit in. They're trying to fit out. If they were even the slightest bit efficient, I might be jealous of their integrity.

Oh, and my feet hurt. A lot.

Anyway, must go. Bit busy atm.

Love
Anji xxx

Send now/send later: send later

CHAPTER TWO
HISTORY'S WHAT
YOU MAKE IT

To Fitz's half-relief, half-disappointment, the girl didn't whisk him off in a TARDIS-type timeship.

She led him down a couple of sandy streets, and then fiddled with something at her belt and a shimmering wall appeared in front of them. 'Come on,' she said, 'You just walk through. You must have done it before – there was a report of a temporary barrier breach. I suppose that's when you got out of your zone.'

She stepped through the barrier, and Fitz followed. 'Oh,' he said, looking at the cobbled streets in front of him, 'this sort of twentieth century. Right. It's not real, is it?'

'This *is* where you come from?' the girl said. 'Let me check your serial number. I know you're not one of mine.'

'No, no,' Fitz said hurriedly, 'this is where I come from. No checking required. Twentieth century is me, definitely.'

'You must just be a pleb, then,' the girl continued. 'Not one of the important characters. I mean, I don't recognise you.'

The enormity of this insult took Fitz aback for a moment. He, the legendary Fitz Fortune, star of the sixties (or at least he would have been, if he hadn't been unexpectedly forced to go on the run through being wanted for murder, and then taken away in a space-time machine), accused of being a 'pleb'. Worse still, 'just' a pleb.

On a nearby wall there was a poster of Elvis Presley. The King. King of Fitz's heart when he was on stage, anyway. He could have been as big as Elvis. (He'd said that to his one-time fellow companion Sam once and she'd made some joke about hamburgers that he hadn't got, so she'd taken him to the TARDIS's film library and shown him. But he preferred not to think about that. Heroes should always remain heroic, in his eyes.)

But anyway. If they wanted twentieth-century 'important characters', he'd give them one. He gave the girl a scornful look. 'You think I'm "just a pleb"? You haven't done your research, darling. I'm Fitz Fortune, of course. Just as big as that guy –' he gestured at Elvis – 'back in the old twentieth century. The printing department must be a bit behind; I expect there'll be posters of me up there any day now.'

'Fitz Fortune?'

'The one and only, baby!' He gave her a few bars of 'Groovy Weekend' on air guitar to prove it.

She seemed stunned with admiration. Then he realised she was staring over his shoulder at a middle-aged woman in the distance, who was inspecting what appeared to be a miniature rocket ship.

'There's the curator,' she said. 'Gotta dash. Not supposed to be able to cross zones; don't want any questions. She'll stick you back in your right place – *Fitz Fortune.*'

And then, with a shimmer of – whatever – she was gone through the barrier again. Back with the mummies and the pyramids. And the barrier vanished, but Fitz tried to follow her anyway. He just ended up on his bum again. So, you needed a sonic screwdriver or whatever that girl had been carrying on her belt to get through. Which meant that Fitz was stuck in the twentieth-century – what did she say? – zone. Twentieth-Century Zone. So that would have been the Egyptian Zone. And the Prehistoric Zone? Some kind of futuristic museum; no dusty cases required, no signs saying DO NOT TOUCH?

There was a sign, though, a big standing sign that read WELCOME TO LONDON – CITY OF SWINGS! So... this was how the people of the future viewed his time, his place, then. He looked around him. On the street corner in front of him was a Coca-Cola vending machine. Oh well, at least he wouldn't dehydrate to death. And you had to admire an advertising campaign that could ensure the product was remembered however far into the future this was. And there were a number of the little rocket-ship things dotted about: maybe he could escape in one of those and hope there wasn't a barrier across the sky. He started walking down the street (ducking down behind a strangely pink pillar box as a giant furry creature wandered past – and what the hell was that all about? What was it, some sort of abominable snowman? What had that got to do with twentieth-century London?), turned the corner, and...

Yee hah! There was the TARDIS! The Doc must have got back to it and managed to do a short hop to pick

Fitz up! Brief dark thoughts about the risk the Doctor'd taken, seeing that he didn't seem to know quite what was going on with the TARDIS at the moment – what if it hadn't worked and Fitz had been abandoned here for ever? Mind you, knowing the Doctor, he might have been flying around the universe for hundreds of years trying to get back to Fitz. He might have lost that stuck-up Anji girl and got a host of new attractive female companions, all dying to meet the legendary 'Fitz' that the Doctor was always talking about. He might have… Oh heck, let's just find out.

Fitz jogged over to the TARDIS. He waved up at the light wherein the scanner eye was located, in a 'hey, it's me, Fitz –let me in!' kind of way.

The TARDIS doors failed to open. Fitz gave them a shove, just in case.

And stumbled forward into a four-foot-square wooden box. Sod it.

He slammed the door shut and banged on it with his fist, frustrated. Might have known it was too good to be true; no easy way out for Fitz. Only half an hour back with the Doctor and he was right in the thick of things already.

'Stop it at once! You're damaging the exhibit!' He spun round. The woman who'd given the Nefertiti girl a shock had managed to sneak right up behind Fitz without him noticing – which just showed how distracted he must have been because they were still on a cobbled street and she was wearing stiletto heels. Sod it times two.

'Who exactly are you?'

Well, it'd worked once, it might work again. 'I'm Fitz Fortune, baby. Obviously. You know, "Groovy Weekend" (da da da da da da dum), "You Broke My Heart, Bikini Girl"?'

'No, I don't know.' Scraped-back grey hair and a snotty manner; this woman reminded Fitz of his old maths teacher. One of the ones who used to say things like, 'that may be how you used to do things in *Germany*' really sarcastically, knowing Fitz'd never been further than the other end of Southend pier in his life. 'What I do know is you're not designated for this section, and judging by your clothing I sincerely hope you're not intended for another zone. Whatever were the designers thinking of?' She took Fitz's lapel in one hand and sniffed in disapproval. 'I don't think even a primitive twentieth-centurion would have worn a coat like this.'

Fitz had spent a long time choosing this coat in London in AD 2001 while waiting to meet up with the Doctor, and was firmly of the opinion that it was (a) the height of style, (b) tiptop quality, and (c) really him. But he supposed that, technically, it was a twenty-*first*-century coat, so he decided not to mention it.

But then the woman sniffed at him again, even more loudly, so he decided to mention it after all. But she didn't seem impressed.

'You've been reprogrammed by one of those little horrors, haven't you?' she said. 'Trying to ruin my sectors with babbling idiots. They just do it to get on my nerves. Jealousy, I suppose.' She took a large – very, very large, and very, very pointy – screwdriver from a pocket of her jumpsuit. 'Just hold still, and let me get to your brain.'

Fitz made an eep sound. And ran.

Behind him – fading fast – he heard the woman give an exasperated sigh. Then there were some beeps. Then a bloody great gold-coloured metallic monster – about twenty foot high (oh, all right, six and three quarters, which was still a fair bit taller than Fitz) – stepped out in front of him and grabbed Fitz's shoulder in a glittering fist as he tried to alter his course at the last second to avoid the horrific thing.

Fitz struggled, alarmed, trying to break its grip without breaking any of his own bones. The woman was approaching, heels click-click-clicking on the stony street. And she was pointing that ruddy huge screwdriver at him, scary end first.

'So why are they executing you?' Anji asked. 'You look rather… young to be terrorists.' Not true of course, but it seemed too rude to use the first word that had come into her head, which was 'ineffectual'. Or the second, which was 'soft'.

'We have a just cause!' said Beezee, angrily. 'Anyway, we're not that much younger than you.'

'But as I'm not a terrorist,' Anji pointed out, 'that's not really relevant.'

'We're not really terrorists,' said Xernic, looking a bit sheepish about it. 'We've not actually done anything. But one of our supporters sent us this stuff, and it seemed a shame not to use it, Jonathan said –'

'Zequathon!' hissed the blond guy.

'Zequathon said (sorry), and so we broke into the centre, and –'

'What stuff?' asked the Doctor.

'Sorry?'

'What "stuff" did this supporter send you?'

Xernic beamed. 'Oh, brilliant things. Really, really brilliant! Devices that let you get through the energy barriers – and this fantastic zappy thing that can disable the androids. Top technology!'

'Fascinating,' said the Doctor. 'I'd have liked to have seen them.'

Xernic reached into a pocket. 'There you go.' He passed a couple of small silvery boxes to the Doctor, earning himself a hard stare from his comrades, who obviously hadn't completely fallen for the Doctor's 'trust me!' act yet.

'The guards didn't confiscate these? That's surprising.' The Doctor began closely examining the boxes.

'They didn't even search us,' said Xernic, shrugging. 'Us just being there was enough for them.'

The Doctor looked up. 'Why? Trespassers will be prosecuted, that's something you hear all the time, but executed? That's fairly unusual on civilised worlds.'

Xernic shrugged again, and didn't meet the Doctor's gaze.

The Doctor turned round and looked inquisitively at the other two. Beezee sneered silently, but Zequathon was no match for the Doctor's stare. 'Well…' he said, defiantly. 'It was 'cos of all the murders, weren't it?'

Fitz was babbling at the top of his voice.

'I'm human! Really I am! Please don't take my brain apart! Ow, that hurts! No, I didn't get here by myself, a girl brought me. I don't know, just some kid! No, that doesn't prove anything, I don't know who these "little horrors" are, but I'm nothing to do with them! I'm human, I tell you! What authorised guest list? What penalty for trespass? No! For God's sake! I am a real live human being from the real live twentieth century and I'm here by accident and I can prove it! Ask me anything about the twentieth century. Anything at all! Well, as long as it's pre-1963. Actually, things after, ooh, say, 1955 would be best, too.'

'Very well,' the woman said, which took Fitz aback a bit. He took a deep breath, psyching himself up, as she continued. 'We'll see how good your programming is. In which year did Earth astronauts first land on Mars?'

Fitz raised a sardonic eyebrow. 'Far too easy,' he smirked. 'Trick question. Never happened in the twentieth century.'

The woman gave him an even bigger smirk. 'Incorrect. As early as the 1960s Earthmen were working, resting and playing on Mars.' Fitz began to splutter his objections, but she continued. 'Question two. Which English politician was well-known for his seaside boxing matches?'

'You're a loony,' said Fitz.

'Incorrect,' the woman told him. 'The answer is Winston Churchill. Question three, who murdered Roger Ack–'

'Shut up!' said Fitz. 'You just don't know what you're talking about! I don't know if you're really thick or trying to catch me out or something, but you're talking serious bollocks. Winston Churchill was the British Prime Minister during most of the war, and when he said "we shall fight on the beaches" he was talking about how if the Nazis invaded we'd never surrender, not running on about a scrap over the buckets and spades. I lived through that, you know, and it wasn't very nice. That was the Second World War, 1939 to 1945. The First World War, also known as the Great War – meaning it was very big, not that it was really good – had been fought 1914 to 1918, and it was supposed to be the war to end all wars, only it wasn't. That man –' he pointed at another of the many Elvis posters – 'had blue suede shoes, not green rubber wellies or whatever stupid thing you've got him down for. And he was a singer – a fantastic one – not a teddy bear or a hotelkeeper or a hound dog. And I don't know who killed Roger Ackroyd – see, I knew what you were going to say – because it wasn't real: it was a book, and I've never read it. I do know who did the murder on the Orient Express, though. And I can tell you about Middle Earth, and the Day of the Triffids, and James Bond. Only none of them were real, either. And I don't know what weird version of twentieth-century England you're talking about, but I reckon it's some stupid fake you've come up with after getting a few details off the back of cigarette cards and chocolate-bar wrappers and scraps from a local library, and then filling in the gaps to suit yourself.'

He paused for a long deep breath, and couldn't quite bring himself to start up again.

The woman was frowning. 'Come with me,' she said. 'We're going to go through this zone together, you and I, and you are going to tell me about everything we see.'

'So you're not going to unscrew my head?' asked Fitz.

'Not yet,' she said – as he knew, from so many movies, that she would.

To: cybertron@xprof.net
From: anji kapoor@MWFutures.co.uk
Date: 14/2/01 13:05
Subject: Fun

Hey babes,

You'll never guess what! Not only are there: (a) dinosaurs and (b) terrorists on this planet, there are also (c) lots of unexplained deaths! Exciting, huh?

Oh well, at least there aren't rats in the cells. At least, not yet...

Love
Anji xxx

PS I miss you.

Send now/send later: send later

The Doctor was talking. He had a lovely voice, soft and

smooth and just deep enough, with that hint of accent that made you think of humour and secret smiles. A stick-on-a-talking-book-in-the-car-and-fall-asleep-at-the-wheel kind of voice. 'Dreamy', even. Funny, she could acknowledge how sexy his voice was – how sexy *he* was, full stop – without actually fancying him herself in the slightest. Just like she could, say, look at photos of Marilyn Monroe or Michelle Pfeiffer and know they were utterly gorgeous, but not be at all that way inclined herself. Not her type. That was it. But what was her type? Oh, yes. Dead. That's what he was.

Focus on the now.

Lots of other people were dead, too, it seemed.

'So how many visitors have died?' the Doctor had asked the boys.

'Don't know,' said Xernic. 'They just said that people had been found dead in the centre. Killed. Wouldn't tell us any more.'

'Because they thought we knew,' added Zequathon, "cos they thought it was us what did it. So they didn't bother to give us the details.'

Xernic looked thoughtful. 'Can't have been that many people, though. The centre's not open yet. Grand ceremony thing's not happened. The only people who go in there are the staff, and advance-guest types.'

The Doctor had jumped to his feet and was pacing up and down the cell. He reminded Anji of a caged tiger – barely suppressed energy, could strike at any moment if they didn't let him out. But there was that hypnotic quality, too, that tigers had – you couldn't keep your eyes off him, had to see what he was going to do next. Hypnotic power – she suddenly had a vision of the Doctor leaning towards her singing 'Trust in me… just in me…' – which was the legacy of a Disney film that she'd both loved and hated as a child. Good film, bad for all the jungle jokes it had inspired in the classroom afterwards (because, of course, there were lots of jungles in Yorkshire where she was born, oh yes). And thinking of *The Jungle Book* and Shere Khan the tiger (who had been the bad guy) made her realise that the Doctor wasn't a tiger after all, because she couldn't imagine him ever being so sneaky. He had to be the good guy – so the nice cat. The black panther, Bagheera. With maybe a bit of Baloo the jolly but incompetent bear thrown in.

When Anji had been taken to see *The Jungle Book* at age six, she had been disappointed by the ending. The boy had had the chance to live a life of adventure with all his friends, and had given it all up to settle down with some girl. She hadn't been able to understand that. Now, she thought she understood it a lot more. But here she was stuck in the jungle, with Doctor the panther-bear and Fitz who was probably the orang-utan, and she couldn't get back to the little human village even if she wanted to.

She reluctantly dragged her mind back from this nonsense to the here and now. What it seemed to come down to was this. This theme park, EarthWorld, was made up of various zones based on periods in Earth's history – or prehistory, in the case of the area where the TARDIS had landed. Earth's history was a very specialist field, as not that many records survived (the boys didn't go into detail why, and Anji didn't ask – the last thing she wanted to hear about was that her world had been devastated by nuclear war or something). The centre was to be populated by androids, built to look like inhabitants of the relevant time and place, and programmed to interact with the visitors as if they were all living in Earth's history together. Visitors could dress up in costume and immerse themselves in Earthlife, forgetting their drab little existences on New Jupiter. The Grand Opening ceremony was due to happen this very week, but a few privileged visitors had been allowed in for sneak previews. And some of them hadn't come out again. There were bodies. Mauled, some of them, apparently. Anji was almost grateful that they'd been arrested. It had got them out of the way, if nothing else.

'And even if we could convince them that we weren't responsible for the deaths,' Zequathon said, 'they wouldn't let us go. 'Cos Hoover's not going to want it spread around that visitors to EarthWorld are likely to end up sliced and diced, is he? If the public don't go, and the off-world tourists don't arrive, he's screwed.'

'We're talkin' ree-voh-looshun,' drawled Beezee. 'Or Hoover'll be forced to abdicate, at least.'

'Which'd be nice,' added Xernic.

'His popularity's soaring since this stupid theme park came along,' said Zequathon. 'They've run competitions and stuff for people to be allowed in before the official opening. It's all anyone's talking about. Can you imagine the reaction if they found out what's going on?'

'So President Hoover is going to cover up the deaths,' said the Doctor, still pacing. Then he suddenly stopped stock still, shouted 'That's terrible!' and sat down.

'So you're going to sort it out, Doctor?' asked Anji.

'I certainly am,' he said. 'This is hugely irresponsible.'

'And what do you think's going on?'

The Doctor didn't answer her directly. He turned to the three boys. 'Your android technology. How advanced is it?'

The boys exchanged 'you what?' glances. 'Pretty standard,' said Beezee.

'But what's that? We've travelled through time and space to get here, we don't know what your standard is.'

Anji saw their expressions and pre-empted what she assumed was coming next. 'He's telling the truth,' she said. 'Just take it as read, it'll make things much easier in the long run.'

The Doctor carried on anyway. 'When we landed in the theme pack, we saw a caveman and a pterosaur, and there were some dinosaurs about too. Were they mechanical?'

''Spect so,' Xernic said, nodding.

'And were they indicative of the general level of historical understanding?' Anji asked, but the Doctor frowned at her. He went on.

'And you say that in general these androids can interact with people. So, assuming we'd landed in some non-prehistoric area, would we be able to tell if we were talking to a human being or an android?'

'No, not really.'

'I spy potential trouble,' said Anji. 'I've seen *Blade Runner*. Well, most of it.'

'So that's pretty advanced technology. And the more advanced it is, the more likelihood of something going hideously wrong.'

Anji frowned. 'How d'you mean, Doctor?'

'You've seen *Blade Runner*. Well, most of it. You tell me.'

She thought for a second. 'Rogue androids? Wanting their own identity? And killing humans?'

'Well, one and three at least, I'd say. It *could* just be a mistake in programming rather than a development of consciousness. But yes, I would think that there's an android revolution going on,' the Doctor said, jumping to his feet again. 'And it's up to us to stop it!'

The three boys cheered. Anji just sighed.

'Well, for a start, the whole of the twentieth century didn't happen at once, you know. If you're gonna have gas lamps and stuff like that, you don't have astronauts. Oh, and those flapper types and the guys with the twirly moustaches? They can talk, you know. They don't have to just mouth "help" or do sinister silent laughs. And all those vampires wandering about? 'Fraid not. Well, not during the day, anyway. And I can't even begin to think what those trundly upright-tanks with the radar things on top are, but they were certainly never in the London I knew.'

The woman – Venna Durwell, she'd said, though Fitz still kept thinking of her as Mrs Taylor, Maths – had kept silent throughout Fitz's rant. Now she finally spoke. 'All of these things came from genuine twentieth-century records. Written matter, filmic matter. Those "upright tanks", for example, are called War Machines. They worked for the General Post Office in the twentieth century, which was an ancient order for the delivery of communications. We have actual filmed records of them on the streets of London, presumably delivering letters.'

'Oh right,' said Fitz. 'And I suppose they had those great thumping arm things to protect their nonexistent ankles from small fierce dogs?'

Durwell was silent again for several moments. She looked almost distraught. If she hadn't been such a sarky cow, Fitz might even have felt sorry for her. 'These things – painstakingly researched – faithfully reproduced on thousands of EarthWorlds all over the galaxy... you're saying that all of it – *all* of it – is wrong?'

'Yes! Take anyone from twentieth-century London and plop them down here and they'll just laugh at you! As I've just proved, actually.' Fitz laughed, to show her he meant it. 'You're lucky I'm here, really. Genuine twentieth-century consultant – thousands of theme parks at fifty quid a time – no, hang on, don't want to price myself out of the market –'

Durrell looked at him pityingly. 'You've just convinced me you're telling the truth. Come with me.'

She turned on her heel and went in the opposite direction, Fitz having to jog a few steps to catch up with her. As it seemed to have done the trick so far, he kept up the running commentary. 'No talking horses. No dancing bears. And that girl's far too young to be dressed like – Hey!' For he recognised her. Early teens, blonde, bobbed hair and big blue eyes (a bit like the Doctor's, said the bit of Fitz that was forever consumed with the Time Lord – and then he mentally kicked himself for not even being able to look at a babe without thinking of the Doctor – and then mentally kicked himself extra, extra hard for thinking of an adolescent as a babe). It was the Nefertiti girl, but now dressed in a flapper outfit of fringed dress, high heels and beads long enough to lasso with. He tried doing a really small wave so Venna Durwell wouldn't notice. She didn't, but neither did the girl. So, was she an android? She hadn't acted like one. But then, he, Fitz, didn't act like an android as far as he was aware, and it hadn't stopped Durwell and her screwdriver. The androids here were obviously pretty good. Maybe this wasn't the girl he'd met before, but they'd just used the same mould or whatever to make her. He thought he'd test the water.

'That flapper kid,' he said. 'She looks a bit familiar. Have you only got, like, a few models?'

Durwell sniffed. 'The infinite variety of the human form is represented in EarthWorld. We have androids of all shapes, sizes and colours, and no two are the same.'

'Oh,' said Fitz. It must be the same girl after all, doubling as a quick-change artist.

'Except for that design,' the woman continued. Aha! 'The President of New Jupiter's daughters –' she sniffed again – 'insisted on making a number of the androids in their own image. The girls are confined to the palace and unable to visit the centre, although they were responsible for a lot of the technical groundwork, so this was understood to be an acceptable compromise.'

'I see,' said Fitz, who didn't really. A few hours later he would be really, really wishing he'd taken the opportunity to ask a few more questions.

'Are we all clear on the plan? First we escape, then I go and find these princess triplets who built the androids –'

'The president's daughters are princesses,' Anji muttered. 'There's democracy for you.'

'– and work out how to stop the robot revolt, while you four infiltrate the theme park using those handy devices your "supporter" so thoughtfully sent you and rescue poor Fitz from the killer androids. Once the park is safe again there'll be no need for the President to execute you, so I'll just give him a quick talk about the importance of maintaining one's own identity, and then we can all meet up back here in the palace for free pardons and tea. All right with everyone?'

The ANJI boys were staring at the Doctor as if Superman himself had come among them. The cynical teen act had fled completely; hero worship was here. 'Yes,' they breathed, awestruck.

'Oh yes,' Anji agreed. 'Fine by me. Just one thing: how do we escape?'

The Doctor's face fell as though she'd snatched his sweeties away. 'I'm not sure.' Then as quick as a flash he was beaming again. 'But I know I'm really good at this bit usually,' he said. 'Let's look for secret passages!'

He began to tap the walls hopefully. The ANJI boys

joined in. After a moment, so did Anji, shaking her head resignedly.

They were at Venna Durwell's office. Fitz knew that, because the door had a big sign saying VENNA DURWELL, CURATOR. PRIVATE on it. They'd gone through one of those energy barriers again to get here – Durwell had used a zappy gadget like the one the Nefertiti girl had had. The office was in the control centre, a sort of reception-cum-control room-cum-gift shop, with nice carpets and a lot of switchboard sort of things. No people there.

Inside the office, Durwell shut the door. 'So,' she said. 'Does anyone know you're here, in EarthWorld?'

That sounded to Fitz like a particularly dodgy leading question, the sort villains always ask to see if it's safe to bump you off. He backed off a few steps. 'Yes,' he said. 'Lots of people.'

'Which means no. Good.'

Fitz backed up a bit more, and fell back over Durwell's desk. 'Don't kill me!' he squeaked.

She snorted. 'Of course I'm not going to kill you. Don't be ridiculous.'

He breathed a sigh of relief, and sat up.

'You're going to give me every scrap of information you know about the twentieth century. And when I'm acknowledged as the greatest academician of our day and can say goodbye to poxy Earth Heritage and its two-bit research grants for good, then I'll kill you, so no one will know I didn't discover it all for myself.'

Fitz lay back on the desk again. He didn't remember

signing a contract when he started travelling with the Doctor, but he reckoned he must have done, and that one of the clauses he'd failed to read was, 'Will get captured by mad bint every three months'.

The Doctor thumped the wall. 'I bate being locked up!'

Anji looked at his face, and saw a flash of an expression that could have been despair. It shocked her.

Perhaps she had imagined it.

'It's an electronic lock,' she said. 'Couldn't you fix it with your sonic screwdriver?'

His eyes gleamed. 'The sonic screwdriver! Of course!' He produced it from a pocket. Anji decided it looked a bit like one of those torches doctors use to see inside your ears. But the Doctor just stared at it.

Then he turned to Anji, and looked at her reproachfully, as if it were her fault. 'Now I don't know what to do. I have to not think about things! It's like...' He seemed to struggle for an analogy that might mean something to her. 'It's like when you go in the wardrobe looking for the strange land. You never find it. But if you just happen upon it, you find yourself in the middle of wondrous adventures.'

Wondrous adventures. Oh yes.

She took the screwdriver from him. 'I think what you actually mean is, don't worry about things and they'll just pop into your mind. Let your subconscious do the work.'

'Oh yes,' he said, a bit disappointedly. 'That's better. Not as picturesque, though. A picture paints a thousand words, you know. I once knew a man who slightly misinterpreted that. He just sat and painted a thousand words. Used the dictionary as his inspiration. He started at "a: singular indefinite article", and it took him all the way to "albumen: the white of an egg". Each word was a slightly different shade of blue. You have to admire someone who can create a thousand different shades of blue, don't you?'

As the Doctor talked, Anji was leading him, step by tiny step, towards the cell door. They halted in front of the locking mechanism.

'Even sky-blue pink?' Anji asked. The Doctor looked quizzical. 'It's a sort of joke. A thing kids say. A mythical colour, because it can't exist. If something's pink, it can't be sky-blue.'

The Doctor smiled. 'But sometimes the blue sky can be flushed with pink. It can be quite beautiful. Maybe that's what it means. Not everything's black and white, you know. Although the sky can be black or white, of course.' (Anji handed him the sonic screwdriver.)

'... or red or gold or sky-blue pink,' said Anji, with a smile.

'... or purple, or green...' continued the Doctor, pulling the front panel off the lock.

'That's taking it a bit far. Far away from Earth?' Anji asked, eyes fixed on the Doctor but gesturing with her left hand to let the boys know that any 'Earth is rubbish' distractions would not be appreciated at this point.

'Mm. I remember a place where the night sky was burnt orange and the tree leaves were silver. Beautiful. I would lie on the hillside gazing at the stars and putting the world to rights.' (The sonic screwdriver was making buzzing noises as the Doctor began to pull wires out of the lock.)

'What world, Doctor? Is this your home planet? Tell me about it.'

There was a loud click, and a buzz from the door. 'What world?' The Doctor paused. And then to Anji's horror he shot her a look which froze her stomach. His eyes suddenly seemed dead. 'I don't know,' he said. 'I don't know.'

'Way to distract the guy!' called Beezee. Anji wanted to hit him.

'I'm sorry, Doctor,' she said, softly.

The look vanished as quickly as it had appeared. 'No no,' he said, smiling at her. 'Nothing to be sorry about.' And to Anji's extreme surprise, he gave her a big hug.

The sonic screwdriver hit her in the small of the back and she gave a grunt. The Doctor let her go and looked at the screwdriver in some surprise.

'You're right, Beezee,' he said. 'That was a way to distract me. Well done, Anji.' But then he looked at the still closed door, and back at the sonic screwdriver, and up at the door again. 'Oh dear,' he said.' I think I need to be distracted a bit more.'

After that *look*, Anji wasn't sure she wanted to give it another go. Of course, she didn't want to stay in this cell for ever, either. But the Doctor – he was supposed to be the good guy. She'd never dreamed that someone like that could suddenly become so terrifying...

And suddenly his face changed again. 'I hate being locked up!' he cried, thumping the door.

And it slid open.

The Doctor's face split in the widest grin Anji had ever seen. He punched the air and gave a silent 'Yes!' to the world. The boys were less quiet, whooping and calling until Anji hurriedly shushed them, fearing guards. 'Well done, Doctor,' she whispered. 'I knew you could do it.'

'I'm glad you did,' he whispered back, looking her straight in the eye. 'I'm glad you did.'

Anji put her blazer back on, picked up her bag, and reluctantly squeezed her sore feet back into her shoes. It was like... like she was popping out after work, not like she was about to venture into killer-robot territory on an alien planet. She felt she should be reacting more. But, just at the moment, she couldn't.

They left the cell, the Doctor almost pantomime with his 'let's creep out quietly' gestures and whispered suggestions. Anji thought she could remember the way she'd been brought to the cell, and could navigate them back; the boys thought they could find their way out of the palace from there. Then there was only the question of whether they could steal – borrow, Anji's naturally lawful mind substituted – a vehicle, or whether they'd have to walk all the way to the complex. She really, really hoped they'd find a car. Then they were going to try to find more or less the same spot where Anji and the Doctor had come out, so they could retrace the route and have a good starting point for locating Fitz. Anji tried to think of some positive things to say about Fitz to motivate them in their task, but, unfortunately, nothing came to mind.

The Doctor claimed to have an unerring sense of direction, and was convinced he could find the three princesses without actually knowing where they were to start with. 'It'll be easy to distinguish the living quarters from the more functional areas like this,' he said. 'And if no one's allowed to see these girls, there'll probably be only one set of guards to get through and then I'm home free.' His face crumpled slightly as he said that, Anji wasn't sure why. 'And,' the Doctor continued, recovering rapidly – if, indeed, she hadn't imagined it to start with, 'I can usually bluff my way anywhere.'

She hoped he could. Anji shot him a secret, pleading, don't-abandon-me look, and he grinned back at her encouragingly. 'It's all going to be fine,' he said, taking in all four of them. Then a special direct look at Anji. 'Don't worry. Oh, and –' he dived into one of his pockets – 'this might come in handy.' He pulled out his hand – and presented Anji with a full roll of Elastoplast. She could have kissed him. And with that, he flew off down the corridor, leaving Anji and the ANJI boys to creep out alone.

Chapter Three
Killing Queens

Three girls sat in a row, each on a golden throne. One wore blue, one wore orange, one wore green. There was no other way to tell them apart physically. Each had bobbed blonde hair and blue eyes; all would generally be considered pretty.

At the bottom of the steps to the thrones stood two figures, a middle-aged woman in fine velvet robes and a caul, and a hooded man. Between them was a wooden block.

The girl in the blue dress stood up from the central throne. 'You have been convicted of treachery; of plotting against us. Do you have anything to say?'

The woman fell to her knees, crying. 'I am innocent! I beg you to pardon me!'

The green-robed girl giggled, not rising. 'Don't think so!'

'You're going to die,' said the girl in orange. 'It's going to hurt. And there's nothing you can do about it.'

'Your Highnesses – please, forgive me!' cried the woman, holding out her hands in supplication.

'Hmmm…' said the girl dressed in green, as if considering the plea. 'Hmm… No!'

'You are a traitor and a danger to us,' said blue-dress. 'We cannot allow you to live.'

'Proceed with the execution!' called the orange-robed girl.

'No!' shrieked the woman, but the hooded man took her shoulders and pushed her towards the wooden block. Shaking, she laid her head down, facing away from the thrones. The man raised his axe –

'Stop!' called orange-dress.

The axe halted. The woman raised her head and turned, sudden hope in her eyes. 'Your Highness?' she breathed.

'I *meant*, stop, I want to see your face when your head's cut off. Turn round, please.'

With a sob, the woman laid down her head once more.

'Proceed with the execution!' orange-dress called, again.

The man raised his axe.

The door of the throne room burst open.

The axe began to fall.

A velvet-coated man dashed through the door and ran towards the scene.

The axe fell. Blood splattered all over the floor as the woman's head was severed, and the three girls cheered.

The running man slipped in the blood, and skidded all the way to the girls. He managed to halt just in front of them, but paid them no immediate attention; instead he hoiked his left foot up to his nose and sniffed. The green-dressed girl giggled.

'Artificial,' the man said. 'You've got the colour and consistency right, but not the smell. Small details are important, you know. I'm the Doctor, by the way. You must be the three princesses.'

'We're not supposed to have visitors,' said the girl dressed in orange. 'Even doctors.'

'We've seen lots of doctors,' said blue-dress, sitting down, 'but they didn't help.'

'Couldn't help,' added orange.

'Didn't want to help,' sighed green.

'Well, maybe I *can* help,' said the Doctor. 'Now, I've introduced myself – why don't you do the same.'

'We don't have to tell you anything,' said green. 'We're princesses and you're not.'

'You don't have to but it wouldn't do any harm now, would it? I'm being friendly. Why don't you be friendly back?'

Blue-dress raised an eyebrow at the others. They shrugged. She turned back to the Doctor. 'All right. I'm Asia.'

'I'm Africa,' said orange.

'And I'm Antarctica,' said green.

'Good!' The Doctor beamed at them. 'What lovely names.' He perched on the steps leading up to the thrones. 'Now, tell me about that.' He gestured to the beheaded figure lying on the floor, and the silent executioner standing beside it.

'That's Mary Antoinette, Queen of the Earth Scots,' Asia told him. 'She's in a book. She had her head cut off. We wanted to see what it looked like.'

'She begged for mercy,' breathed Africa.

'If that's Mary Stuart you're talking about, no she didn't,' said the Doctor, cheerfully. 'She met her fate with courage and resolve.'

Africa sniffed, disappointedly.

'And,' the Doctor continued, 'they didn't cut off her head in one clean stroke. It took several before the head was severed. Little details, you see, little details.'

'Cool!' said Africa, cheered again. She turned to Asia. 'I want to do it again. Now.'

Antarctica rolled her eyes. 'We need to repair the Queen first, silly.' She made a tutting noise.

Asia looked at the Doctor thoughtfully. 'Or we could just find someone else to execute,' she said.

Surprisingly, Anji and the boys had made it out of the palace easily enough. Anji was getting the impression that the whole planet was just basically incompetent. Guards wandered about lazily, never checking around them, never noticing feet sticking out from under alcoved curtains or heads ducking hastily back round corners. She'd often shouted at the screen at the implausibility of TV guards; now she realised that the portrayal of stupidity was fully justified. She wondered whether, if she were to creep up behind one and chop him lightly on the neck, he would be rendered instantly unconscious, but unharmed. Possibly not a good idea to check that out unless entirely necessary, though.

The black car – ground-car, the boys called it, as if there were things to drive a car on other than the ground – was still outside the palace. Unguarded. Unlocked. Anji kept checking for ambushes or secret cameras, but had to finally concede that it really was a gift. Under these circumstances, she felt rather embarrassed to have been captured at all in the first place. And these boys must have done something pretty damn stupid for all three of them to have got nicked. She considered asking them how it had come about – but she did want them on side, so maybe now wasn't a good moment. Save it for later.

With Zequathon behind the wheel (he insisted and she didn't argue, though she was convinced in her mind that she'd be perfectly capable of driving a future-car), Beezee beside him and Anji and Xernic in the back seat, they sped off towards EarthWorld.

At a gesture from Asla the hooded man had raised his axe, but the Doctor had just shaken his head. 'You really wouldn't want to execute me,' he told the three girls.

'Yes, we would,' Africa insisted. 'We really, really like executions. There's lots of blood and they plead for their lives and sometimes there's screaming.' Her eyes were alight. 'I like the screaming best of all.'

'I never scream,' the Doctor said.

'Oh, you would,' said Africa, inching forward involuntarily on her throne. 'You would. After you've pleaded for your life.'

'Really?' said the Doctor. 'What, like this?' He sank to his knees, arms stretched towards the girls imploringly. 'Spare my life! I beg you to spare my life! I know that I am only a humble subject and you are great and important, but I beg you to show your mercy and let me live. If you do this, it will prove how powerful you are – how mighty. Let me live, let me live!' His voice raised into an anguished cry, and he clasped a hand to his chest as he gazed pleadingly into Africa's eyes.

She was on the edge of her seat by now, transfixed. 'Yes!' she cried. 'Oh yes, yes!'

'Sorry, no,' said the Doctor, picking himself up off the floor and dusting himself down. 'You'll never get me to do that, I'm afraid. Not if you're threatening to execute me, anyway. If, however, you agree to stop threatening me… well, let's just say that the only way you'll get me to plead for my life is by promising not to kill me. Is that a bargain?'

Africa's look of exultation had faded, but she shrugged unenthusiastically when Asia turned an enquiring eye to her. 'All right.'

'Mmm,' agreed Antarctica.

'OK, we won't kill you, then,' said Asia. 'Well, not yet. So, what did you want to talk to us about, anyway?'

'Oh,' said the Doctor, casually, 'I'd just like to ask you a few questions about androids, if you'd be so good.'

'We don't know anything about androids!' yelped Antarctica.

The Doctor looked pointedly at the severed head of Mary, Queen of Scots.

'What my sister means –' Asia glared at her – 'is, why should we tell you anything about androids?'

The Doctor began pacing the room. 'Because I'm interested? Because I understand from everyone that you are the planet's experts? Because –' he swung round to face them – 'people are dying and I think you can help.'

Africa's face lit up. 'Oh yes! We can help people to die! Just tell us what you want!'

*

It was as the ground-car drew to a halt that it suddenly hit home for the first time. Really hit home.

Anji was alone.

The Doctor had left her alone. Yes, all right, she wasn't *literally* alone, but…

She was on another planet, in the future, and the Doctor had sent her off with three… *children* that she'd known for a few brief hours! What if she didn't find Fitz? What if, in the meantime, the Doctor disappeared? She had no one here she could turn to. She was also, to all intents and purposes, an escaped criminal; she couldn't enlist any official help. Her only links to her home – to her whole life – were the Doctor, Fitz and the TARDIS.

What if they left without her? It wasn't like being abandoned in a foreign country – she couldn't seek refuge in the twentieth-century embassy.

No, she'd known the Doctor only a very short time, but she didn't believe he'd leave without her. But he was still in the palace – as far as she knew – and so were the men who had sentenced him to death. And while she might be sure he wouldn't deliberately abandon her, she was less certain that the Doctor was immortal.

Fitz had told her all sorts of stories about the Doctor. He'd hinted that he was virtually indestructible. Anji really hoped he wasn't exaggerating. What she wouldn't give to hear Fitz telling one of his tales right now. And that was something that she never thought she'd say.

Fitz had been sitting in a locked room for about twelve hours. Admittedly, his watch thought it was considerably less than that, but it was probably slow. Very slow.

The door was controlled electronically, and despite vast exposure to strange futuristic devices and having picked up a rudimentary working knowledge of video recorders, mobile phones and time machines, he still didn't have the first clue about how to deal with this sort of thing. He'd met a guy in 2001 who'd had a set of lockpicks, and Fitz had been impressed. Apparently this guy had had to get someone to send them from America, and Fitz decided that next time they went to Earth he'd have to persuade the Doctor to stay in one place long enough for Fitz to get some lockpicks sent from America too. Or just go to America and find the lockpick shop, that would do. Fitz knew that in spy thrillers a simple hair grip worked just as well as any professionally crafted instrument, but unfortunately he didn't have any of those, either. Maybe something else to shop for. That and a homing device to stop him continually losing the Doctor. Though the Doctor would be bound to find him soon, anyway. Wouldn't he?

One minute Fitz was staring at the wall, counting the seconds until the Doctor turned up to rescue him. The next he was staring at the hole in the wall where one of those blooming great six-and-three-quarter-foot golden humanoid robots had punched its way in. Fitz suddenly realised – and it rather shocked him – that he was so used to this sort of thing these days that instead of becoming a quivering wreck hiding in a corner, his first thought was a weary, Oh, what *now*?

The robot spoke in perfect – if slightly slow – BBC received pronunciation. 'You will accompany me to my mistresses. They wish to see you.'

'More than one mistress? Lucky old you,' said Fitz. 'You must be exhausted.'

'You will accompany me to my mistresses. They wish to see you.'

'No sense of humour,' said Fitz. 'All right, I'll accompany you, then. You've probably got orders to kill me if I don't or something like that, haven't you?'

'I am authorised to use necessary force,' the robot confirmed.

Fitz sighed. 'Fair enough, Robbie. Lead the way.'

The robot walked back through the jagged hole it'd made. Fitz scrambled after it, catching his coat on a sharp piece of masonry, which irritated him considerably. 'This is brand new!' he complained to the uninterested robot. 'It cost loads! I don't suppose we could stop off in that twentieth-century zone and see if there's a decent clothes shop in the High Street?'

The robot clamped a metal hand round Fitz's arm, but otherwise ignored him.

'How about getting me one of those mending kits like you get in hotels, then?'

The robot kept ignoring him and kept striding jerkily forwards, dragging Fitz after him. Fitz, reflecting that he wouldn't know how to thread a needle anyway, stumbled miserably on.

Anji was standing by a cross-link fence that looked more appropriate for keeping stray dogs off an allotment than saboteurs out of a hi-tech theme park. They were apparently near the spot where the Doctor and Anji had exited, but had decided not to go to that exact place – it was an official gate, the boys had said, and they didn't want to risk their luck any further. Zequathon was systematically chopping at the fence with a pair of wire-cutters, but there was nothing on the other side anyway, so it seemed, just a continuation of the earthen waste they were currently in.

'The fence is just symbolic,' explained Xernic when she questioned this. 'There's an energy barrier the other side, through the hologram, and we'll have to get through that too.'

Anji shuddered slightly, not relishing the prospect of going through a barrier again.

Xernic was still speaking. 'This is just to indicate the line not to be crossed, you see. The whole idea of the walls is that you can't see them – they reflect the image you expect to find in front of you.'

'And I suppose it's a form of psychology,' Anji mused. 'A natural human reaction not to breach obvious barriers.'

'Unless you're a rebel, like us,' said Beezee. ''Cos it's a natural rebel reaction to breach obvious barriers wherever possible.'

Anji sighed. She was perfectly aware that someone had to go and get that idiot Fitz out of whatever trouble he'd got himself into, and that she was probably the best person for the job. She also acknowledged that she needed some technological assistance. But a trio of rebel children was not her idea of ideal companionship.

She'd never been fond of the youth-club type of culture when she'd been a teenager herself, so their company didn't even have the appeal of nostalgia.

She did like Xernic, though (birth name James, he'd confessed earlier in the cell). Anji actually thought the way they'd adapted alien names was quite sweet, and wondered quite how anyone could think this freckle-faced boy could be a threat to national security. He was clearly bossed around by Zequathon and Beezee, but he seemed to take it all in good humour. Anji suspected he'd had to be persuaded – probably bullied – into jumping into action by the other boys. She thought he'd be more at home setting up a rebels' website or distributing subversive pamphlets from a basement somewhere. Zequathon – né Jonathan – had probably turned down the idea of subversive pamphlets because he couldn't read. Oh, bitchy, Anji, she thought with a smile. She wondered if Zequathon's definitely-not-natural blond hair had been one of his first acts of rebellion, and then wondered if anyone had ever told him that it really didn't suit him. Probably not. So she amost certainly shouldn't mention it. Best to keep on his good side, seeing as these three boys were the only ones she'd met so far on the whole planet who hadn't wanted to arrest or kill her.

And she definitely wanted to keep on the good side of Beezee – otherwise known as Timothy – who was clearly the power behind the throne (assuming Zequathon to be the throne) in this set-up. He gave her the creeps – one of those slimy kids who didn't really say much and what he did say was sarcastic, but you just knew he was watching you all the time, taking it all in, waiting to use it to his advantage. So she wasn't going to give him any ammunition. He'd probably become a rebel because he thought they were allowed to pull the wings off insects or something.

Anji stopped herself. Even if she had reservations about these boys personally, the facts remained that not only were they helping her out (and they had no need to do so, less honourable types could easily have dashed off on their own agenda after the Doctor had freed them), but she actually did understand their cause, and had an admiration for those who had the guts to do something about what they believed in rather than sitting at home moaning about it. Speaking as the person who always had to take the initiative and arrange the parties/pay the bills/sort out collections for leaving presents or else they'd never get done, Anji felt that anyone who actually bothered to get off their bottom and do something was automatically several points ahead.

Zequathon had by now managed to create a metre-square hole, big enough for them to crawl through easily. Xernic crouched beside it and flicked a switch on the getting-through-barriers device. Instead of the barren waste ground on the other side of the fence, the water-wall barrier appeared, just as before.

'Yee-hah!' cried Beezee. 'Here we go!'

Anji's stomach lurched – she really wasn't looking forward to this. Should she warn them?

'It might be a good idea to hold hands,' she said, after a moment's thought. 'It's not pleasant, and if you wander the wrong way you could be in there for ever.'

Beezee gave an incredulous snort. 'We *have* done this before, you know. And it's hardly what I'd call difficult – walking in a straight line for a few metres.'

'Fine,' said Anji. 'You go first, then. OK?'

Beezee shrugged, and knelt down to crawl through the hole. Zequathon followed him.

Anji looked at Xernic, still holding up the device. 'Are you OK to get through? You're not going to get left behind?'

He smiled shyly at her. He was probably unused to people worrying about him specifically, rather than him as representative of an oppressed culture. 'I'll be fine,' he said. 'The hole'll hold up for as long as I keep the machine switched on and in range. I can just go through and close it up the other side.'

'That's all right, then,' Anji smiled back at him.

'But – if you like…'

'Yes?'

'Well… I'll hold your hand if you want.'

Anji's smile got broader. She was pretty sure he needed the reassuring human contact as much as she did, but she was grateful for the offer anyway. 'Thanks,' she said. 'Oh – and I won't tell the others, OK?'

He grinned, and held out his hand.

She'd seen the Prehistoric Zone before, obviously, but there hadn't been a brachiosaur in her bit of it back then. She was totally taken aback by its size. Skeletons in museums and giant cinema screens still hadn't prepared her for this. You stood next to an elephant in a zoo and it was huge, but you could feed it buns and peanuts, and, theoretically, imagine climbing on its back with a bit of help. This thing… no way. She'd heard it said that the human brain couldn't visualise numbers above a hundred. It was now patently obvious that it couldn't comprehend animals larger than a double-decker bus, either. She just stood and stared, open-mouthed.

'It's all right,' said Xernic reassuringly, coming up from behind her. 'You don't have to be scared. As long as you keep out of its way it won't bother you. I've read the guidebook: it's what's known as a herbivore. That means it'll only eat you if your name's Herb.'

Anji considered several responses to this, and finally decided to hope he was joking and ignore it. 'How near are we to the border where we lost Fitz?' she asked.

'From what you and the Doctor said,' said Beezee, pointing, 'it's a few kilometres over that way.'

A few kilometres! Thank goodness for the Elastoplast.

'Of course,' Beezee went on, 'I'd have more faith in the estimate if either of you had bothered to notice what was on the other side of the barrier there.'

Again, Anji decided that it wasn't worth the hassle of responding. She set off in the direction he'd indicated – still limping slightly, but nowhere near as badly as before – and the boys followed. The brachiosaur lifted its head from the grass it was munching, and watched their progress.

Fitz was slightly fed up. The robot, obviously not

programmed to cope with Fitz's attempts to lag behind/wander off/stop to smell the roses, was now carrying him over its shoulder. With every clunking step, Fitz's rather long nose was bumping painfully into the robot's solid back.

This uncomfortable position also meant that Fitz had been more or less unable to observe exactly where he was being taken. A strange tingly sensation told him they'd crossed a barrier somehow and were in one of the zones, but quite which he didn't know. There were no motor sounds and he detected a distinct aroma of vinegar, but that could mean anything from the Fish and Chip Shop Zone to the Land of Pickled Onions. Which reminded him that he was starving. The robot finally came to a halt. Good. Maybe it was tea time. Next time Fitz left the TARDIS, he'd have to remember to bring a packed lunch. Ham sandwich. Packet of crisps – the proper sort, with a little blue bag of salt inside. Couple of tomatoes and a big wedge of fruit cake. Yep, that'd go down a treat right now.

Lost in snack-related dreams, Fitz didn't realise the robot was dropping him until he was on the floor. Now he had bruised knees and elbows to add to his sore nose. He was really getting fed up. Groaning, he rolled over and sat up.

The Nefertiti girl was standing in front of him, hands on hips. Only she wasn't dressed Egyptian style any more, or in flapper gear: she wore a sky-blue Roman dress-thingy, with her hair piled high on her head and fastened with tortoiseshell combs.

Fitz shifted his gaze to the right. There was the

Nefertiti girl again, dressed Roman-style again, only this time her dress was orange. And to her right, there she was in green, a small crocodile with a pink ribbon around its neck clasped to her chest, as though it were a pet cat or rabbit. Fitz looked to that girl's right. There didn't seem to be any more of them, but he swivelled right the way round anyway to check. He reached the one in blue again, and decided that there were just the three of them. None of them were saying anything, although there was a faint ticking noise coming from somewhere. He couldn't tell where.

Obviously up to him to break the ice. 'Hi,' he said. 'I'm Fitz.'

'We know,' said one.

'Fitz Fortune,' said the next.

'You're our very favourite singer,' sighed the third.

Fitz blinked, wondering if he really was in a parallel universe after all.

'We were just going out for a treat,' said the first – blue – girl.

'You can come with us,' said orange to her right.

'Uhhh?' said Fitz. 'Um, you must be the President's android daughters, right?'

The girl in blue looked scathingly at him. 'You should choose your words more carefully for greater accuracy,' she said. 'How could the human President have android daughters?'

'I meant,' Fitz replied, sensing it was going to be a really long day, 'that you're the androids of the President's daughters. The ones they made to look like them. How many of you are there?'

Green-dress giggled. 'There is only one of us. We just happen to be divided into three parts. I'm Antarctica.'

'What, where the penguins come from?' asked Fitz.

'This is Africa –' she indicated the girl in the orange dress – 'and this is Asia. Asia is the oldest of us.'

'Weren't you all built on the same day, then?' said Fitz, who had already forgotten which girl was which.

'Don't be silly,' said, um, penguin-woman… Antarctica. 'We weren't built at all.'

'You're rather slow, aren't you?' said Asia. 'Don't you get it?'

The last girl, Africa, walked slowly around Fitz. She ran a finger down his cheek. 'I could explain it to him,' she breathed sensually. Fitz struggled to remember that she was only about thirteen years old. 'I could carve the answer slowly into his flesh, so he feels his stupidity with every drop of spilled blood.' Fitz's excitement died as fast as it had arrived.

'Africa…' said Asia, warningly. She seemed to be the one in charge.

Antarctica took her sister's hand and dragged her away from Fitz. 'You're not to hurt him!' she scolded. Fitz breathed a sigh of relief. 'He's my pet and I'm going to keep him for ever and if he's naughty and has to be punished *I'll* do it.' Fitz's relief left him. What was this? Did they think he was a lapdog or a hamster (or a tame crocodile) or something? Obviously another rule in the Doctor's little companion contract: if thou art rescued from a mad woman, the ones rescuing you shall be yet more loony still.

'You know, I'm really grateful to you girls – or

whatever you are – for rescuing me from that mad researcher woman, but I really ought to be getting back to my friends now...'

The golden robot moved a step closer. Even without any facial expression, it still appeared suddenly menacing.

Antarctica giggled. 'Don't be silly, Fitz Fortune! You don't need any other friends now you've got us. Now, you have to dress up for our treat.'

Fitz looked down at his ripped coat. 'I suppose I'm not very presentable,' he said, resigning himself to hanging around for a bit until a chance to escape from these scary teenagers presented itself (please, God, make that soon). 'What did you have in mind?'

It had taken Fitz three goes before he'd managed to get the sheet thing to resemble the toga it was supposed to be, and not a do-it-yourself Hallowe'en ghost costume. His legs were a bit too skinny (and hairy) for comfort, but he'd happily wandered around in shorts back on Earth in the old days, and this wasn't really that much different in terms of flesh exposure. The laurel wreath actually quite suited him: he thought he looked aristocratic. Or at least, more so than usual. He probably wouldn't have gone out like that by choice, but he could cope. Until Antarctica put the collar and lead on him.

She'd only laughed at his protests. He was her pet, and he was coming with her on their 'treat', and she couldn't possibly let him run free, could she? The indignity of this really hurt. The only plus side was that he'd mentioned that pets needed to be fed, and she'd agreed. But then she'd looked at her crocodile, so it was potentially not such a good thing after all.

After what had happened last time, Fitz had decided not to point out to the girls the incongruity of wearing wristwatches with their Roman-style outfits – and then he looked and realised they weren't actually wearing wristwatches, so why had he thought that? Maybe memories of *Ben Hur* at the cinema. No, it was because he could still hear that stupid ticking. What was that all about?

Anyway, so now the four of them were sitting on deckchairs, looking down on a Roman arena, with a tray of goblets on a trestle table in front of them and a heaped plate of food on each lap. So that was good. Unless they were fattening him up. But the crocodile had a plate of its own. Some bits of the dish were definitely chicken, or at least some sort of bird, and it tasted quite good; Fitz was shovelling it down. Asia then explained that all their ancient-world recipes came from a book about a genuine Greek chef called Aristophanes. Fitz, who had once got accidentally trapped in the classical section of the TARDIS library for two days, and had as a consequence formed an appreciation of Greek and Roman plays upon discovering that they contained a hell of a lot of sex and violence (especially sex), remembered that Aristophanes, as well as writing a play called *The Birds*, had also written ones called *The Frogs* and *The Wasps*, and so decided he wasn't that hungry after all. He picked up a goblet and took a swig of wine instead. And then realised why the zone smelled so much of vinegar, and wished he hadn't. Hopefully the entertainment was better than the catering.

Over the opposite side of the arena, a gate thudded open. A skinny man stumbled into the ring, dressed in gladiatorial costume. He was holding a trident in one hand, awkwardly, as if not quite knowing what it was. There were distinct big-cat-like roars coming from somewhere behind him. 'And this is the treat, is it?' asked Fitz.

Antarctica nodded. 'Isn't it fab? Ancient World Zone is my second favourite zone of all; after Twentieth-Century London of course. But it's Africa's most favouritest zone, and she got to choose the treat this time.' She leaned towards him and whispered conspiratorially, 'She likes to see the blood, you see.'

Fitz did see, and didn't like it. Didn't like any of this. Typical: they re-create Earth for entertainment and fixate on the nastiest, most bloodthirsty bits. He now understood why his dates – and yes, he'd had a few, although admittedly they were mostly first dates – didn't want to see *Dr No* and preferred some Cliff Richard let's-do-the-show-right-here guff instead. There really was enough violence in the world – worlds – without having it in your leisure time, too. He didn't *want* to see a lion tear some poor little Christian apart; given the choice he'd have Cliff and the gang sweeping in in their double-decker bus any time. And he never thought he'd say that.

The man in the ring had backed as far away as possible from the lion sounds. Fitz stared down, and even from such a distance he could see the horror in the man's face. He turned to Antarctica, his face impassive. 'That's not an android, is it,' he said – statement, not question. 'Everyone here is supposed to be androids, but no one is – not me, not you, not that poor man down there.'

She rolled her eyes in an exasperated but amused fashion. 'Well, *they're* androids, silly,' she said, pointing to the golden giants just behind Fitz. 'And the lion is, of course. Cutesy, cutesy lion!' The last was called into the arena, as another gate thudded open and the magnificent beast prowled out on to the scattered sand. It didn't look quite right – legs too long, and the tail was more like a horse's – but the teeth were spot on.

The man in the arena raised the shaking trident. It didn't look very effective.

Antarctica was cooing to the lion; Africa was leaning forward, eyes gleaming with bloodlust. The third triplet, Asia, cooler than the others, smiled slyly over at Fitz. 'This is our world. They made us build it for them, but now it's ours and we're going to keep it. If people insist on coming in, they have to play our games. That's the price of admission. So don't try to rescue him. You're not allowed.' She gestured at the menacing golden robots.

And Fitz realised with a horrific sudden-stomach-collapse feeling that he hadn't even been considering rescuing the man. Had it been the Doctor down there, now, then he would have jumped into the ring in a second and sod the lion and its huge teeth. But it just hadn't occurred to him to risk his life for this weedy-looking stranger. Damn, there went his patting himself on the back in the TARDIS later on for all the heroic deeds done today. But – yes, of course – surely the trips weren't serious about killing this bloke. They wouldn't be loony enough to commit murder out in the open like this, would they? Or – this was even more likely! – maybe the gladiator man was an android after all and they were just joking. Ha! A funny joke! That's what it was! Or, maybe, just maybe, the man would win.

But he didn't.

The camera reluctantly panned away from the blood-soaked corpse, leaving the skinny man lying there, eyes wide open and staring, the look of disbelief and horror frozen on his face by death. The Doctor and Asia had watched the whole performance in silence; the other two hadn't. Antarctica had been cheering for the darling lion; Africa had been letting out a series of almost sexual moans at each tear of flesh. Now she was panting, eyes shining, a grin of victory and fulfilment.

The Doctor asked casually, 'Does she tear the wings off butterflies, too?'

'My sister,' said Asia, 'finds enjoyment in many places.'

'How odd,' said the Doctor. 'Considering she's an android.'

Africa and Antarctica were suddenly silent, swinging round to face the Doctor.

'What makes you think that?' asked Asia.

'I have a gut instinct in these matters. I've been watching you, watching that –' he gestured to the screen – 'and it wasn't *quite* right. Ninety-nine per cent there, but that's not near enough. Perhaps I've met too many androids before.'

'Have you?'

The Doctor frowned. 'Yes, I expect I have. Anyway, it seemed the sort of thing I'd do, if I were a mad teenager. The triplets were obviously brought up in a restrictive atmosphere, with a father who cares more about a distant planet than about people. Do you have a mother, by the way? I don't mean you, of course – the circuit board's your mother – I mean the real triplets.' There was a stony silence. Then Antarctica burst into tears. 'I see,' said the Doctor. 'Don't ask about the mother. You really have been programmed with all the responses, haven't you? They create their own tiny Earth here in the palace – madness often goes hand in hand with genius – and then are asked to engineer entire worlds, for real. Probably not asked, told.' He began to pace up and down in front of the three. 'They'd be torn between exultation and resentment. Creating whole worlds of their own – a dream come true. But having done so, how could they return to the little prison of their world here? Natural enough for them to want to create androids in their own image – a common form of narcissism. And I'm sure the people round here had got complacent in their security procedures – after all, who'd expect young girls to want to live in a park instead of a palace? After so many years locked up, they must have thought they were institutionalised. Didn't expect them to escape. Didn't expect them to start killing people.'

Asia sneered at him. 'You're so stupid. That's exactly what they *did* expect. Why do you think they kept us locked up all these years? They *knew* we'd keep killing people. After we'd killed our own mother.'

'My turn my turn my turn!'

After the man's death throes had finally ceased, and the battery-operated lion had gone back to whatever electric jungle it had come from, the trips had started to row. Antarctica seemed to think it was her turn for a treat now. Africa was obviously quite happy to gaze at the corpse for a bit longer. She'd probably go down and start prodding it in a minute. Asia was regarding them both in a scornful, yet strangely indulgent way. The Big Sister. Fitz thought she was probably the most stable of the three. But then that was rather like saying that the Pacific was probably the least wet of all the oceans.

In the end, in the manner of foot-stampers everywhere, Antarctica got her own way. She was to have her treat. What would it be? Fitz wondered. A re-creation of the St Valentine's Day massacre (romantic yet blood-soaked)? The English Civil War (possibly a problem: Fitz'd place the trips as Roundhead by inclination, but they'd undoubtedly prefer the Cavalier costumes)?

Fitz tried to put on a mask of eager anticipation while Antarctica decided. He didn't really succeed. The look of shock when he heard what she had to say was perfectly genuine, though.

'I want a Fitz Fortune concert!'

'Pardon?' said Fitz.

Antarctica ignored him. 'I do I do I do! I want a Fitz Fortune concert by Fitz Fortune *now!*'

'Do I get any say in the...' (glare from Antarctica), 'no, obviously not.'

'Fitz Fortune is my favourite singer ever and I love him and I want a concert *now.*'

Fitz marvelled at his successful self-publicity. How come he'd never got this sort of attention from teenage girls back home? Of course, they had actually heard him sing. And they weren't, on the whole, homicidal lunatics.

'Ladies, ladies, I'd love to oblige, really I would, but I'm afraid I don't have my guitar with me – and Fitz Fortune sans guitar is just not Fitz Fortune at all...'

Antarctica glared at him. Asia turned to stare. Even Africa tore her eyes away from the gladiator's bloody remains. And Fitz realised that saying 'ha-ha, they're homicidal lunatics' in his thoughts was one thing, but for goodness' sake he'd just seen them have a man ripped apart and just because they looked like the babes in the wood didn't mean they were any less likely to kill him than any of the other homicidal lunatics he'd met (and there'd been a few). 'Um, do you possibly have a backing tape?' he asked.

Africa had wanted to hold the concert in the Roman arena, because then if Fitz wasn't very good they could set the lion on him and at least have fun that way. Fitz had tried a half-hearted 'my friends will be looking for me' defence, but it didn't seem to worry them.

Antarctica had ridiculed her sister's suggestion that

her beloved Fitz Fortune might be a bit poor, because he was 'the greatest pop star in the whole world'. Fitz, however, did not find this comforting.

Asia had remarked that the twentieth century was probably the best setting for a twentieth-century act, and Antarctica had jumped up and down going 'Yes! Yes! Yes!', so off to the Twentieth-Century London Zone they went. They rode in a horse-drawn chariot to the border, but Fitz barely noticed. He didn't even twitch when Antarctica's crocodile wandered over and sat down on his foot. For the first time in his life, he had real head-pounding, butterfly-stomach, eyes-staring, legs-frozen stage fright.

The trips must have some major publicity machine going. No more Elvis: every Twentieth-Century London Zone wall had a 'Fitz Fortune' poster pasted on it. Fitz was pictured in purple crushed velvet, raising a knowingly sexy eyebrow to the unseen crowd; full-length in black leather, microphone in hand; in high-necked Beatle suit (and, more disturbingly, a Beatle haircut in place of his scruffy locks), and with an all-girl blonde backing group who looked suspiciously familiar. The first was Fitz's favourite: he thought the unknown artist had definitely managed to capture the essential him. He wondered if he could half-inch one for his room back in the TARDIS. If he got out of it all alive, of course. At least the posters didn't say FOR ONE NIGHT ONLY.

The concert hall was superb, a far cry from Molly's in Soho, where he used to strut his funky stuff when he was much younger and another person. He had a dressing room with a gold star, and a big bowl of lavender-scented talcum powder (he assumed this was another historical detail they'd misinterpreted somehow, but didn't want to enquire too deeply – or perhaps stars really did have talc in their rooms, you know, in case of pop star's foot or something, and he just didn't know about it 'cos he hadn't been one). He flirted briefly with the idea of escape, but there were giant gold robots outside the door. And they'd given him a Fender-Stratocaster with FITZ! painted on it in glitter, so if he had to go, this was as good a way as any.

He'd changed into a gold lamé suit and black silk shirt, all a perfect fit. He looked in the mirror before he left the room. Cool. Damn cool.

The gold robots led him out to the stage. He was expecting to feel ridiculous – him in front of an audience of three. But the lights were shining so brightly into his eyes that he couldn't tell who was out there. And the atmosphere – it wasn't the echoing silence of a near-empty room: it was the hush of anticipation. He stepped forward to the microphone, and played his first chord. And suddenly, to his great surprise, Fitz Fortune lived again.

He gave them 'Groovy Weekend', 'You Broke My Heart, Bikini Girl' and 'Upside Down in Venice', his all-time classics. He gave them 'Song for Sam', which he'd meant as a romantic gesture, but she'd said the title sounded like a serial killer. Then a medley of his personal hit parade: 'Shakin' All Over', 'Three Steps to Heaven', 'Chantilly Lace' and, in a brief moment of desperation, '(I wanna be) Bobby's Girl'. He finished the whole thing off with a frantic, sweat-soaked, shimmering rendition of 'Twist and Shout', and yelled his thanks to the audience.

The crowd went wild.

The lights dimmed. There were robots to each side of the stage. Fitz dived into the audience and began to run as fast as he could towards the far end of the hall. To his surprise, there actually was a bit of a crowd in the auditorium – perhaps some of them were even real. They were on their feet; a standing ovation. Boy, how they'd loved him. But he had been good. Better, he'd been great. A happy memory to while away his time when safely back with the Doctor. Which would be soon, soon, soon…

He was halfway down the aisle now, and he could hear a triplet screaming in rage – Antarctica, his mind said, but he wasn't turning to look. The screams were picked up all round – but hey! They weren't screams of rage, they were screams of. delight, screams of worship… The crowd was surging towards him, arms outstretched, crying out its love for him. He pushed his way through, not caring if he was breaking hearts as he went. They grabbed at his clothes, his hair, tearing out bits from the roots. How come all pop stars weren't bald? Nearly there, nearly free. The triplets' voices were distant, the crowd was preventing them getting through. He was going to make it. Fitz 'Freedom' Fortune. Nearly there.

Two yards from the doors, and Fitz was brought down by a gang of howling girlies. He was really embarrassed.

Back in his dressing room, changing into a non-ripped suit (purple velvet), Fitz sighed. It wasn't just that he'd been recaptured and locked up. For the first time ever, he'd been wanted desperately by a horde of screaming women, and he wasn't allowed to capitalise on it. They wanted him so bad. Lying on the ground, he'd been grabbed and stroked and touched and, oooh, don't start thinking about it all now because he'd be close to tears. One of the audience – a stunning redhead of twenty-ish, who, you never know, may not have been an android – had thrust her address and contact number in his pocket. A gold robot, acting on orders from Antarctica, had removed it and scrunched it up. Fitz, Antarctica had said as he was carried away from all the hot babes, was her pet. No one else could have him. And she wanted a Fitz Fortune concert every single day and no more naughty attempts to escape. Fitz didn't think he'd be able to oblige concert-wise, even to save his neck – now the adrenalin had gone, he wanted to sleep for a week.

But he had been so good. In many ways, he didn't blame her. They'd recorded the concert, and left him with a Walkman-like device (despite having travelled all round the universe he still felt dead clever when he recognised future-Earth gadgets) so he could listen to how fab he was and psych himself up for next time.

He'd been good before, back in the old days, and he'd

known it – not in any big-headed way, but he wasn't one for false modesty, either. In the wannabe rock-star league, he'd been one without the opportunities rather than without the talent. After a few years gadding about the universe, though, with not all that much time for practice, he'd expected to be a bit rusty, not bloody-hell-better-than-ever.

And then he realised.

It wasn't him.

One of the things that Fitz had been trying to shut from his mind was his recent discovery that he – well, that he wasn't Fitz. It was a bit complicated, and his understanding of it was hindered by the way his mind automatically stuck its fingers in its ears and yelled LA LA LA CAN'T HEAR YOU every time the subject threatened to come up.

What had happened was: Fitz had been replaced with a copy; the real Fitz whisked off elsewhere. Over the years, memories of the copy were imprinted on to a lump of biomass, until only a Chinese-whispers version of the Fitz-copy remained. The Fitz-copy had then been taken to the TARDIS, and the TARDIS had 'remembered' it into the Fitz it'd known in the first place. Neither the new Fitz nor the Doctor had realised he'd only been a copy to start with. And the real Fitz – the biological, born-on-Earth, went-on the-run-with-the-Doctor Fitz – well, he grew old waiting for the Doctor to rescue him; he lived for thousands of tormented years, and then he was killed.

Fitz was dead. Long live the Fitz-copy.

Real Fitz had been good at the guitar; Real Fitz could

sing. The TARDIS had known that, and remembered him thus. Not as a guy who hadn't played for a while and needed a bit of practice, but as somebody who was bang-up-to-date, right-that-second damn good.

He wasn't real. This wasn't him. No, it was *him*, but he wasn't Fitz. He wasn't really anybody. Not an actual person at all.

Fitz – the Fitz-thing – threw off the headphones and curled up in the corner of the dressing room, hugging its knees. It suspected that the real Fitz would have cried. But it wasn't the real Fitz, so that wasn't allowed.

Chapter Four
A Man is the Sum of His (False) Memories

While still cursing her heels, Anji tried to count her blessings, and thanked goodness that she'd chosen casual slacks yesterday – was it only yesterday? No, surely not – she'd have to get out her Psion and work it out. Anyway, whenever it was, she was glad she'd not gone for a suit. It might have given her a psychological advantage in the earlier cross-examination, but a restrictive skirt would have made things twice as bad as they already were – her feet would be hitting the ground twice as often for a start. Mind you, now she came to think of it, she couldn't keep wearing the same outfit for ever, could she? Did the TARDIS have a wardrobe? Or at least a laundry? Thank goodness she'd kept spare knickers and a roll-on deodorant in her bag. She tried to surreptitiously sniff her right armpit. Still bearable. How much longer it would stay that way, though, with all the to-ing and fro-ing she was doing... She wasn't particularly keen on walking in general – fifteen minutes to Canary Wharf tube in the morning, up and down the platform a few times, and then three minutes to the office at the other end. Same in reverse in the evening, with only a stroll to a restaurant or sandwich shop in between. Strictly A-to-B functional stuff. No time for blisters to develop. And definitely no dinosaurs.

She was dealing with it now in an 'it's not quite real' sense. She was outside her body, watching herself as though she were in a movie or a dream. There she was, just there, dressed in designer casuals, a Gucci bag over her shoulder, trekking across a future-prehistoric plain with three adolescent boys. There were monsters all around, and yes, theoretically they could kill her and she should be terrified, but she couldn't shake the feeling that if they did attack, a sign would spring up saying GAME OVER and real life would begin again.

At the same time, her relations with the three boys seemed real and direct. Zequathon and Beezee tended to lead the way, with Anji and Xernic paired behind. She was feeling very protective of the red-headed boy. And she'd revised her opinions of the others, too – they were loud and a bit aggressive, but basically 'good kids'. Even Beezee, who still really wasn't her type of person but was winding her up less now. Because they had to get on. These boys were all risking their lives to save someone they didn't know. So she had to like them.

She'd asked Xernic to tell her about life on this strange, past-obsessed, White Anglo-Saxon Protestant-type world. She still didn't really get it. It didn't seem that different to her Earth in a lot of ways – fairly impersonal, with the welfare of a few more important than that of the masses, though the few preached the opposite (yup). Those in power were tolerated if not respected by most citizens (definitely yup), but even when the people disapproved of something, only a few – like the ANJI boys – actually did something about it (yup – and signing the odd petition at university didn't count, she told herself ruefully). A reasonable percentage of New Jupitans (she extrapolated from Xernic's impassioned ANJI sales pitch) thought that Earth was revered too much, moaned about it a bit in bars and thought it was a bit much that Earth didn't even send them the odd aid package, and if they had to choose they'd be happy to go with the whole New Jupiter/own-identity thing. But no one was forcing them to choose, so they merrily plodded on their own sweet way and abided by the President's rules (still sounding very familiar). There had been a few more rumblings than usual lately – and yes, it was possible that rebellion had been in the air – but the promise of EarthWorld and the revenue it was expected to bring had successfully crushed them. Bread and circuses, thought Anji. People didn't change.

The details were different, though. There were worries about the Presidential succession (it being a hereditary position, and the President's children apparently insane and confined to the palace); and the attitude to death, as seen in the casual acceptance of capital punishment, seemed medieval too. And she hadn't seen anyone apart from herself who looked other than white in appearance, which was a bit worrying. Terrifying thought: were they all extinct? No, that was silly. Because thinking about it, there had been no comments, no pointing, not even a question. And that implied (a) she wasn't the future equivalent of a dodo, and (b) a degree of generic tolerance here that she was very pleased to see, and actually a far cry from her own time, where one was always aware of differences, whether in a positive or negative or an 'of course it doesn't matter' kind of way. This was obviously just a white-dominated area. The New Jupitan Buckinghamshire or Surrey, rather than its North London.

There was a teenage blonde girl watching them from under a tree.

Anji was suddenly back in the game. The girl looked rather like a young Drew Barrymore, but wearing a leopard-skin leotard.

The three boys stopped dead in their tracks. 'Oh, gosh,' said Xernic. 'That's one of the mad princesses.'

'No,' said Anji, 'it's an android built to look like one of the mad princesses, remember? It thinks it's a cave person, it won't bother us. And if it does, you can zap it with that android-zapper thing. Come on.'

They carried on towards the girl. Anji was almost amused to see that the three boys, even the bluff Zequathon, seemed more nervous of a replicant adolescent girl than they did of the dirty great full-of-teeth dinosaurs they'd passed earlier.

The girl sauntered from under her tree to meet them. 'Ug ug,' she said in a cultured voice not befitting a cave person at all. 'You're not supposed to be here. Are you Fitz's friends?'

Anji's stomach did a strange leap. The game had changed.

'Who wants to know?' said Zequathon.

'I do.' She opened her hand, showing them a device that looked like a TV remote control. 'See this button here? That will summon all the androids in the area to this spot. And this red one? That will enrage them.

They'll tear apart anything in their paths.'

Anji did not like being talked to like this, especially by stuck-up children. 'Then you'll be torn apart too. Or does that not worry you? You can just go into a garage for repairs?'

The girl laughed, raising the device.

Anji turned. 'Xernic, quick! Zap her!'

The boy fumbled desperately with the silver box, pointing it at the girl. She froze, finger still poised over the controls. Anji waved a hand in front of her face: no reaction.

'Thank goodness for that,' she said. 'Now, the question is: what was all that about? And how does she know about Fitz, anyway?'

'He's our pet,' said the girl. 'Ha-ha, fooled you.' And she pressed all the buttons at once.

'So the triplets' mother's not actually dead?' said the Doctor. 'I don't think it technically counts as matricide, in that case.'

'Doesn't matter,' said one of the triplets gloomily. 'Still our fault.'

'And you can hardly call her "alive",' said another. 'So Father doesn't care what it technically counts as.'

'Hmm.' The Doctor pondered. 'Their father – forgive me if I don't refer to him as "your father" – seems to have singularly failed to be paternally understanding about this. I'm a great believer in showing people the errors of their ways, rather than just locking them up, you know. The triplets were very young, and if they didn't mean her harm…'

'We loved Mother,' said android-Asia, simply.

'Tell me all about it,' the Doctor said.

'Mother was a scientist,' she told him. 'They say we inherited our technical abilities from her. But her field was genetics, not robotics. Hanstrum was the one who taught us robotics. Hanstrum? You really don't know anything, do you. Hanstrum is Father's chief technician. He was the only person apart from Father who was allowed to visit Mother in her imprisonment. No, she hadn't done anything wrong, silly. It's an old Earth custom. A woman who wants to have children is kept in confinement until she has them. Mother was in confinement for years before she had us. We were allowed out, for a while, when we were young. We don't really remember it.

'We don't like New Jupiter, though. We wish we'd been born on Earth. We've read every book and seen every film about Earth that Father owns, and we think it's wonderful. Hanstrum says there are people on New Jupiter who don't like Earth. When we're the President, we're going to have them all killed. Yes, Father says he's going to execute them, but he never does. And anyway, he can only execute them if they've broken one of his laws. We're going to make lots more laws when we're the President. Mother didn't want us to be President, though. She didn't like us killing things. She was going to tell Father not to let us be President; that's why we killed her. We were very young, though, we don't really remember what happened. Mother was calling us... then she was lying on the floor. Father and Hanstrum found us with her. And she hasn't woken up since. We miss her.'

'You don't have feelings,' said the Doctor. 'You only feel as if you do.'

Anji cursed her heels and her short legs again. She'd been here before. This was level two of the game. Level one: caveman and pterosaur. Level two... well, she didn't know what half these things were. Not that she was a dinosaur expert, but she was fairly confident that several had more basis in animation than in prehistoric reality. The bright pink polka dots were a bit of a giveaway. That detached bit of her mind was still telling her that being chased by cartoonlike monsters was just ridiculous. She was running away from things that wanted to kill her, and she was more irritated than scared.

She could tell the boys were scared, though, and she – the token grown-up – had to deal with it. Poor Xernic was desperately trying not to show his terror in front of the other boys, and valiantly zapping any android that got too close. It was working, too, but there was only one of him and lots of them. What was really annoying Anji was that she could still see in her mind that smug blonde kid laughing at them as she pressed the buttons.

'Why didn't the zapper work?' Xernic had gasped as they had begun to run.

'It must be a pile of junk,' Zequathon had said. 'Ditch it.'

'No!' Anji had dived back and rescued it 'Don't just give up! Try it again!'

And, as the dinosaurs began to close in on them, he had done so. And this time, it had worked.

'Try to clear a path away from the barrier,' Anji had instructed. 'They're trying to herd us towards it so we'll be trapped.'

And again, brave Xernic had done his best. But inevitably, with monsters closing in from all sides, they were getting closer and closer to the invisible barrier. The Edge. The Point of No Return. Game Over. You Have No Lives Left.

Closer and closer. And then there they were.

The creatures were slightly wary of the barrier. They must have been programmed to avoid it – or perhaps, as electrical beings, they could sense it; like forces repelling, or something like that. That – and the zapper – were giving Anji and the boys the tiniest degree of breathing space. Or, to be more accurate, the tiniest space in which to carry on breathing. Life – for a limited time only, Anji thought. Hurry! It won't be here for long.

The dinosaurs moved in on them. And in the distance, Anji could see the blonde girl approaching, laughing.

The android-Asia had seemed subdued after telling her tale. She'd wandered off on her own, as the other two told their versions of the same story. They seemed to expect sympathy. They didn't get it.

'I came here because I thought there was some sort of robot revolt in progress,' said the Doctor. 'Obviously there isn't – just your ridiculous selfish doubles causing mayhem. So I really don't think there's much point in me spending another few hours while you lie on a completely unnecessary psychiatrist's couch. I have friends who may be in danger.'

Then android-Africa began laughing.

Android-Antarctica tried to shush her, but it was too late. The Doctor had spun round to see what was so funny over his right shoulder – and saw the screen.

'That's Anji!' he cried. 'What are you doing?'

'A dinosaur can break a person's arm with a single blow,' said Africa.

The Doctor frowned. 'I think you'll find that's swans.'

'Can I get a swan?' Africa asked Asia, who'd returned.

'Call those monsters off!' the Doctor ordered.

'Shan't!' said Africa.

'Can't,' said Asia.

'Or won't?' asked the Doctor. 'How do the triplets get through the force barriers between zones?'

'We have our ways.'

'You have your ways or they have their ways? You really should stop confusing yourselves with the real things, you know.'

'They have their ways,' said Asia, reluctantly. 'Devices.'

'Oh, they have *devices*. Well, why didn't you say so?' The Doctor moved closer to the images of Anji and the boys, nose almost touching the screen. 'Of course, if they have *devices* that makes all the difference.' He spun back round to face the triplets. 'But you can control things from here. I know you can.' Direct to Asia: 'Where did you go?'

'I'm sorry?'

'You left. Went into another room. Not long after the real princesses left the Roman arena. And now –' he indicated the screen again – 'at least one of them is in another zone. I'm sure they do have devices enabling them to walk around at will, but I doubt they'd leave it to chance in the event of, say, loss of device or risk of discovery. Now I admit I'm skipping a number of steps between first premise and conclusion, but I think you are able to control the barriers from here. Excuse me.' He darted past the girls, behind the thrones. And there was a door.

He found himself in a control room. A very small one, but the banks of switches, dials and levers were unmistakable. A small screen showed a diagram which he presumed was a map of the EarthWorld zone barriers, and another echoed the scene that was shown in the throne room. 'You didn't hide this very well,' the Doctor called back into the throne room. 'Anyone could just walk in, and where would your secret identities be then?'

'But no one ever visits us,' said Asia, coming through to join him. 'And as there are no big signs reading "we are really androids", it's irrelevant anyway. What could anyone tell from this?'

The Doctor gave her a hard stare. 'That you have rather more of an involvement in the centre than you should. Which, considering all the suspicious deaths and so on, is quite enough to call for a further investigation, I should say. Now, tell me how to call off those monsters. Or shut down the barriers.'

'No,' said Asia.

'Why not? What use is it to you if my friends are killed?'

'My sister obviously has her reasons.'

'And how long do you think your "sister" will last once I've told people exactly what's going on here?'

'And how long do you think *you're* going to last now you've said that? Africa!'

But it wasn't Africa who came through the door. It was the sixteenth-century executioner, complete with axe. Africa was behind him, though, laughing excitedly. A glimpse at the small screen showed the Doctor that Anji and the boys were being herded against the barrier, prehistoric monsters approaching from all sides. He darted to the control bank, and began to flick switches and swivel dials at random.

'No!' cried Asia, and leapt on the Doctor's back. He threw her effortlessly to the ground, and continued his work. The executioner stalked closer.

'Kill him!' called Africa. 'Chop him into bits!' The Doctor carried on pulling levers. 'Little bits!' Africa added.

The axe was raised above the android's head, and began to sweep down. With all the time in the world, the Doctor flicked a final switch, looked up at the plan to see one of the white lines wink off, glanced at the second image to watch the barrier shimmer into visibility and Anji and the boys breaking for freedom, and stepped to one side as the axe fell.

Sparks flew from the desk. On the screen, more white lines disappeared, one by one.

The Doctor admired the blue flicker that surrounded the android momentarily, then stepped over the fallen Asia, putting out a hand to help her up as he went, dodged round Africa in the doorway, and bounded through the throne room past a stricken and shrieking Antarctica. Once in the corridor, he began to run.

Fitz. Fitz.
Fitz?
Confusion.
Are you Fitz? Answer: yes, no, unsure.
Unsure.

Anji and the ANJI boys were running as fast as they could. The dinosaurs hadn't followed them immediately – confused by the breakdown of the barrier (could androids get confused? Some sort of signal breakdown?) – and had given them a head start.

If this was what Fitz had seen earlier, Anji could understand his enthusiastic reaction. Golden sun shone down on to fantastically sculpted sand dunes, filling some tiny inner part of Anji with a desperate longing for a bucket and spade. There was a massive pyramid just over there – just how much of the planet did this theme park take up, anyway? Or could they possibly have bigger-inside-than-out technology, like the Doctor's TARDIS? The boys were looking less stunned – they'd probably been here before on one of their sabotage missions.

'This is incredible,' Anji said. 'Just incredible.'

'It's the Eggy-put Zone,' Xernic informed her.

Anji gave him a look. '*Ee-jipt*. It's pronounced Ee-jipt. And don't stop running!'

A cat streaked across their path, followed by another, and another. That was either lots of good luck or lots of bad luck, but Anji couldn't remember which. Maybe it didn't count if they weren't black cats. And she didn't believe in superstitious rubbish. And anyway, surely her luck couldn't get any worse so it *must* mean good luck. In which case, she decided she would believe in it after all.

The dinosaurs, recovering from whatever confusion they may have suffered, were starting to chance their luck in this new environment. Would it be too much to hope they'd get distracted by the cats? Probably. And once they started the chase again…

'Head for the pyramid!' Anji yelled. 'We can't outrun them, we have to get somewhere they can't reach us!'

The three boys followed her lead obediently. 'Won't the dinosaurs just follow us in?' Xernic gasped, running beside her as fast as he could. Anji half reached out a hand to help him along, but remembered at the last second that these were teenage boys and Xernic would probably prefer to be eaten by a dinosaur than endure teasing from his mates.

'Big pyramid, small door,' Anji said. 'I hope. Built strong enough to withstand dinosaur attacks. Also "I hope". And if they're going for the full mythical experience, we can also expect riddles and traps. And when was the last time you saw a dinosaur solve a logic problem?'

'They're catching us up!' cried Zequathon. 'Hurry!'

The pyramid was close now. As they approached, Anji could see a large – almost dinosaur-large – creature guarding the entrance. It had the body of a (very large) lion, the wings of a (huge) eagle, and the head of a (giant-sized) woman. Its nose was missing.

The dinosaurs were gaining on them as they reached the sphinx. The creature opened its enormous mouth and began to speak. 'Wha-'

'It's a man!' yelled Anji, without slowing down. 'The answer's "a man"! Let us in!'

The sphinx, slightly confused, lumbered to one side. A stone door slid open in the pyramid, and the four tumbled through, just as a velociraptor gained the path.

They sank gratefully to the cold stone floor, catching their breath. Through the wall, they could distantly hear a booming female voice asking: 'What walks on four legs in the morning, two legs in the afternoon, and three legs by nightfall?' and some faint answering growls. (So obviously android dinosaurs could get confused after all.) 'I said, what walks on four legs – ow! There's no need to bite just because you don't know the answer! You could just ask for a clue! Right, you've asked for it! These claws aren't just for decoration, you know.'

Anji looked at the boys. 'I'm on another planet in the far distant future, trapped inside an ancient Egyptian pyramid with three young terrorists while a sphinx fights it out with a load of dinosaurs outside.'

They looked back at her enquiringly. 'Um…' said Xernic.

'It's all right, you don't have to say anything.' Anji reassured him. 'I just had to say it out loud, see how it sounded.'

'What was all that guff about "a man"?' Beezee asked.

'Do you *neeeeed* a man?' Zequathon laughed.

'I had one,' Anji said. 'He was killed yesterday.'

Silence.

'Come on,' she said after a moment. 'With any luck there'll be a secret exit somewhere and we can get on with finding Fitz without princesses or rampaging monsters getting in our way.' She looked round the bare stone chamber, realising as she did that it was lit by a single bare light bulb, which slightly ruined the atmosphere of the place.

'I can't see any secret exits,' said Xernic, after a few minutes.

'They wouldn't be secret if you could, would they?' said Beezee, sarcastically.

'Perhaps I'm wrong,' said Anji. 'This might be all there is. In which case, we can either wait till the fighting's died down outside and hope the dinosaurs have got sick of looking for us and left, or we could try to creep out now in the confusion, and hope they're too distracted by that sphinx to notice.'

'But how do we get out again?' asked Xernic.

Beezee rolled his eyes. 'The same way we got in. Poor little Xernic, doesn't understand doors –'

'The door's gone,' Zequathon interrupted. 'It ain't there any more.'

Anji looked. The stone door had slid back into place after them. And now there was no sign that it had ever been there. The wall fitted together perfectly, no hint of a join; no lever, no handle, nothing. Four people, fifty cubic feet, no doors.

Those cats would be meaning bad luck, then, after all.

The Doctor had made it down three corridors and two flights of stairs before he was caught.

Now, flanked by guards, he was standing in front of another throne. Upon it sat a dark-eyed man wearing a golden jumpsuit with a heavy-looking bejewelled crown on his dark head. The Doctor held out a hand. 'Hello,' he said. 'I'm the Doctor. It's very nice to make your acquaintance; we didn't meet last time I was arrested.'

'Silence!' yelled a guard.

'Why?' asked the Doctor. 'Do you have a headache? I'm so sorry, maybe there's something I can do to h-'

'Si-*lence!*' yelled the guard again. The Doctor was silent.

A blond man, probably in his late thirties, stepped out from the shadows of the throne. He was tall and slim, and wore robes of deep-green velvet that clashed with his bright-blue irises. 'So, you're the Doctor,' he said.

'Yes,' the Doctor answered. 'I said so a minute ago. I hope you don't mind my saying so, but I do like your dress.'

The man ignored him. 'You are a known terrorist –'

('No I'm not,' muttered the Doctor.)

'– and have already been condemned to death. You

have now added escaping lawful custody to the charges against you.'

'Oh dear,' said the Doctor, 'does that mean I'll have to be executed twice? I didn't meet you last time I was sentenced – in fact I didn't meet anyone last time I was sentenced – in fact, I wasn't actually aware I *had* been sentenced: some men just shouted at me for a bit and then threw me in a cell. Not a very sophisticated system. Earth would be ashamed of you. Trials on Earth take months, sometimes. Anyway, I take it you –' to the man on the throne – 'are the President, Mr John F Hoover, which means you –' to the blond man – 'are probably Hanstrum. Am I right?' He didn't wait for an answer. 'Now, before you sentence me to death again, could I just point out that there are some enraged prehistoric monsters rampaging around your star attraction, and all the barriers have gone down – irretrievably, I'm afraid. I was just on my way to sort it all out, but maybe you'd like to do it instead?'

'What lies are these?' asked the man who was almost certainly Hanstrum. 'Undoubtedly this is some saboteur's trick.'

'No, it isn't,' the Doctor said, patiently. 'There are a lot of mad androids in your theme park that are probably killing people. Or they undoubtedly will be soon, if they're not already. And there's nothing holding them back. I was just off to the centre to attempt to shut them down.'

The President spoke for the first time. 'Impossible. Hundreds of off-worlders will be arriving for the opening ceremony any day now.'

'I don't think you mean "impossible",' the Doctor corrected him. 'It's perfectly possible I'm sure; you just don't want me to do it. You'd rather people died.'

'This is ridiculous!' the President cried. 'You are a saboteur; this is some sort of trick! You wish to ruin EarthWorld for your own selfish reasons. Your story is patently absurd: you cannot possibly know what is happening in the centre.'

'Hmm. You don't visit your alleged daughters much, do you?' said the Doctor.

Hanstrum visibly jumped, and for a moment it looked like he was going to hit the Doctor. '"Alleged"?' he roared. 'What in the name of Earth are you implying?'

The Doctor gazed steadily at him, as if daring the man to take another step towards him. 'I mean,' he said, 'that they are not the President's daughters.' Hanstrum opened his mouth again, but the Doctor continued before he could speak. 'They're not anyone's daughters. They are androids constructed by the President's actual daughters, and they have a full control panel for the centre, and also screens on which they can watch the mayhem their real-life counterparts are creating in EarthWorld. Unfortunately, the control panel has been seriously damaged, which means that not only are the people in EarthWorld in danger from the triplets, the triplets – the real, live girls – may well now be in danger from the marauding androids.' He swung round to stare at the President. 'How much do your daughters mean to you? Will you risk disrupting your precious opening ceremony to save their lives?'

The President held the Doctor's gaze, but when he

spoke it was to Hanstrum. 'Go and check the girls. Find out if what he says is true.'

Hanstrum left the room.

'This is meant for tourists, right?' Anji said, tapping a stone wall. 'It shouldn't be that hard to figure out, then.'

They'd been tapping their way round the room, all four of them. It had turned out that the boys were fairly knowledgeable on the subject of secret passages, trapdoors and what they called 'beast holes' – apparently concealed spaces where, in the olden days of Earth, animals could hide from religious persecution. Anji had completely failed not to laugh.

It was Xernic who found the clue, and he got quite excited about it. In a dim corner of the room, he'd discovered a frieze of hieroglyphics. Anji was examining them, and trying to be encouraging.

'This'll be easy to work out,' she said. 'Now, I'm assuming they're not genuine Egyptian hieroglyphs, because even in my day the average person wouldn't be able to interpret those, so the chances of your lot managing to sort that out when they've even lost the knowledge of what a priest-hole is... and anyway, there aren't any eyes or eagles or men with their arms stuck out in funny ways. And they're unlikely to be a letter-substitution code, because I assume if you're having off-worlders to visit they'd speak different languages. So I would think that they're general pictograms, or ideograms, rather than a form of alphabet. I mean,' she clarified as the boys looked bemused, 'that we have to interpret what the pictures are, and that'll tell us how to get out of here. So, let's see. Circle with lines coming out of it – looks like a classic sun representation to me. Next one – some sort of plant? Sun plant?'

'It's got a flower,' pointed out Xernic.

'OK, sun… flower. Hey, sunflower! That's actually a word! Can't quite see how it would be relevant, but… what's the next one. A hand? Sunflower hand? Marigold gloves. We have to do the washing up to get out of here.'

The boys looked at her anxiously.

'No, no, I'm just being silly. OK, sun… flower… hand. What's next? A curly thing. Looks like a pig's tail. Sunflower handtail. That makes no sense. Oh, I know, it's a spring! Do sunflowers come out in the spring? Or perhaps it is a plant after all, and we have to plant sunflowers in the spring. By hand! That's it, of course! Plant sunflowers in the spring, by hand!' She looked triumphantly round.

'That's really good,' said Xernic doubtfully. 'Very clever. How does it help, though?'

'It must be a cryptic clue,' Anji said. 'Double-layered. Once we've solved this, it'll tell us how to get out.'

'… Only,' continued Xernic, bashfully, 'I was just thinking: if it's not a double-layered cryptic clue, and accepting that visual puns don't work in all languages, but… well, I wondered if it might mean "light bulb five twists". The sun gives light, you see, and that plant does seem to be growing out of a bulb, and –'

'Oh yes,' said Anji, feeling a bit silly. 'Um, could someone give the light bulb five twists, please. And be careful not to burn yourself.'

110

In the end, Beezee had to give Zequathon a leg-up, in order for them to reach the light bulb.

One.

Two.

Three.

Nothing seemed to be happening; Anji made a surreptitious visual check of the room just in case there really were some sunflowers that they'd failed to spot earlier.

Four.

Was that a faint creaking sound from somewhere below them?

Fi—

And the floor suddenly tipped sixty degrees, and with shrieks of shock – the loudest from Zequathon, who was suddenly suspended in midair – the four were careering down the cold stone surface towards the black depths below, as if it were the biggest, scariest slide in the world.

I am not Fitz.

If I am not Fitz, what is Fitz?

Fitz is dead.

The Fitz thing told himself – itself – that it had to pull himself – itself – together.

The real Fitz hadn't been much of a one for philosophy – apart from 'if it looks female, try to shag it' – but he had been aware of the dictum 'I think, therefore I am'. And he – well, not he, but the Fitz-shaped object – was definitely thinking, mainly about how he wasn't a real person. So the very act of thinking about not being real made him real…? Did that make sense?

Analyse it (oh, God, no…). If he (until knowing otherwise) had thought he were Fitz, and had Fitz's memories, and Fitz's attitude to life, and basically had been made to be as exactly like Fitz as made no odds, in what way *wasn't* he Fitz? He lived and breathed and needed food and oxygen and – hang on, did he (it)? (the Fitz-thing managed to hold its breath for thirty seconds before deciding that it did) – and was an actual living being.

No, he – it – was a made thing, a construct.

But everyone is a made thing. Some are made by a mummy and daddy loving each other very much, and others are made by someone plonking down a whopping great lump of biomass and telling it, 'be like Fitz'. If you'd never known otherwise – or if someone had stuck rotten old 'real Fitz' Father Kreiner to a lie detector and proved he was fibbing for reasons unknown – then you'd be Fitz now. The real Fitzgerald Michael Kreiner. No worries.

Yeah, ignorance had been bliss. But the Fitz thing wasn't ignorant any more. He knew exactly what he was.

Hang on, he'd just thought of himself as 'he' again. Oh, and again!

Old habits dying hard.

Or an acknowledgement that he didn't have to have been physically born of Fitz's mother to be a person, not a thing.

His earliest memory was of a trip to the zoo. He'd laughed at the monkeys, and his dad had bought him a paper bag of peanuts to feed to them. There was a man with a monkey on the beach, and the monkey'd sit on your shoulder and you could have your picture taken – no, that was a different memory. But he remembered the photo, black and white with a white border, a bit creased, showing the small Fitz in his school blazer, scruffy curls and cheeky grin, the monkey in its little hat gripping his collar – the monkey's hat had been red, although you couldn't tell that from the photo, obviously. His mum had kept that photo by her bed, right up till when she'd gone off to be a test case for Dr Roley.

He remembered Roley's place, too, and how he'd met the Doctor there, and the girl called Sam (who he'd fancied), and how the police thought he'd killed a man, so he'd hitched a ride in a time machine to get out of North London, 1963.

He *remembered* all these things.

And he knew exactly how Fitz'd act in any given situation. That is to say, sometimes he didn't, but that was because he was frequently useless and faffed around a lot, which was probably what Fitz would do too, so in a way he did.

He thought he was Fitz – deep down inside. The Doctor, he was pretty certain, thought he was Fitz.

But what did the Doctor know?

They were back in the TARDIS. 'I wonder what Sam would have made of all this,' Fitz had said, casually. 'You wouldn't get a Volkswagen Beetle in here now, would you?'

'Sam?' the Doctor had said, in an 'oh yes, just give me a minute' tone.

'Someone you were travelling with when I met you,' Fitz had prompted.

The Doctor had given him an 'of course!' look, and slapped his forehead theatrically. 'Oh, Sam. Of course. What a guy, eh... always tinkering around with that Beetle...'

And Fitz had realised that things definitely weren't back to normal, not by a long way.

Anji. Anji thought he was Fitz, because she'd never known him otherwise. And he was willing to bet that if he'd looked up Sam while he'd been waiting for the Doctor to pick him up, she'd have thought he was Fitz, too. After all, Sam had had identity crises of her own, and she'd come through them OK.

When Fitz had been James Bond, or Simon Templar, or Frank Sinatra, he'd still been Fitz. Surely it would be much easier now to still be Fitz, when Fitz was the person he was pretending to be too? (Did that make sense? Shush, we're nearly on the brink of a decision.)

Fitz was this guy who liked a laugh and a joke, fell in love far too often but pretended to himself he didn't feel that deeply really, played the guitar like a dream, hid from the world behind other personalities because in them he could be more confident, more alive, more cool, more the kind of guy he wanted to be. He'd laugh in the face of danger, but only if it was impossible to run away. Though he'd found he'd risk things for the Doctor – the only person in the world, really, he'd do that for.

He was this guy.

Therefore he was Fitz.

Whatever he may have been before; however he had been created; he was Fitz.

(Yes!!)

Then he imagined how he, Fitz, would feel if he'd been abandoned for two thousand years because the Doctor had found a copy just as good as the real thing, and ended up whimpering in the corner again.

Hanstrum came back into the throne room. 'It's true,' he told the President. 'The girls are gone. There are only androids.'

The Doctor gave the President an 'I told you so' look.

'I never dreamed their skills were so far advanced,' Hanstrum was saying. 'Oh, they've been able to build realistic androids since they were tots, and we saw the astounding specific physical resemblances they could create when they built their doubles – as we thought – for the centre. But these… the simulated personality… add a copy of the memory, and you've got something that is in essence indistinguishable from the real thing.' He seemed to be half talking to himself, worried.

'It *is* astounding, isn't it?' said the Doctor. 'Downloadable memory, very impressive. But now we've all been astounded, could we just pop to the centre and turn off the rest of the androids? Before they kill anyone?'

The President waved a hand. 'If my daughters are in there, then… Yes, Hanstrum, go to EarthWorld and bring the girls out. Do whatever you have to do.'

The Doctor waved at him. 'What about me?'

The President turned. 'Guards, take the prisoner back to the cells.'

'Hang on!' The Doctor was most indignant. 'You need my help!'

'Hanstrum,' the President said, 'is my chief technician. I am quite sure he does not need the help of a saboteur.'

The Doctor produced his trump card. 'How about the help of a saboteur with a sonic screwdriver?' He pulled the metal wand triumphantly from his pocket like a rabbit from a hat. 'I can make things much easier for you, I'm sure. Besides, I have friends of my own to rescue.'

The President snorted. 'I'm already agreeing to you ruining EarthWorld – the greatest achievement this planet has ever seen; the only thing that's given us any hope. Why don't I just let you get on with doing a thorough job of destroying it? Hanstrum, take the Doctor with you. I'm going to visit my wife, to tell her –' He stopped for a moment, then visibly pulled himself together. 'To tell her about our daughters.' Hoover stood up, suddenly looking older than he had done before.

The Doctor grinned his thanks and slapped Hanstrum companionably on the back.

Hanstrum seemed to be thinking of something else.

The door banged open. 'Hello, Fitz Fortune!'

'Leave me alone.'

'That's no way to talk to your fans, Fitz Fortune. And you don't want to upset your fans, do you?'

'I don't care,' said Fitz. Then he remembered the

man being ripped apart by the lion, and the look on the triplets' faces as he'd died, and said, 'No, I don't want to upset my fans. Sorry.'

He sat up. The trip in the room with him was wearing a green FITZ FORTUNE IS FAB! T-shirt, and so he was pretty damn sure it was Antarctica. 'Listen, I'm not who you think I am. Really.'

She giggled. 'Don't be silly!'

'I'm not. I… I wasn't really a star back on Earth, you know. I wasn't as big as Elvis. I wasn't even as big as Elvis's smallest toenail. I played once or twice a week in a small club in Soho, and never even pressed a disc. That was it.'

Antarctica giggled some more. 'You *are* funny, Fitz Fortune. I *know* that can't be true. Because if it was, I'd have to let Africa have you, and that wouldn't be very good, would it? After all, you are my favouritest singer of all time ever.' She gazed off into the middle distance. 'Africa puts knives under people's tocnails. She likes that.'

Torture. Honesty or torture. Self-discovery or torture. Which to choose?

The Fitz thing, now Fitz again, became once more Fitz Fortune. 'Ha-ha! Just kidding ya, baby! Tell you what, I'll dedicate my next record to you, OK?'

Antarctica beamed. 'Did you hear the alarm earlier, Fitz Fortune?'

Fitz hadn't. In serious introspective mode he probably wouldn't have heard a bomb go off under his nose.

'We think it might be your friends' fault.'

Fitz's heart jumped.

'So we've sorted things so they won't get you.'

His heart sank again.

''Cos you're going to stay with me for ever and ever!'

Fitz's heart reached his boots.

'And I'm going to leave Princess Leia to keep you company until we're ready.'

'Who? Ready for what?' cried Fitz, his heart jumping up slightly at the idea of a princess who wasn't one of the triplets sharing his room. But it sank down even lower than he thought possible when Antarctica dropped her crocodile in his lap, and locked the door on them.

And there was that ticking sound again! It was coming from the crocodile. Was it a crocodile-bomb? Were they trying to blow him up? He pushed the animal on to the floor hurriedly. It just sat there, gazing up at him in what was really quite a cute way for a reptile, and… ticking. Fitz thought about crocodiles, and about the loose grip on the realities of history that most people on this planet seemed to possess, and then shook his head in recognition. He picked up the little crocodile and gave it a rueful, if somewhat wary, hug. 'They're quite mad, aren't they?' he said to it.

CHAPTER FIVE
POWERPLAY

Hanstrum didn't seem to be particularly interested in what the Doctor had to say, but the Doctor didn't let that discourage him.

'I find androids fascinating, don't you? Androids. Hmm. From the Greek *androeides*, manlike. Man seems determined to set himself up as a creator of life, and as he can't do it in any real sense he contents himself with these strange approximations and pretends that's enough. I knew a man – should I call him a friend? Yes, I think I should – I had a friend, many years ago, called Alan Turing. A very, very clever man. He predicted that computers would one day be able to think like humans, and he came up with a test that would prove it. He said, if you had a computer and a human hidden from view and asked them a series of identical random questions, there would one day be a computer who could not be told apart from the human by its answers alone. The trouble is, that's not a finite test. When do you stop asking questions? It could always be the very next question that shows the difference. You'd have to spend your whole life asking questions, and you still couldn't come to a decision. And imagine how boring that would be for the human in the test. And the computer too, of course, if it really did think like a human. Your whole life spent answering random questions. Except the computer wouldn't grow old and die, like the human. Which is another difference between them. Should you cry when an artificial intelligence dies? Is there any difference between a dead AI and a broken watch? Of course, that's another area in which Turing's theories differed from Descartes'. Can a computer have a soul? one side would say – and the other would say, Ah, but does a human being? And then there are all those in between – who believe a human has a soul and a computer does not, but neither does a dog, or a creature from Mars. For those who think computers can have a soul, do they think dogs do? What about a computerised dog? An android dog. Except it wouldn't be an "android", would it. A canindroid? A candroid. That's a good word. That would mean that a computerised cat would be a feldroid. And a computerised bear would be an ursdroid. And a computerised wolf would be a lupdroid. And a computerised sheep would be an ovoid. No, that's not right. An ovdroid. That's it. Though I'm not entirely sure why anyone would want a computerised sheep. How would you tell an Artificial Sheep Intelligence? What sort of questions could Turing ask it? "Is that grass nice?", perhaps. Oh, are we there?'

They were there. The banner read: EARTHWORLD. SO REALISTIC, YOU'LL THINK YOU'VE TRAVELLED IN TIME AND SPACE! The Doctor smiled knowingly.

Hanstrum keyed in a few numbers on a security pad, and the huge double doors slid open. Here in the foyer, they were treated to spinning holo-images of dinosaurs, medieval maidens, Egyptian mummies and, taking up most of the space, an elephant. There was also a booth where one could buy EarthWorld T-shirts (I'M AN EARTHLING – ARE YOU?); EarthWorld badges in the shape of pyramids or rocket ships; EarthWorld personal datapads and pencils; boxes of EarthWorld Genuine Earth Recipe Fudge (small print: made in Alpha Centauri) and EarthWorld Genuine Earth Recipe Coca-Cola ('with Real Earth Cocaine!'). Posters invited visitors to book now for An Audience with Julius Caesar (includes Gladiatorial Show), A Night with Elvis Presley (featuring Genuine Earth Songs!), and Robin Hood: The Outlaw Experience (Bows Not Included). A keypad invited visitors to input their details if they wished to receive further information about Earth Heritage, and noted that they may be sent information on other organisations from carefully vetted galaxies. The Doctor went over to it and typed, 'The Doctor, The TARDIS, The Universe' and was slightly disappointed to find that he'd failed to fill in six of the required fields and this was therefore Insufficient Data.

Hanstrum, however, ignored all of this, and crossed to an insignificant door behind the elephant, labelled PRIVATE. STAFF ONLY. He knocked.

As the Doctor joined him, a voice from the other side of the door shouted, 'Go away!'

'Miss Durwell, this is Hanstrum. You will kindly open the door.'

There was an audible sigh of frustration, and then the door slid back. On the other side was a bank of viewing screens, instrument panels and keypads – a

121

much more sizeable version of the triplets' control room. A grey-haired woman was sitting with her back to them, frantically copying numbers from a screen on to a personal datapad. 'This had better be important,' she said, without turning to face them. 'I'm extremely busy.'

'I should think you would be, with all the barriers down and your robots on the rampage,' commented the Doctor carelessly.

She turned then. 'How do you know about that?' she demanded.

'Well, look!' The Doctor pointed at one of the viewing screens, where a horse-mounted knight in armour could be seen charging a small stegosaurus. 'Or are you telling me that's one of your floor shows?'

Hanstrum shook his head contemptuously. 'We found out about it at the palace,' he told the woman. 'There have been... complications. We think you should shut down all the automatons.'

'Oh, really,' she said. 'I'd never have thought of that. Thank you so much. Would you care to tell me exactly how I'm supposed to do it, given that none of the controls are responding?'

Hanstrum snorted. 'You're the curator. Think of something.'

She glared at him. 'You're the President's chief technician. You think of something.'

'Children, children!' cried the Doctor. 'Let's talk about this like rational beings. Now, Miss... Durwell, was it? Miss Durwell, are there any people in the centre?'

'Some. Not many. Advance passes, competition winners, that sort of thing.'

'Do you know where these people are?'

'No! How can I keep track? Especially with these monitors behaving so erratically.' She gestured to the viewing screens, several of which showed nothing but static.

'Ah. That could be helpful. It's extremely likely that the girls carry some sort of blocking device to prevent you seeing where they go and who they kill. If you can tell us exactly which locations those disrupted monitors represent...'

Durwell turned away from the Doctor. 'Mr Hanstrum, why exactly have you brought this lunatic here? What is he talking about?'

'There's no time to explain! If the controls in here don't work, we have to find a way of adapting them!' cried the Doctor. 'And to give us time to do that, we need to evacuate the centre. You must have a... a loudspeaker system or something.'

'No. It would hardly be an authentic part of the experience for most of these zones.'

'But you have cameras set up...'

'Which aren't intrusive – and don't carry sound.'

'Don't, or can't? Mr Hanstrum here, being the chief technician, can undoubtedly wire them for sound. I'm just slightly worried, having seen your general level of historical accuracy, that most of your visitors won't realise they're not meant to meet a charging rhino in the streets of renaissance Italy or a tyrannosaurus in twentieth-century England unless someone tells them.

So, Mr Hanstrum, please set up a sound system for the centre and tell the patrons to evacuate. Miss Durwell, work out which areas have disrupted monitors and locate the homicidal triplets. They may be able to shut the place down. And now I'm going in there to fetch Fitz and Anji.'

'Are you mad?' asked Durwell.

'No,' said the Doctor. 'I've met a great number of people who were clinically mad, and I can honestly say there's little resemblance. Now, could you show me the way in, please? Oh – and I should probably take a guidebook.'

Anji and the boys, after getting their breath back, had examined their new surrounding – made possible by yet another bare light bulb hanging from the ceiling. Zequathon was all in favour of twisting it straight away to see if anything happened, but Anji reasoned that surely they wouldn't use the same trick twice in a row, and there wasn't a diagram this time. It all turned out to be much simpler than that, anyway – Xernic found an actual door. What it revealed wasn't that promising, though – a dark corridor (with no light bulbs).

'I suppose we have to go down there,' Anji said, unenthusiastically. 'Would a few EXIT signs really have been too much to ask for?'

'I'll go first, see if it leads anywhere,' said Xernic, bravely. Anji was getting very proud of him. A real little trooper. Just needed a few brushes with death to bring him out of his shell, obviously. And she really wasn't that keen on the dark, so she agreed.

He hadn't been gone very long when they heard him call back, 'I'm just going round a corner.' Then a bit later, and, 'I've come to a fork. I'm turning left.' And a few seconds after that, 'It's a dead end.'

'Come back, Xernic,' called Anji. 'You don't want to get lost.'

The redheaded boy returned to them, looking shyly pleased with himself. 'Your eyes adjust to the dark really quickly,' he said. 'But there's nothing to see. Just stone.'

'I think it's a maze,' said Anji. 'I thought they were Greek, but maybe they were Egyptian too. Anyway, I expect we have to find our way to the centre if we want to get out of here. Anyone got a compass?' No one had. In fact, none of the boys actually knew what a compass was. 'Well, has anyone got a really good sense of direction?'

'Yeah, 'course,' said Zequathon.

Xernic nudged Anji. 'Zequathon gets lost getting out of bed in the morning.'

The blond boy glared at him, but didn't argue. Anji took that as a no from all three of them. She sighed. 'Has anyone got a ball of wool?'

'What do you want that for?' asked Beezee.

'In the legend of Theseus and the Minotaur,' said Anji, meeting blankly uncomprehending looks all round, 'when Theseus goes into the labyrinth – that's a sort of maze – he unwinds a ball of thread as he goes, so he can find his way out again, and so he doesn't cross his path. If you don't know where you're going, you can end up walking round and round the same bit for hours. That happened to me at Hampton Court once. Still, never mind that now.' But no one had a ball of wool. Or a bag of pebbles, or even breadcrumbs (cue much explanation of fairy tales – which the boys dismissed as kids' stuff, but Anji could tell they found quite fascinating really).

'Um, Anji,' said Xernic, when she'd exhausted all options, and was calculating how many disposable marker items they had between them (she'd got as far as three ANJI badges and a pair of gold hoop earrings), 'your top's made of wool, isn't it?'

'No,' said Anji, looking down at the black fabric peeking out from under her blazer, 'it's knitted cotton.'

'But… it would unravel…'

'But it's Harvey Nicks!'

'But we have to find our way through this maze, you *said* so.'

She thought for a moment. 'Can't you unravel your jumpsuit thing?'

'Fused plasti-thread. Sorry.'

Anji looked suspiciously at him. 'Did you just make that up, or is it a real future thing?' she asked.

'It's real,' said Xernic, apologetically.

'Oh, all right. But turn your backs,' Anji sent up a brief prayer that she was wearing a good bra, rather than an old grey I'm-not-seeing-my-boyfriend-tonight one, which reminded her that she didn't have a boyfriend any more, anyway. She hurriedly brushed that thought aside as she took off her top – although she did note that the bra was a sensible black cotton one, which wasn't too bad. And she was able to do up the buttons of her blazer so it hardly showed, anyway. She wondered if every tourist who came here was expected to sacrifice a piece of clothing, or if there should be a ball of string but one of the ANJI boys had hidden it. OK, so they were supposed to be working together to get out of a potential life-or-death situation, but she'd known teenage boys go further for a potential glimpse of underwear. Or maybe she'd just overlooked something obvious again. Whatever, the top was sacrificed now.

She tied an end of black cotton around a convenient nail (which rather gave credence to the 'missing string' theory), and they set off.

Xernic was right: it took no time at all for their eyes to adjust to the dark. With Anji's extremely expensive thread to guide them, they managed not to cross their own path, and despite a fair number of dead ends, eventually reached the centre of the maze. Anji couldn't suppress a shiver. This was scarier than dinosaurs. Which was ridiculous, because they'd been an actual, real danger, and this was just a horror archetype.

It was a crypt. On either side of the room stood a large stone sarcophagus, each bearing a humanoid image – one of a jackal-headed man, the other with the head of an eagle. 'I don't think that's quite right,' said Anji – and then realised she hadn't spoken aloud at all. She couldn't possibly be frozen with fear, could she? Did that really happen? Oh, this was stupid – she, the grown-up, worldly, experienced member of the group, was actually gripping the arm of one of these… children! She let go hurriedly.

'I didn't mind,' said Xernic, shyly.

And then she heard the sound. The slight, creaking sound that brought back memories of every mummy flick she'd ever seen. One of the sarcophagi was opening.

Anji – deep inside noting she was going to be really, really embarrassed later – screamed.

'Hello, Anji, everyone,' said the Doctor, stepping out of the sarcophagus. 'Oh dear, did I – yes, I think I did, didn't I. Sorry, I didn't mean to scare you. I like the new outfit, by the way.'

'Um, she's fainted,' said Xernic.

To: <u>cybertron@xprof.net</u>
From: <u>anji kapoor@MWFutures.co.uk</u>
Date: 14/2/01 19:31
Subject: Oops

You know how we used to laugh at films when the heroine fainted at the slightest thing? Well, I've decided it's not funny.

Ax

Send now/send later: send later

It was a deeply self-conscious Anji that the Doctor finally led into the sarcophagus. 'Look, it's really a lift!' he said, far too enthusiastically. 'Just press the UP hieroglyph, and it takes us back to the surface. Not exactly authentic ancient Egyptian I'd say, but there again they were very clever people and knew all about quite complicated things like embalming, so maybe there was more to them than met the eye. In any case, I've found you. You don't seem to have Fitz, though.'

'No, we haven't really had much chance to look! Some teenage bimbo decided to try to kill us when we were only halfway there!'

The Doctor looked concerned. 'I wasn't blaming you. I've been kicking myself for sending you in here. Of course, I didn't know quite what was going on back then.' And, seeing they were a captive audience, he told them everything.

The Doctor was very adept at dodging robots. With directions from the ANJI boys, it took them no time at all to reach the Twentieth-Century London Zone, described in the guidebook as 'The Age of Discovery: marvel at the wonders of the time that gave us space flight and moving pictures; gaze on extinct beasts such as the tiger and the whale in their natural habitat: London – the city with the swings! Feast on authentic twentieth-century cuisine: fishy chips, Coca-Cola and cheese on toes!'

Anji had leafed through the book, and was being very disapproving. Not just at the level of historical inaccuracy (which she was feeling less smug about now, after the Doctor had casually mentioned that getting past a ferocious sphinx by answering its riddles was actually from the Greek myths, not the Egyptian ones, and wasn't it lucky that neither Anji nor the EarthWorld people had realised that), but at the assumption that the only bits of Earth's culture that were important enough to feature were the sort that would be found in a history text book from an English middle-class school before the advent of the National Curriculum. Ancient Romans. Ancient Egyptians. Medieval England (incorporating the Dark Ages and Myths and Legends), and the Second World War. The nearest they got to Asian culture was the Japanese Zone, which seemed to be all kimonos and raw fish, anyway. How her grandparents would wail and gnash their teeth: all the insistence on holding on to their cultural identity and it was all for nothing. Of course, the whole of the future might not be like this. But it was scary how such important things could dissolve into nothing. An entirely different perspective. Like how she'd been worried for ages about her annual review coming up next month, and now she just had to concentrate on staying alive long enough to even have the chance of getting home again. Made all those deadline/report/conference crises seem quite ridiculous. Had she really used to have sleepless nights about that sort of stuff? It was like looking back on your teen crush from the happiness of a stable relationship, and wondering how you could ever have cried yourself to sleep because Robert Fordham asked Joanne Davies to the end-of-term disco, or your fave pop star turned out to prefer boys. Relationship stuff. Don't go there. Pay attention to your surroundings.

'Hmm,' said Anji. 'In which version of the twentieth century was there a top pop star called Fitz Fortune?' She pointed to a poster pasted on the side of a bright-pink pillar box.

'Fitz!' The Doctor's face split into a huge grin. 'Well, he has made a success of himself.'

'We've been here before,' said Beezee. 'These weren't here then. Just ones of some other old-time bloke – Elvers or something?'

'Elvis,' said Anji. 'Elvers are baby eels. So did they have an Elvis impersonator? Or an Elvis android?'

'We were here to sabotage the place, not visit the attractions,' Beezee told her with a sigh, as if it were perfectly obvious. Anji noticed that he reverted to being the rather less attractive snotty kid now they weren't pulling together in extreme circumstances. Or maybe it was just that now the Doctor was back, she didn't feel the need to persuade herself she was part of a team.

The Doctor read from his brochure again. '"Why not take in a show? King Elvis performs every night of the week at the Alhambra Theatre, City Centre Street". Well, shall we assume that that's where Fitz Fortune is now performing if he's the new Elvis?'

'Sounds as good a place to start as any,' agreed Anji.

They ducked behind the pillar box as a giant, caterpillar-tracked metal monster trundled past, with what seemed to be a postbag hooked over its, for want of a better word, shoulder, and steam-shooting guns blazing away.

'What on Earth's that?!' hissed Anji to the Doctor. 'It certainly doesn't come from twentieth-century London!'

'No idea,' said the Doctor cheerfully. 'It's probably crossed over from another zone. Just keep out of its way.'

They continued on their way, helped by the map in the Doctor's guidebook, darting between pillar boxes, double-decker buses and miniature rocket ships to make sure they weren't spotted by the roaming monsters. Finally they reached the theatre. TONIGHT: FITZ FORTUNE!!!!! screamed the posters outside.

'This looks like the place!' said the Doctor. 'Now, where is he likely to be?'

'We could go to the stage door and pretend we're autograph hunters,' Anji suggested, not entirely seriously.

'Good plan!' cried the Doctor. 'Come on.'

The five of them strolled casually round to the side of the theatre, but as it turned out, no pretence was needed. There was a door, no one was guarding it, and it wasn't locked.

'Doesn't look like he's being held against his will,' said Anji. 'Are you sure he's going to want to be rescued? If he's a big star and everything…'

'Even big stars can be hurt by rampaging dinosaurs,' said the Doctor. 'I don't think he'll mind.'

They crept down a carpeted corridor, past doors marked ELVIS (DRESSING ROOM), ELVIS (TROUSERS), ELVIS (BLUE SUEDE SHOES) and ELVIS (WIGS) until they came to the one with a big gold star proclaiming FITZ FORTUNE (DRESSING ROOM). The Doctor knocked; there was no answer. He tried the door; it was locked. 'Aha!' he said.

'Maybe he's not in there,' suggested Xernic. He needn't have bothered.

The door was secured with an electronic lock ('Very

twentieth-century,' muttered Anji), and the Doctor whipped out his sonic screwdriver – obviously, and thankfully, having forgotten that he'd forgotten how to use it. In a few seconds, the door buzzed open.

Fitz was sitting in a corner of the dressing room, arms round his knees and eyes staring, rocking to and fro. Anji was moved to compassion despite herself. She ran over and knelt beside him. 'What is it, Fitz? What have they done to you?'

He turned soulless eyes to her. 'I'm not Fitz,' he said.

'What do you mean? Of course you're Fitz!' The Doctor was beside them now.

'I'm not the real Fitz. I'm not a real person. Just leave me.'

'There's something definitely wrong,' said Anji. 'He hasn't looked at my cleavage once. You don't think he's a replicant, do you?'

'Don't be silly, Anji. And don't be silly, Fitz!' The Doctor took hold of Fitz's left arm and began to help him up. Anji took the other arm. 'Come on, we're going to get you out of here.'

Anji preferred to draw a blank over the rest of their journey. Concern for Fitz – he might be an irritating slob, but he was her only link to her own world and, sort of, time, and that created some sense of solidarity at least – and residual embarrassment from her earlier faint, combined against another retreat into unreality as the Doctor, armed with his guidebook, negotiated their way through a medieval village and the Japanese zone, passing the triplets (definitely androids) dressed as three little maids from school. The dinosaurs didn't seem to have reached this far yet, but the absence of barriers was obvious from the mixture of costumes on display. They also passed several elephants, none of which were in their natural habitat. If anything got too close, Xernic blasted it with the anti-android zapper. The Doctor scooped up a number of visitors on the way, who were disposed to argue until a voice boomed out at them: 'Evacuate! Evacuate! All visitors must return to the control centre immediately. Danger! Danger! Evacuate! Evacuate!'

'Very subtle,' said Anji, struggling to hold up her bit of Fitz. 'Guaranteed not to cause undue panic.'

They got back to the control centre eventually. The loudly complaining visitors ('Been looking forward to this for months!', 'Disgraceful, absolutely disgraceful!') were left in the foyer while the Doctor, Anji, Fitz and the three boys went to find Hanstrum and Durwell.

'Well done on the announcement,' said the Doctor, striding into the control room and seemingly taking charge instantly. 'I knew you could do it. Now, any luck in locating those girls? We didn't see them, and Fitz doesn't know where they were.'

'You didn't search for them?' asked Hanstrum.

The Doctor looked puzzled. 'No. I went in to fetch my friends, Anji and Fitz.'

'I'm not Fitz,' muttered Fitz, as Anji dropped him into a chair.

Miss Durwell looked slightly alarmed. 'It's all right, he's not dangerous,' said Anji.

'No, no... but he looks ill... I'll take him somewhere he can rest quietly, shall I? It must have been quite an ordeal.'

The Doctor was busy consulting with Hanstrum, so Anji took it on herself to agree. 'Thanks. I'm sure he'll appreciate it.'

As Durwell led Fitz from the room, the Doctor beckoned the ANJI boys over to him. Anji followed to see what was going on.

'Can I see that device of yours, please?' the Doctor was asking.

Xernic produced the anti-android zapper. 'This?' he said, offering it.

'That's the thing!' The Doctor turned to Hanstrum. 'We need something like this, but on a massive scale. Oh, hello, Anji. Bit of a crisis, I'm afraid.'

'I know!' said Anji

'No, more than that. It seems that the barriers really can't be set up again – the whole mechanism's fused. So the robots can just wander around at will. And although at the moment only a number of them are hostile, it's entirely possible that more will follow. Enrage an elephant, for example, and there's no stopping it.'

'But at least we're out of there now. I mean, they'll only be attacking other robots.'

'Hmm. Interesting thing, it seems now the internal barriers have collapsed, the main external barrier – the big thick one we went through? The one keeping the robots out of the streets of New Jupiter – is having difficulty coping with the power load. And we can't turn the power off. It could go at any minute. So it's probably a good idea to shut the robots down.'

'Oh yes,' said Anji. 'I can see why it would be.'

'Of course, the feedback may well cause this entire centre to explode. But at least we won't have robots roaming the streets afterwards.'

Anji felt strangely uncomforted.

'This doesn't have a big enough range,' Hanstrum said, indicating the zapper. 'But if we could boost its power...'

'I'm assuming the androids all have their own internal power supplies – yes?' The Doctor was taking apart a control panel as he talked. 'So the greatest single power source is that being used to uphold this main barrier.'

'The one you can't switch off,' added Xernic, helpfully.

'That's right. So, what we have to do is wire in this excellent device, increase its range, and then at the very moment the power load becomes too great and begins to surge back, we switch it across, so the power surge goes through the device instead. If I'm right, the magnetic waves should blast out just strongly enough to knock out all the robots, before the device burns out. The diversion of power will stop the centre exploding, and the people of this planet will be safe once more!'

'And if you're wrong?' asked Hanstrum, obviously unconvinced.

'Just keep your fingers crossed that I'm not,' said the Doctor, with eyebrows raised.

Anji, who poured scorn on all forms of superstition, quietly crossed her fingers behind her back. 'Doctor...' she said.

'Yes?'

'When you've wired that thing up and saved the planet... could we please leave?'

He flashed her that incredible heartbreaking smile that she was so thankful she was immune to. 'Yes, of course we can.'

Behind her back, she crossed two more fingers.

Venna Durwell led Fitz into her office and sat him down on a chair. 'We need to talk,' she said, narrowing her eyes. The idiot just kept sitting there. 'Have you told anyone what happened earlier?'

No response.

'Have you forgotten our bargain, Fitz? You were supposed to tell me everything you knew about the twentieth century.'

Sightless grey eyes turned up to hers. 'I'm not Fitz.'

'Will you stop spouting that rubbish? Look –' she pulled open a desk drawer and took out a gun – 'obviously I don't want to have to harm you. But this time I'm not going to give you a chance to get away from me. Start talking!'

The young man just stared. 'I'm not Fitz,' he said.

'We've got about five minutes, I think,' said the Doctor. 'It might be an idea if you all left. Just in case.'

'Just in case we want to be savaged on the streets by rampaging robots instead of being blown up?' asked Anji.

'Yes,' said the Doctor. 'That's right. Where's Fitz? Could you go and fetch him, please? It took me over a hundred years to find him – I'd rather he wasn't killed now I'm just getting to know him again. Now, Zequathon, Xernic, Beezee, would you lead all the visitors out of the centre, please?'

Zequathon looked at the other two. 'It's not that we don't want to help…'

'But?'

'But if we go out there we're probably going to get arrested. Stuck back in the condemned cell.'

The Doctor gave him a hard stare. 'I thought you were fighting for the ordinary man in the street.'

'Well, we are… sort of thing.'

'Those people out there *are* the ordinary man in the street. In fact, some of them are probably quite influential men in the street, I would imagine, as they were privileged guests to this place. Go and rescue them, and I would think you'll gain friendships in useful places. As well as possibly saving a number of lives, which obviously isn't as important to you as your leafleting campaign, but give it a go, you might like it.'

Zequathon looked like he was going to argue. The Doctor sighed. 'Mr Hanstrum?'

'Yes?'

'Would you please go with these boys and not arrest them?'

The man shrugged. 'Why not?'

Beezee grabbed Zequathon's arm. 'Come on, Zeq. We're not going to get a better offer. Xernic?'

'Um…' said Xernic. 'Um…'

'Are you coming or what?'

It looked like Xernic was ready to cry. 'No, I'm not. I might be able to help the Doctor if I stay.' But he was looking at Anji, not the Doctor.

'Have it your own way, then,' said Beezee, shrugging and leading Zequathon out of the room.

'I'll see you later!' Xernic called desperately after them.

'Whatever,' came floating back.

'I'm not a very good rebel,' said the redheaded boy, forlornly.

Anji put her arm round him. 'Yes, you are. You're a lovely rebel. Come and help me to find Fitz.'

He smiled then.

'I'm not Fitz.'

'Stop saying that!'

Venna Durwell was getting more than irritated. She was fast approaching furious. (a), This kid was getting on her nerves. (b), She had to find out if he'd blabbed to anyone, because it could ruin her reputation if he had. (c), Oh yes, and she could get arrested for kidnap and threatening behaviour. (d), She needed information from him in order to get out of this lousy job and off this lousy planet, and gain her rightful place in academia. (e)… She just wanted him to *shut up*.

'Shut up!'

'I'm not Fitz.'

'Shut up or I really will shoot you! If you're not going to tell me anything, at least I can safeguard my reputation and stop any of my rivals getting at you!'

'But I'm not Fitz. I'm not.'

'This is a real gun you know!'

*

'Where would she have taken him?'

'Don't know,' said Xernic. 'She's probably got an office down here somewhere.'

They were hurrying down a corridor, not unlike the one backstage at the theatre. Actually, Anji thought it may well have the same carpet. How cheap.

'Look, here we are. VENNA DURWELL. CURATOR.'

Anji knocked on the door. No answer. She tried it. Locked. 'Must be somewhere else,' she said.

Xernic was frowning at the door. 'No, I think I can hear something inside.'

As one, they both placed an ear to the door.

'*I warn you, shut up or I shoot! My reputation's more important than your stupid life!*'

'*I'm not Fitz.*'

'*I'm going to shoot!*'

Anji and Xernic looked at each other. 'She's flipped,' said Anji. 'Try to break the door down. I'm going to go and get the Doctor and his sonic screwdriver.'

She ran back towards the control room.

'Doctor!'

'That was quick!' he called, head stuck in a control panel muffling his voice. 'Now can the three of you wait for me outside, please? This thing's got less than a minute.'

'Doctor, we didn't get Fitz! That curator woman's threatening to shoot him!'

'What?' The Doctor straightened up too quickly, knocking his head on the underside of a monitor. '*Ow!*'

'You've got to come and unlock the door. Please.'

140

The Doctor looked from her to the control panel, then back again. And again. 'All right! This should work on its own. Come on.' He grabbed a small LCD timer. 'Look! Thirty seconds!'

They ran down the corridor, Anji leading the Doctor by the hand. 'Twenty seconds,' cried the Doctor as they reached Durwell's office.

'They're still in there,' gasped Xernic, stumbling away from the door. 'She's really lost it. And the door just won't open.'

'We'll see about that.' The Doctor handed the timer to Anji, and produced his sonic screwdriver.

'Ten seconds,' read Anji.

'Not a problem!' said the Doctor, unconvincingly.

From the other side of the door, they heard: 'I'm not Fitz.' 'This is your last warning! I'm counting down from ten, then I shoot!'

'Nine seconds,' said Anji.

'Nine!' Venna Durwell's voice.

'Easy!' said the Doctor.

'Eight seconds,' said Anji.

'Eight!' echoed Venna Durwell, inside the room.

'I'm not Fitz,' said Fitz's voice.

'Seven seconds.'

'Seven!'

'Six.'

'Six!'

'Nearly there,' said the Doctor.

'Five.'

'Five!'

'Four.'

'Four!'

'Three.'

'Three!'

'Hold on to your hats... here it comes –'

'Two.'

'Two!'

'Hurry, Doctor! One!'

'One!'

The door beeped open.

The gun went off.

There was a massive explosion – but... not from the control centre: it was here, in front of them, and as the door slid back all they saw was a flash of blinding white light as they were hurled to the ground.

The Doctor, Anji and Xernic staggered to their feet, and peered into the room through the clouds of grey smoke. Venna Durwell was lying on the floor, not a pretty sight, gun still in one hand and... (was their vision distorted by the fog?) a detached hand buried deep in her head...

'Fitz!' gasped the Doctor.

'Oh dear,' said Xernic. 'I think your friend's exploded.'

'So that Fitz was a replicant after all,' said Anji, later, sitting gingerly down in a control-room chair. 'He did *say* that he wasn't Fitz, Doctor.'

'Anyone can make a mistake,' said the Doctor, seemingly unconcerned.

'Just as well for Fitz that you did! That woman would have killed him!'

'Had it been the real Fitz,' the Doctor assured her, 'he

would never have let that happen.'

'At least the Doctor's plan worked,' put in Xernic, nervously. 'All the robots are out of action. And... and nowhere exploded.'

'Apart from that woman's office,' said Anji

'And that woman,' added the Doctor. 'In a way. Still, she was a potential murderer.'

Anji was about to remark on his callousness, but she was distracted by a bleeping from somewhere near her feet. She bent down and picked up a small box. 'What's this?'

'Communicator,' said Xernic. 'Someone must have dropped it.' He pressed a button and the beeping was replaced by a voice.

'Hanstrum! Is that you, Hanstrum?'

Xernic shot a worried look at Anji. 'Um, no...' he said.

'Well, where is he? Hurry! the President's wife has flat-lined. We need him here now!'

'Sounds like they need a doctor,' murmured the Doctor. He took the communicator from Xernic's hand. 'Hello, this is the Doctor. I'm on my way. Over and out.' He pressed a button and handed the box back. 'Anji – sort things out here, will you? We still have to find Fitz. Meet you back at the palace.'

And before Anji could say a word, he was out of the door.

CHAPTER SIX
ELVIS LIVES!

Fitz was trying hard not to look at any of the corpses in the cell where a gold robot had thrown him. Some of them were just lying there in a could-almost-be-asleep way, but others were... well, let's just leave it at the trying-hard-not-to-look thing. And, although the cell was extremely cold, the refrigeration obviously wasn't sufficient to stop... Look, there was a smell, all right? And not a nice one.

Fitz wasn't sure which bit of a twentieth-century theatre this was supposed to represent. Maybe they'd heard of the Chamber of Horrors, but hadn't realised it was a waxworks exhibition. Or they'd watched *The Phantom of the Opera* a few too many times. The walls were whitewashed stone with manacles hanging from them, some occupied (don't look!), and a few rats, which admittedly had turned out to be robotic, but that didn't mean he had to like them.

He had brought Princess Leia with him. The robot hadn't seemed to notice, and after his initial apprehension Fitz had decided he actually quite liked the little reptile. It was tamer than most cats he'd known, and was happy to sit in his lap. He'd given it a tiny tap on its nose when it had tried to nibble him playfully (its teeth looked extremely sharp), and it hadn't tried that again. And it had been company, but now it was off examining corpses, and Fitz didn't really want to watch. But anyway, he had another distraction now.

Fitz was sitting on the floor with his hands cupped round either side of his head, so he could look directly at the only other living thing in the room (apart from Princess Leia), with no decomposing distractions. 'And you really know all his songs?' he said.

'Well, I guess I do,' said the other living thing, a man in his sixties dressed like Elvis Presley. '"Jailhouse Rock", "Hound Dog" – you name it, brother.'

'So, the people of this time think gun-toting robots delivered the post, that we colonised Mars in the Edwardian era, and that "going to work on an egg" was talking about a new form of public transport, but they know every single one of Elvis Presley's hits? Loony. Completely loony. Wacko! Crazy-daisy!'

'Well, hey, man, he was the King o' Earth, know what I'm saying?'

'Yes…' said Fitz, tentatively. 'I mean, you know he wasn't *actually* the real King of Planet Earth, don't you?'

The elderly Elvis-alike looked shocked. Fitz half expected him to yell, 'Burn the heretic!' but thankfully he didn't. 'What in tarnation are you sayin'?' the man eventually said. 'I know there's a few of yoose sceptical types out there who don't worship the very ground the King walked on but I don't know of nobody who doubts that he was actually the King o' Earth!'

'Sorry,' said Fitz, deciding that his accurate historical knowledge had got him into enough trouble for one day. 'Of course, you're right. I meant no disrespect. Long live Elvis! Er, that is, if he wasn't dead already. Sorry.' He thought it would be a good idea to change the subject. 'So, how come you're locked up, then?'

The man flicked back his quiff with one heavily bejewelled hand. 'It was those crazy chicks, man! Those little girls! They look sweet as sugar, but I'm telling you they sure ain't, no sir.'

'I'd noticed,' said Fitz.

'Well, it happened like this. I travel about a bit, do a little show, few numbers, few hip swings, few "uh-huhs", catch a bit of the underwear thrown on stage, that sorta thing. Goes down well with the chicks –'

'And their mothers,' suggested Fitz, who, despite having found out in one of his earliest realisations of the horror of time travel, that the fresh-faced GI chart-topper of his time would become a big-collared overweight living legend in the next decade, just couldn't picture his fifty-something cellmate with the sequinned pants and the dodgy accent in the role.

Elvis shrugged this off. 'Anyways, got a call from a Miss Venna Durwell, curator of this here show. They wanted to have a concert from King Elvis here, two, three times a day. Big attraction, you see. Get the chicks in. O' course, I would a liked to've helped, but I got my public to think of. Can't restrict myself to just one planet, no, sir. Why, I just could not have all those sobbing girls on my conscience.'

'Right,' said Fitz, who imagined that this was a slight exaggeration, and that this guy probably hadn't been asked to do all the shows in the first place.

'This Durwell chick was a mite disappointed, and that's no lie. But she had this rootin'-tootin' –' (Fitz shuddered) – 'idea, that she would get these three pretty kids to make a model o' me, and get me to sing my whole darn repertoire into some fancy tape machine to stick in its head. Then they could have the pleasure o' my performance, so to speak, without me actually having to be in the same galaxy. Well, seemed a mighty good idea, and I did just what she asked for. Only trouble was, these chicks have got to be the maddest fans o' the King who ever walked the face of any planet in this system. Oh, they made their machine man and no mistake, but they got it into their twisted little heads that they liked the real thing a bit more. So what d'ya know but they decoyed me away down here and here I stay unless they decide they want a bit of a concert. It's that Antarctica kid – she's the one. I'm her most favourite singer of all time, she says; I'm her pet, and if she wants a concert she has to have one. Mind you, guess I should consider myself lucky. These poor guys –' he indicated in a direction Fitz had no intention of looking – 'were the pets of the Africa chick, and she don't seem that keen to treat people right. Heck, talk o' the devils…'

There were high-pitched voices rapidly approaching, three of them. Fitz couldn't tell which voice belonged to which trip.

'It's not fair!' cried voice A. 'How could they shut down everything? What are we supposed to do now? It's no fun without our robots.'

Fitz and Elvis exchanged glances.

'There are other ways of making entertainment,' said voice B. 'I told you, we should have a death match.'

'I don't want a death match! Death matches are boring! Anyway, all the silly people have run away now,' said voice C – or, actually, it was probably voice A again.

'Do you have another suggestion?' That was – well, it might be B, but this time it was fairly likely to be voice C.

'A concert! A concert from my pet! A lovely, lovely concert from Fitz Fortune!' Yes, that was voice A, and it was undoubtedly Antarctica.

'You got bored of King Elvis soon enough,' said, erm, B or C. 'Always said he'd be a five-minute wonder.'

(Next to Fitz, Elvis gave a massive 'hmmph'.)

'Oh!' cried Antarctica. 'I'd forgotten about my lovely King Elvis! Maybe I'll have a King Elvis concert instead.'

'Well, make up your mind. If I can't have a death match, I'll have the one you don't want for a game.'

Fitz felt his buttocks clench involuntarily. Not that he wished any harm to this old Elvis impersonator, but if it was a choice between singing for a couple of hours and being involved in one of the triplets' games – and he was betting that it was Africa who'd had that idea – then he knew which he'd prefer, exhausted though he was.

Then the third voice spoke. 'I have a better idea, something that we can all enjoy.' There was an attentive silence. 'Antarctica wants a concert – King Elvis or Fitz Fortune, but she can't decide who. Africa wants a death match. So why don't we have a death match between

King Elvis and Fitz Fortune? Then the survivor can give a concert.'

'Oooooh yes!' squeaked Antarctica. 'Yes yes yes yes yes! That would be brill. I'll go get some costumes.'

'Africa?'

The triplets were so close now that Fitz could even hear Africa's answering 'Mmmmmmmm'.

He thought quickly. 'Hang on,' he whispered to Elvis, who looked petrified. 'They're three little kids. Without their muscle we can take them any day!' Elvis seemed confused. 'No robots! If there're no robots, then we can jump them as they come in! Stick the manacles on 'em and we're out of here!' He pointed to one side of the door, indicating where Elvis should go, and stationed himself on the other. There was the bleeping sound of an entry code being inputted. The door slid open. Fitz stood poised... he flexed his knees... he sprang... and bounced off a golden robot.

'I thought you said there weren't any robots!' he said accusingly to Asia, who followed the metal monster in. Possibly not a good tone of voice to adopt in the circumstances.

'All our personal automatons have intrinsic shields,' she said. 'Now, put these on –' Antarctica hurried in and threw some clothes at them, patted Princess Leia on the head and then ran out again – 'and then you will come with us. You too,' she added to Elvis, who was still cowering on his side of the door. The coward hadn't even tried to escape.

The Doctor swept through the door, handing his coat

to one of the guards in passing, without looking at him. The room was a cross between a regally appointed bedroom and an infirmary – presumably it had been the one and converted to the other out of necessity. It was pink and lacy; pastel drapes were hooked back on a four-poster and the pale carpet pile was so deep the Doctor's shoes were almost hidden. A machine stood next to the bed, half concealed by the falling fabric. What could be seen of it was dead – no noise, blank screen, lights dim. And then there were the people. Lying on the bed, arms folded across the pink coverlet and dark hair floating over the pillow as if underwater, was a woman: the President's wife, Elizabethan. She was not moving, and her face was as pale as a ghost.

Kneeling next to the bed was the President, Hoover, crying his eyes out.

The Doctor was at the bed in an instant, looking here, there and everywhere – at the woman, the machine, finally lying flat on the floor to examine the leads that joined the one to the other. The President, still weeping, barely looked up.

'Who switched off this machine?' the Doctor asked. The President didn't answer. The Doctor turned to look at the door guard, still clutching his coat, and raised his eyebrows enquiringly.

'Er, the President did,' said the guard – and then, obviously unsure of the Doctor's place in the scheme of things, added 'sir', just in case.

The Doctor didn't lower his eyebrows.

'Um, it was no use. She was –' the guard lowered his voice – 'she was dead, sir.'

The Doctor turned back to the bed, and whipped back the covers, eliciting a concerned gasp from the guard. The Doctor lifted the woman's arms, letting them drop back on to the bed. He looked up again. 'Could everyone leave the room please,' he said, gesturing for the guard to help up the President. Bewildered, the guard came forward and did so. The President allowed himself to be led away.

As the guard turned to shut the bedroom door behind them, he saw the weird man with the long curls take a small metal rod from his pocket and kneel down beside the bed.

Half an hour later, the Doctor found the President in the throne room. The man wasn't crying any more, but staring sightlessly into the middle distance. The Doctor pulled up a chair and sat down beside him.

'Tell me what happened,' the Doctor said, quietly. 'Tell me what happened all those years ago. How did she become like that?'

The President frowned and looked up slowly, as if noticing the Doctor's presence for the first time. He didn't look at the Doctor as he began to speak.

'Elizabethan was from one of the first-wave families of New Jupiter – a direct descendant of an important Earth family. They were geneticists, and Elizabethan had followed the family tradition. It was a good match, but it wasn't just that. I… I was very fond of her. There was only one problem – she could not fulfil the most important duty of a presidential consort. For a long time, she bore me no children. You understand, the succession is of vital importance. The crown must stay with those appointed by Earth to rule – we cannot risk it falling into the hands of the un-Earthly masses.'

'Of course not,' said the Doctor.

'After some years, much as I… cared for her, I feared I would have to put Elizabethan aside and take a new wife, to ensure the succession. However, to our great delight, at last she bore me an heir. In fact, three heirs. Beautiful children, Asia, Africa and Antarctica. Oh, you've met them, of course.'

'Not exactly.'

Hoover was already back in the past. 'It was then that Elizabethan changed. She – she worried about our children, I think. Why? I don't know exactly why. She sensed, even then, that they were not ordinary girls, I suppose. She didn't talk to me about it.

'We decided early on that the girls should be kept from the public – for their own safety. Daughters of the President – a prime target for the dissidents of our society. Kidnap, assassination…'

'A useful fiction,' said the Doctor. 'Actually, of course, you had noticed the children's antisocial tendencies and didn't want to risk letting the people see them, as it might prove a public-relations disaster. However, isolating them only exacerbated the problem to an insane degree. The obsession with Earth, for example – force-fed your views, were they? Allowed nothing but books and films about Earth for entertainment? Until they started making their own, of course. Tell me about the androids.'

Hoover took a deep breath, and shook his head unhappily. 'Androids. The early settlers used them when they first came here. Common to use them for the heavy work. Drones and so forth. Some of the senior families brought humanoid replicants as servants. We used those for the girls. The only... people they saw were their mother –' he stifled a sob – 'and my chief technician, Hanstrum.'

'And you?' enquired the Doctor.

Hoover looked slightly ashamed. 'And me,' he agreed. 'Sometimes.' The Doctor said nothing. 'I have a planet to run!' the man cried. The Doctor still said nothing. He only looked. After a moment, Hoover continued. 'The girls are brilliant technicians – they inherited their mother's scientific skills. They liked games. They wished – well, they wished they lived on Earth, not New Jupiter. They modified the replicant androids to play their games; be their friends. Act out their fantasies, pretend they were on Earth. And so when the EarthWorld people contacted me –'

'Yes yes yes,' interrupted the Doctor. 'That's not what I asked you. What happened to your wife?'

'They killed her.'

'The triplets did, yes, but how? Why?'

'"Why?" You expect me to understand what goes on in those girls' minds? Let me tell you...'

'Doctor.'

'... Doctor, that those girls are mad! Not responsible for their own actions.'

'Really? Nature, not nurture, you're saying?'

'They're not normal! They've never been normal!

154

Are you saying what they did was my fault? We had hoped there would be improvements as they grew older – their mother said she was making progress with them. But then they killed her… I had no choice, I had to keep them locked up.'

The Doctor laughed, quietly. 'Not that you succeeded, in the end… And I haven't laid any blame. I was just interested to hear what you had to say on the matter, that's all. You don't seem to be very aware of the reality of the situation. Not very perceptive at all, in fact.'

Hoover thrust out his chest. 'How dare you, Doctor whoever-you-are! I am the *President* –'

The Doctor was continuing with no regard for Hoover's blustering. 'So unperceptive, in fact, that you never noticed your wife was an android. Now, perhaps you will tell me the facts that I asked for?'

But Hoover just stared at him.

After a long walk – a very long walk – they were now in a roped area that Fitz presumed was meant to be a boxing ring – with just one slight error.

'When is a ring not a ring?' Fitz asked the elderly Elvis, but just got a blank look in response – unsurprisingly, as the ring in question was actually perfectly circular.

Fitz was feeling incredibly self-conscious, dressed only in boxer's shorts (green and shiny) and boots, although they had also given him a towel, which he'd draped round as much of his skinny upper body as he could. Elvis was in shorts too (white with sequins), and his belly hung over the top.

The gold robots had picked them up and thrown

them inside. A tracksuited trip – Asia – had pushed a button and the ropes of the ring had hummed to life. No one had mentioned whether or not the barrier was fatal to touch, so Fitz was playing it safe by staying in the middle. Antarctica seemed to have appointed herself Fitz's second; she had a towel round her neck and was wearing a big green FITZ! rosette. Africa – with an orange ELVIS! ribbon – was over the other side. Both had armfuls of weapons. Oh joy.

Asia – no ribbons, no allegiance – trotted over to the ring and blew the whistle that hung round her neck. 'The rules!' she cried. 'King Elvis versus Fitz Fortune, to the death! Any weapon is allowed, including all forms of unarmed combat. No body area is off-limits. Participants can only leave the arena once their opponent is dead. Seconds should not get involved in the fighting, even if they really want to. And I've got your popcorn – buttered for you, Antarctica, salted for Africa. Come and get it!'

Antarctica pushed her truckload of weaponry through the barrier, and trotted off to take her pink-striped cardboard box of popcorn. As the barrier obviously didn't kill people, then, Fitz decided to take advantage of the distraction to nip out. He landed back in the middle of the ring on his bum, nursing a tingling hand, and watched dazed as Elvis half-inched a big swingy spiked ball on a chain – a flail, was it called? Something like that – from Fitz's pile, and, with some difficulty, on the third go began to whirl it round his head.

Pulling himself rapidly together – and ignoring

the cry of 'Naughty, naughty, Fitz Fortune!' from his second – Fitz dodged the swinging blow and picked up a polearm. With dexterity born of fear, he tangled the chain of the flail and yanked it out of Elvis's hand. 'Don't do that!' he shouted, alarmed. 'We've got to work together, find a way out of this!' He then fell backwards on to his backside again, having failed to take into account that a polearm plus a flail weighs a good deal more than a polearm alone.

'No way, kid!' Elvis shouted back, staggering slightly too. 'Only way out is if you're doing the dead thing. They said that, an' I bee-leeve them.' To Fitz's dismay, Africa had returned with her popcorn, and was stockpiling nasty pointy-looking stuff in Elvis's corner. Elvis grabbed something that Fitz didn't know the name of, but it was long and sharp. 'Now stop crying like a dirty hound dog and face me like a man!'

'Who are you calling a hound dog?' muttered Fitz, scrabbling in the pile for something with which to defend himself. 'I certainly ain't no friend of yours!' he yelled defiantly, picking up a similar pointed thing and waving it wildly in front of himself. 'Just hold back a second, so we can talk about this!'

'Nothing to talk about, boy! You gonna be lonesome tonight – in the grave!'

'And stop with the song-lyric references already, unless you want me to stamp right down hard on your blue suede shoes!' called Fitz, parrying desperately. Elvis, although presumably considerably older than Fitz, and probably about six stone heavier, hadn't recently done a three-hour concert. And he obviously actively wanted to kill Fitz, whereas Fitz really just wanted to avoid being hit. Though if this guy was going to keep on at him like this he wasn't going to pull his punches, oh no.

'If we work together we might be able to think of a way out of this!' Fitz tried again. Elvis dived at him; Fitz only just ducked out of the way in time. Fitz attempted to appeal to Elvis's sense of reason. 'Do you really want to murder someone for the amusement of three batty teenagers?'

'I got my public to think of! You die – what, you got your momma and poppa grieving? Well, that's too bad. But me – I if bite the big one I got several thousand suicidal chicks on my conscience.' He lunged at Fitz, who dodged again.

'They're not going to let you go, whatever! If you stop trying to kill me for a second, we might be able to think of a way to get us both out of here. You kill me – you just stay locked up in that cell for a while longer, and wait for the day when they get bored with you again and you're dead meat. Escape, or stay of execution – which sounds the better deal?'

'Uh huh?' Elvis dropped the pointed thing and picked up a long leather whip. 'So what exactly is your great escape plan, my friend?'

Fitz yelped and dropped his weapon as the whip flicked his hand. 'I don't know yet!' he cried. 'If you'd just stop trying to kill me for a minute I might be able to concentrate long enough to think of one!'

Elvis took no notice. The whip cracked against Fitz's thigh and he yelled again, stumbling backwards. Why on Earth would anyone think that something that horribly painful was a turn-on? Stupid, stupid people.

Africa was yelling at Elvis through their side of the barrier. 'More blood!' it sounded like. 'More blood! Use the scourge!'

Fitz didn't know what a scourge was, but if it was likely to bring about more blood he doubted he'd like it very much. Antarctica was no help, jumping up and down too, calling, 'Stab him, Fitz Fortune! Stab him!'

Elvis picked up the weapon that Africa passed through the barrier. Fitz's eyes widened. It was... oh God, it was worse than he could possibly have imagined – he couldn't even think of the words. With desperate hope he launched himself at the barrier, just in case they'd happened to switch it off for a moment. Of course, they hadn't. But luck was on his side – in the manner of a wrestler launching himself off the ropes, Fitz was repelled by the barrier with such force that he smashed into Elvis and the fat bloke dropped the scourge. Fitz grabbed it and backed away. The scourge was like a short whip with five whippy bits, each with metal barbs tied along its length. That wasn't a weapon, it was a torture device. No wonder Africa wanted it used. Fitz kept hold of it in his left hand, not because he wanted to use it, but because he damn sure didn't want Elvis to get hold of it again. With his right hand he grabbed a five-foot spear. He was keeping the guy at as great a distance as possible. Who'd have thought a self-important old club singer could become so homicidal?

'Kill him, Fitz Fortune!' Antarctica was calling.

'Give me a gun and I will,' Fitz yelled back. Unfortunately, no gun was forthcoming. 'Couldn't we at least have a time out?' he tried.

'Asia needs to blow her whistle for that, and she's gone off,' Antarctica told him. 'She was a bit bored.'

'Oh dear,' said Fitz, sarcastically. 'I'll try to make my final moments more entertaining in future.'

'How can she be an android? We – she had children!'

'Not for a long time, though, did she? You were going to put her aside.'

It had taken about two minutes for Hoover to speak after the Doctor's revelation. He had stared at the Doctor, as if willing him to take back his words – then turned and gazed away, a puzzled, hurt look in his eyes. His hands were balled into fists. When he finally opened them, four white crescent moons showed on each palm where his fingernails had dug in.

He turned again to the Doctor, now. He was speaking quietly, unnaturally calm. It didn't seem quite real. 'You're saying that the girls – they're not mine? Not ours?'

The Doctor shrugged. 'Rather a hasty assumption. That woman – she was human once. She may have borne children.'

The President was rocking back and forth in his seat, eyes still fixed on the Doctor. 'I don't understand. I don't understand. What are you telling me?'

'She's been – well, cybertised, that might be one way of putting it. Parts replaced by android components. Electronics making her appear to breathe. Mechanics keeping the blood pumping round her body – keeping the body alive. An expert job – and fascinating, absolutely fascinating. I don't know how long she's been like that, of course. I can't tell if there are any brain components without opening her up – things that may have made her seem human when she wasn't. That's why she appeared to die now, obviously – the blocking waves I sent out interfered with her workings. The question now is, was she really murdered? Are you justified in having had those girls locked up for all these years? Or did your wife merely break down?'

The President began to cry again. Racking, heartbreaking sobs of loss and pain.

The Doctor sat there, and watched.

CHAPTER SEVEN
SEVERAL SINGALONGS

This was really creepy. Anji had never been keen on waxworks – long-dead people stuck in one position, staring forward for ever…

This was worse. Half an hour ago, these people had been walking around, talking, to all appearances living. And suddenly, they were as good as dead. Had they felt anything as the magnetic waves had flooded through them? Was there a second of realisation, of horror, or did things just stop? Was it just like switching off a computer? (A computer didn't feel anything as you switched it off – did it?)

But the quiet was the worst thing of all. The only sound was her and Xernic's footsteps. Anji was trying to walk as softly as possible, which was quite ridiculous if you thought about it, but it somehow made her feel more comfortable. They were talking in whispers, too.

'How are we going to find your friend?' Xernic asked her. 'He might not even be here still.'

'I'm sure he is,' Anji whispered back. 'He's not clever enough to have got out on his own. Wherever those girls are, that's where Fitz will be. And there's nothing else living in this whole place except them and us. We'll find them. We'll start back at that theatre, and – Oh!' She gasped and came to a sudden halt.

'What is it?' Xernic hissed worriedly.

Anji let out her breath. 'Nothing.' She gestured at a frozen policeman. 'I thought it moved. That's all. Just my imagination. All these androids – it's getting to me a bit. We don't have things like that where I come from.'

Xernic looked at her, frowning. 'You're nothing like how I imagined Earth people would be. I mean – I hate Earth people. I really do. It's not just some teenage bandwagon: they're really taking advantage of this planet.'

'People take what they can get. I think it's human nature. Not that I'm defending that, you know, but…'

'Oh, you're right. But being told we ought to be grateful to them – that we should *worship* them for it…' His voice was getting louder.

Anji shot him a smile, and answered at a normal volume. 'I know.'

He smiled back, sheepishly. 'I know you do. Sorry. I won't start. But… I really don't understand how you don't know about androids. Earth's where the technology was developed.'

'Yes, but…' She thought he already knew this. 'But it's long after my time. We're time travellers. The closest there was to interactive androids in my time were toys that had a dozen prerecorded phrases that they'd trot out in a random order. Or baby dolls that you'd feed at one end and they'd wee on you from the other. Quite why children are meant to find this amusing I never found out, but…'

Xernic was staring at her. 'Really? I thought – well, I don't know what I thought. That you were joking, or something. Pretending you weren't from this Earth 'cos of us. Something like that. You mean it's real?'

'It's real.'

'You're from… the past?'

She laughed. 'Yes, I'm from the past!'

'But I thought – well, you're not very primitive. I mean,' he said hurriedly, 'you're not primitive at all.'

'Thank you,' she said. 'I'll take that as a compliment. And not give you a student-union talk about how my world was primitive in many ways, in its attitudes to race, and women, and might making right.' She smiled. 'You don't deserve that.'

Xernic probably didn't understand, but he smiled back.

'Let's get on and find Fitz. Now, he really is from a primitive time. The 1960s,' she added, in response to Xernic's quizzical look. 'Free love, racial intolerance and bad haircuts.' She sighed. 'At least we're not whispering any more.' She gestured at a nearby frozen gladiator. 'It's not as if any of these things can – *Aaaaaaaaagh*!' She grabbed Xernic's arm. 'Something moved!'

The boy frowned. 'I didn't see anything. They're all switched off now, really.'

Standing on a London street, surrounded by statue-like men and beasts, back to back with a teenage boy, frightened of her own shadow. Not an image she'd wish to promote. If the guys at the office could see her now… cool, collected Anji, never a hair out of place, as unflappable as they come, the biggest ball-breaker of them all. Why was this happening to her, of all people? But then she realised. They'd laugh at her now, the men in the office: poor Anji, little girl lost, crying 'cos the nasty world was mean to her. But imagine them here. Every single one of them relied on something, whether it was their Porsche or their corporate charge account or their old-school-tie network or their coke or their pulling power with cute young trainees. Whereas what Anji relied on was herself. She didn't like what was happening to her now but she was dealing with it, and they wouldn't be able to. Because they knew only one world and that's all they were equipped for, and she – she'd had to work to fit in, and so she could do it again. She was – *Aaaaaaaaagh!* 'It moved! Over there, something definitely moved!'

Xernic was whispering again. 'I thought I saw it too – Oh.' Because someone had stepped out from behind an elephant, and it was that guy who'd been with them back at the reception centre: Hanstrum.

'What on Earth do you think you're doing?' Anji cried angrily. 'Were you trying to scare us to death or something? Do you get off on lurking around mysteriously?'

Hanstrum snorted derisively, walking towards them. 'I'd be careful what you say to me,' he said. 'Two convicted saboteurs insulting the President's chief technician – not a sensible move.'

Anji opened her mouth to tell him where to go, but Xernic's fingernails were pressing agitatedly into her arm. He was right. It probably wasn't a sensible move. 'What are you doing here?' she asked instead. 'I thought you'd left.'

'Did you?' he said. That was all.

Anji turned to Xernic. 'Come on,' she said. 'Let's leave Mr Mysterious to his little games. We've got to find Fitz.'

Hanstrum was suddenly in front of them. 'I think you're going my way. We might as well all go together.' He smiled. 'That's not a problem, is it?'

'N-n-no,' squeaked Xernic.

'I suppose not,' said Anji. 'As long as you don't slow us down. What do you want with Fitz, anyway?'

'My dear young lady,' said Hanstrum (how patronising could you get?), 'I don't want anything with Fitz. Why should I? I didn't even know of his existence until half an hour ago.'

'So... ?'

He gave her a scornful look. 'The princesses, on the other hand, I have known for thirteen years; I am the chief technician to the President, and it is my duty to protect the heirs to the throne. I am, of course, perfectly capable of finding them on my own, having been here many times, whereas you, as far as I am aware, have only skulked around in the shadows for a few hours. My offer was, therefore, entirely for your benefit.'

'Oh,' said Anji. Then, 'Thank you.' The first words that had entered her head had been 'sod off', but loath as she was to admit that the smarmy git was right, unfortunately, the smarmy git was right. He would be helping them.

Hanstrum took the lead now, as they worked their way past peasants, dinosaurs and a giant mouse that was definitely, Anji thought, a copyright violation.

'So, these princesses are the heirs to the throne, yes?' she asked.

'Yes.'

'And you think they're fit for the job?'

He half smiled. 'What does that have to do with it?'

'Well, it's fairly important, I'd say!'

'Would you?' He seemed to be amused. 'Would you really? How lucky, then, that you have little saboteurs like James here to overthrow the centuries-old system and make New Jupiter a better place.'

'We *are* trying to make it a better place,' muttered Xernic.

'How sad, then, that there are only three of you.'

Anji was getting wound up. 'It only takes one person to start a revolution, if it's the right person,' she said.

'Yes,' agreed Hanstrum. 'You're right.'

She was surprised. 'I am? I mean, I know I am, but you agree?'

'Yes,' he said again. 'That's why I've been feeding these ANJI children information and providing them with equipment.'

Anji and Xernic just gaped at him.

Several guards had rushed in – independently of each other – to see what was happening in the throne room. The Doctor had shooed each one out again. There were several doors to the room, so he'd made it into a bit of a game, trying to anticipate which entrance a guard would come through next and be stationed there ready. So far he'd had a one-hundred-per-cent success rate.

Six guards later, the President was sitting upright and silent again. The Doctor abandoned his current door and went to sit on the steps to the throne again.

'They might have been innocent all these years,' said Hoover. 'And I had them locked away.'

'Yes, well, what's done is done,' said the Doctor. 'You can't –' and here he began to speak more slowly – 'turn... back... time...'

'No.' The President nodded. 'Doctor – can you... that is, would you... Doctor, find out what happened to her? Whether she was ever my Elizabethan or just... just an android?'

'Would it matter to you now? You thought she was a person back then. Would knowing change anything?'

Hoover shook his head despondently. 'I don't know. But I think I have to find out. Will you help?'

The Doctor took his sonic screwdriver out of his pocket. 'Apparently I can do wonders with this,' he said, turning it over in his hand. 'So I could do with some more practice.'

The Doctor had persuaded Hoover that he really didn't want to see what was going to be done to his wife's body, and as Hoover felt that, in that case, the guards shouldn't be looking either, the Doctor was now on his own. He'd been provided with piles of medical equipment, and, having whispered privately to a guard in an attempt to spare the President as much as possible, a hacksaw. Then he'd got down to work.

Now he was just sitting by the bed, looking at the woman lying there. And she was – or at least had been – definitely a woman. Most of her was still flesh and blood. He could reassure Hoover of that, at least. He could also see how the electronics worked, and exactly

169

what he had to do to isolate the circuit, let it run on its own power, and block out any waves of interference. Quite how he was going to do that was another matter.

He examined the sonic screwdriver. He could see the principles it worked on – but what he didn't know, without an instruction manual – and there wasn't one – or handy labels (also absent), was exactly which bits did what. For example, if he twisted it here...

'Ow!' he cried, dropping the red-hot metal on the floor. Gingerly, folding his coat over his hands, he picked it up and twisted it back again.

There was a banging on the door. 'Are you all right in there?' a guard called, beginning to open the door.

'Yes!' shouted the Doctor, not wanting to be disturbed. He hastily triggered the electronic lock with his sonic screwdriver.

Ah.

Anji had been right. He knew exactly how to use this thing, despite having never to the best of his knowledge seen it until very recently. His conscious mind was saying he didn't have a clue; his subconscious was leaping up and down giving him clues aplenty. A distraction was required again. But – and this was the important bit – he was going to have to pay attention to what he was doing while he was distracted.

He tried to dredge up the memory of one of the older songs from his time on Earth. He'd heard it enough times during the war. Yes...

'It's a long way to Tipperary,' sang the Doctor, moving over to the bed, 'it's a long way to go. It's a long way –' ah, yes, press that button 'to Tipperary, to –' touch wires

– 'the sweetest girl I know… Goodbye –' adjust the frequency – 'Piccadilly, farewell… where was it now? –' hands faltering 'Aha! Farewell, Leicester Squaaaaare… It's –' twist – 'a long –' connect – 'long –' cut – 'way to –' feed wire – 'Tipperary, but my –' fuse together – 'heart's –' charge up – 'right –' switch – 'there! –' power on…

The President's wife's chest began to rise and fall. The Doctor grinned, and squeezed his sonic screwdriver happily.

'So, she… she was… real?'

'As far as I can tell,' said the Doctor, 'the android components were introduced after she was dead. I'm sorry.'

'But she wasn't dead…'

'I'm sorry,' the Doctor said again. 'She was. The electronics resurrected her body, have kept her heart beating and the oxygen pumping through her veins, but she would have been braindead by then – just a shell.'

'But you've resurrected her!'

'No. I set the machinery in motion again to see how far the damage extended. But she's just like –' he looked round for inspiration, and settled on a grandfather clock in the corner – 'like a clock with no hands. She'll tick when you put the battery in and stop when you take it out, but she can't tell the time.'

Hoover was quiet for a few minutes, thinking. Then he said, 'Why would the girls do that to their mother?'

The Doctor shrugged. 'To keep her alive? Or at least, a semblance thereof.'

171

'It doesn't make sense.'

'Do you have the death penalty for murder? You seem to have for everything else.'

'Yes.'

'Then perhaps,' the Doctor suggested, 'that's your answer. If she's technically alive, it's not murder.'

'It doesn't make sense,' the President said again. 'They wouldn't think like that.'

'And you know them so well?' the Doctor queried.

Hoover didn't answer. He stood up and sleepwalked down the throne steps, past the Doctor, and across the room to the grandfather clock. He stood looking at it for a moment. Then he reached up and violently wrenched off the hands. He turned back to the Doctor, blood dripping from his fingers. 'I can still hear it ticking,' he said. Then, as if struck by a sudden thought, he turned back to the clock again, and grabbed hold of the slowly swinging pendulum. 'Now I can't.'

And scrunching his face up, he jerked out the pendulum, then strode out of the room.

'You're the power behind the throne, but you want a revolution?'

'Not *a* revolution. *My* revolution.'

Anji looked at him. 'Can I just check,' she said, 'that you're not just telling us your masterplan before you kill us?'

He gave her a condescending stare. 'No. Why should I kill you?'

'My question was rather, why are you telling us this?'

Xernic was open-mouthed. 'You sent us all that stuff? The gadgets and codes?'

Hanstrum was smug. 'Yes. You're surprised?' He hadn't answered Anji.

'Well, I certainly am,' Anji interrupted. 'I admit I'm judging on more or less first impressions here, but you don't seem the altruistic type to me. If the people overthrow Hoover, won't you lose your job?'

He smiled. 'But I don't want Hoover overthrown, not now.'

Anji was surprised. 'You don't? Surely that's what a revolution's all about?'

'If the President is overthrown, anything could happen. Anarchy would reign. But if the President were to hand over the reins of power to a more suitable candidate…'

'Oooh,' said Anji innocently, 'I wonder who that could possibly be. Is he likely to do this, then, do you think? He seems to have worked hard enough to hold on to power all these years.'

'Oh yes,' said Hanstrum. 'Now I am certain he will find he has finally had enough. Soon.'

The Doctor followed the trail of blood spots down the corridor. It was quite easy at first, but after a while he had to look hard for the next droplet, and explore several turnings before he found it. Eventually, he found himself in a corridor he recognised, and was able to abandon his Hansel and Gretel search and head straight for the place where he knew Hoover must be.

The room was essentially the same as when he had

first seen it, but the whole atmosphere had changed. It felt eerie, abandoned, lifeless.

The headless queen still lay on the floor, but the blood had dried to a sticky mass. Now, only one of the thrones was occupied. A green-robed girl – Antarctica – lay curled up on the right-hand seat, eyes staring fixedly ahead. The Doctor went over to her. It was a broken-down android, but for a second, in his head, it was a dead blonde child, and something deep inside him hurt.

After a moment, he left her, and went through to the tiny secret room. The blue-robed triplet – the Asia android – was caught in mid-action, the killing wave reaching her as she leaned over a control panel. The third girl, the orange-dressed Africa, was perched on a chair, staring up at the screen, her rapt expression captured for ever. The Doctor looked at the screen. It was still working, but the scene it showed was empty and dull – a plain white corridor with no signs of life at all.

He went over to the far side of the room where the President of New Jupiter was shivering in a corner. The Doctor reached out a hand and helped him up, wordlessly. The President winced as the Doctor took hold of his lacerated hand, but allowed himself to be led out into the girls' throne room.

The Doctor sat the President on the central throne. When Hoover turned to look at his dead daughter – what seemed to be his dead daughter – by his side, the Doctor removed his velvet coat and laid it over the android. He then fetched a flask of water, took a clean handkerchief from his waistcoat pocket, and began to bathe the President's wounds. Neither of them spoke for a while.

Then, when Hoover's hands had been cleaned and bandaged, the Doctor said, 'Tell me about that day. Tell me what happened when you found your wife's body.'

For a moment, it seemed as though Hoover hadn't heard him. But finally he spoke.

'We were happy together, my beautiful wife and I. But I cannot say it was a perfect marriage. She did not always understand what it meant to be married to an important man: that sometimes the planet must come first. Please don't look at me like that. I did love her. Even when she did not give me children, I did not put her aside. Surely that proves it? Though it was a relief when she fell pregnant. I would not have enjoyed making the choice between my wife and the succession, because I know which I would have had to choose in the end. I know this isn't what you asked for, but please bear with me. I will get to that day in time. All too soon.

'It was a blessed day when she bore me children – and three times the blessing we could have hoped for. I named the girls to show that they were part of Earth, that their destiny was to rule.

They were brought up knowing this.

'But bringing up our daughters did not seem to bring Elizabethan the fulfilment it should have done. She grew distant from me. I should have noticed more, found out what was troubling her. But I had a planet to run.

'The girls were shown what a supreme honour was ahead of them. They were shown the Earth, what a great world they had to look up to. And I know they appreciated it. Perhaps, as things have turned out, it was not wise. But how could I know?

'There were signs, I found out later. No nurse would stay with them, they tormented people so. One of them had a kitten – I'm not sure which. Elizabethan said the girl loved that kitten. I discovered later that one day it was found in one of the girls' beds, dissected. I don't know if it was the cat's owner who killed it or one of the others. And apparently there was more. Dead animals. Smears of blood on the walls. But people hadn't wanted to worry me. Hadn't wanted to tell me what sort of hands I was going to leave my planet in.

'Their mother – you know she was a geneticist? – she taught them science, no doubt hoping it would prove a distraction. Hanstrum – yes, as my chief technician he was allowed access to Elizabethan and the girls too – taught them about technology. Even at such a young age they excelled. I was told about their achievements, and I was so proud! I was so stupid, so blind.

'Then… that morning. Hanstrum and I were just starting our daily conference. A servant came in, and told us that there were screams coming from Elizabethan's room. We rushed straight there. There were guards, servants everywhere, panicking and yelling. And there, in the room – my beautiful wife lying on the floor. Her eyes – her beautiful dark eyes – still open. They seemed to be looking straight at me, begging, pleading for something. The girls were there.

They were all screaming. They were all covered in blood. They said, later, that they'd been trying to help her. They said she'd called for them on a communicator, and they'd come to her. But she was dead when they arrived.'

'And did she make that call, do you know?' the Doctor asked.

'Yes, she did. Hanstrum had been with her at the time. She was unhappy, didn't want to be alone. He was leaving for his meeting with me, and she called for the girls to join her. It wasn't that unusual.'

'And it must be true, if Mr Hanstrum says so?'

The President frowned. 'Hanstrum is completely trustworthy. My right-hand man.'

'And did anyone see your wife after Mr Hanstrum left her? Before the girls arrived?'

'No. There were guards outside her room all the time. No one else went in.'

'Really? I see.'

'But they heard her. No one else went in. She – she used to sing. It was one of the things I loved about her. When she was happy she couldn't stop singing!'

'When she was happy. But she obviously sang when she was unhappy, too.'

'No... no, that wasn't like her...'

'You're beginning to see, aren't you?' said the Doctor. 'It doesn't make sense. You don't have to relive the rest. I'm sure I can guess. Dragging the girls away, locking them up – for their own safety, as much as anything, I'm sure you kidded yourself. They said they didn't do it, but who was going to believe them? They were known to be violent and unbalanced. There was the evidence against them. And as they were young and impressionable, and irreversibly damaged by the loss of the one person who cared about them, they probably even came to believe it themselves. Just one more thing. With your wife in a coma, why didn't you put her aside? Take a new wife, have some less homicidal children, maybe pass the succession on to them?'

Hanstrum looked confused. 'I couldn't. It would be against Earth law. Elizabethan had fulfilled her wifely duties, she had provided me with heirs – however undesirable. It would be unlawful to put her aside.'

'But if she had died – that is, if you had known she was dead? Then you could have remarried? Had more children?'

'Yes.'

'Thank you,' said the Doctor. 'That's all I wanted to know.' He got up. And then sat down again. 'Oh, just one more thing…'

'Yes?' said Hoover, not quite meeting the Doctor's gaze.

'You say your wife was a geneticist?'

'She was. A very great one.'

'Hmm.' The Doctor looked interested. 'I'd have liked to have asked her if she'd studied the works of Gregor Mendel.'

The President shrugged. 'I'm sorry, I don't know who you mean.'

The Doctor smiled reassuringly. 'Oh, he's no one to worry about. I suppose his name's been lost to history with so much else. But he was generally considered to be the father of genetics on Earth. The eyes have it, you might say.'

'You don't think they did it, do you?' Hoover was frowning, but still seemed miles away, haunted.

'No, I don't.'

The President didn't respond.

'I'll be back in a minute,' said the Doctor, getting up and heading back to the tiny control room.

The Doctor looked at the screen again. It was still showing the same blank passage.

The Asia android had obviously been trying to fix the control panels, but hadn't got far. The Doctor sat down and examined the desk. He twisted a dial that he thought should operate the scanner, but it came off in his hand. Flicking a few switches produced no effect, either: the picture remained static. He took his sonic screwdriver from his trouser pocket and began to take apart the nearest panel. A few minutes later he tried turning the dial again, and to his delight images began zipping across the screen. Adjustments brought him the sight of a small, coffee-skinned young woman walking with a tall blond man and a redheaded boy by her side. The Doctor frowned. Then he realised he'd used the sonic screwdriver without having to think about not thinking about it, and grinned instead.

The door opened, and Hoover came in. 'I have to see them,' he said in a low voice. 'I have to see the girls. Speak to them.'

'You can come with me,' said the Doctor, jumping

179

up. He called back over his shoulder as he left the control room. 'I'm going that way.'

Hoover followed the Doctor out of the door and through the throne room. Outside, the Doctor asked him to wait for a moment. He nipped back in and reclaimed his jacket off the android's body. This time he didn't give the green-dressed figure a second glance.

Fitz was really tiring now. He had darted, dodged, ducked and dived, swerved and skipped, and he didn't know how much longer he could keep going. Elvis seemed to have more stamina, though he was puffing and panting a bit. It seemed that doing a concert a night must keep you fitter than adventuring round the universe, which was a bit unfair. Or maybe it was because Elvis was used to having young girls screaming at his every move and didn't find it quite so distracting.

Having exhausted most of the weaponry, the two were facing off each other with big sticks, circling round and round the ring, neither making a move. To either side, the girls were rummaging in boxes, trying to find something to give their chosen one an advantage. Africa suddenly stood up straight. 'I've got the gun,' she called, holding it up on the other side of the barrier.

'Then give it here, kid!' yelled Elvis, lumbering around the ring and trying to hit Fitz with his long stick.

'No, don't!' squeaked Fitz. He desperately called out to his only possibly ally. 'Antarctica!'

'I don't have a gun,' she called back cheerfully. 'We've only got one.'

'That doesn't help!'

'Oh, she won't give it to him – will you, Africa? – 'cos it's much too quick.'

'Then why's she waving it around like that?' Fitz yelped.

It was all too much for Elvis. He turned to Africa. 'Give me the goddamn gun, baby doll!'

It took Fitz a fraction of a second to realise that Elvis was no longer facing him. This was it! His moment of golden opportunity! Big stick, back of head, unconscious Elvis: problem, if not solved, then at least temporarily suspended. Yes!

Fitz launched himself across the ring towards Elvis's back. And – and as he fell he knew that this would be immortalised for ever as his most embarrassing moment, and how embarrassing to die embarrassed – his pumping arms brought forward the scourge, all but forgotten in his left hand. One of its thongs whipped up and caught round the end of his own big stick, yanking it out of his grip. A barb from another thong caught on his shiny shorts in mid run, jerking them down to his knees and sending him crashing to the floor.

Elvis was turning, was above him, and he'd dropped his big stick and had picked up a sword…

Fitz was scrambling to get up, get out of the way, but he was all tangled up with strips of leather and shorts at half-mast and couldn't manage it. He was going to die with his trousers down.

Elvis was raising the sword above his head. He seemed to be posing. In the background, Fitz thought he heard a door swishing open. Were the gates to heaven electric?

'As a crowd gathers round an angry young clown, Face down on the floor with his pants falling down, In the ghetto,' crooned Elvis, bringing the sword down.

'Stop him! Save Fitz!' Beautiful words. The cry of an angel? Then the long, drawn-out screech of a whistle.

And then there was a bang, and there was blood on Fitz's chest. And Elvis slowly toppled forward, sword still raised. Fitz rolled aside. The ring shuddered as Elvis's body hit the floor. And Fitz, lying panting on his side, saw Africa lowering the gun.

He wanted to ask her why, but this was a murderess and he perhaps shouldn't question her motives while she was still holding a smoking gun.

The other two triplets had come to stand by their sister. Three of them? Asia had returned. Had it been her voice, then, the angel's voice? Had she saved him?

She spoke again, this time to the golden robots. 'Take them back to the cells. We –' she gestured at her sisters – 'have things to discuss.'

There was a fizzing sound all round Fitz – which presumably meant the energy barriers had gone down. Fitz couldn't even bring himself to make a run for it. There was no point. Two robots were coming towards him, and he hadn't forgotten the gun. For some reason the trips had decided they wanted him alive, but no one had mentioned anything about his being unhurt.

The two robots climbed into the ring. One effortlessly picked up the corpse of Elvis, the other bent down and grabbed hold of Fitz. He didn't protest. He just asked, as politely as he could, 'Could you just wait while I pull up my shorts?' And when he'd done that, the robot led him away.

CHAPTER EIGHT
IF YOU PRICK ME,
DO I NOT BLEED?

Fitz sat there and looked at the body of the man who had been Elvis. Alone. He was alive, but alone. Which should be a relief, but wasn't, because he didn't know what was going to happen next and it might well be worse.

He was in a tiny stone cell that wasn't very pleasant but at least wasn't as full of corpses as the last one he'd been put in: only one this time, and it wasn't rotting yet, which was something. And he couldn't see it very well, as the only light was coming though the door grille from the flickering torch on the other side, so he could try to pretend it wasn't there. A trepidatious feel around the floor brought to light a couple of robot rats and, fantastically, his old (well, new, but it seemed old now) coat in a heap in the corner, but there was no sign of the rest of his clothes. He put the coat on over his shorts anyway, after he'd wiped as much of Elvis's blood off his chest as he could. He wondered why they'd bothered to throw Elvis's body in with him too. Maybe they were just keeping it out of the way. Maybe this cell was like the cupboard under the stairs, where you stuck old rolls of wallpaper and broken chairs that you might fix one day and buckets and spades waiting for the next summer holiday, oh, and anyone you'd killed recently that you weren't quite sure what else to do with.

Elvis hadn't wanted to die. Oh, he'd been a bit of a bigheaded prat, but bigheaded prats had feelings too and they didn't deserve to be shot down just like that, even if they'd been trying to kill Fitz a few seconds beforehand. And what a way to go. Those were not cool last words. Mind you, they were not, in Fitz's opinion, cool words at all, but Elvis had presumably thought them amusing. Fitz wondered if he'd dreamed them up on the spot, or if he'd been spending half his time in the ring composing some dodgy lyrical parody. If so, not time well spent. Fitz tried to take his mind off his possible impending demise by thinking what his own last words should be to ensure adequate adulation after his death. Strangely, it didn't work.

He scooted his bum to one side as the puddle of blood crept closer. Shouldn't it start to clot soon and stop doing that? Fitz shivered. The sight of other people's blood wasn't quite as disturbing as the sight of Fitz's own, but it still wasn't good. Thinking of that, Fitz did a quick top-to-toe survey of his own injuries – or, rather, lack thereof. Not a scratch. He'd been very lucky.

Or… had he?

He was still made of flesh, wasn't he? Therefore he could bleed. Couldn't he?

He thought back. With all the running around over rocky plains and being attacked by strange monsters that went on in his everyday life with the Doctor, he must have shed some blood at some point since he became bioconstruct-Fitz. It was just that for the life of him he couldn't think of any examples right now. Maybe he couldn't bleed. Maybe his future future-flesh was strong and impervious. Maybe he couldn't even *die*. He'd been worried for nothing! The fake Fitz body would just go on functioning whatever they threw at it. Not that he wanted to risk testing that out, but... well, a nice thought to carry around with him. Might just about make up for not being a real person any more.

The blood puddle spread a little further. Fitz crab-crawled away a bit more. And put his hand slap bang right on Elvis's sword, still clenched in his death grip. He yelled in pain, snatching his hand away, and whipped out a handkerchief to staunch the bleeding. So much for that theory. Guess he could die too, then. Bummer.

And while he was thinking these comforting thoughts, the triplets came in. Great.

Fitz leapt to his feet, narrowly avoiding tripping over Elvis. He backed away as far as he could before the wall got in his way.

Antarctica rushed forward. Fitz somehow managed to back away a few inches more. 'Fitz Fortune!' she cried. 'You're hurt!'

Fitz waved his hankie-bandaged hand in the air without taking his eyes off her. 'Just a scratch,' he said. 'It's not like I've been, oh, I don't know, shot dead or anything.'

'Good,' said Asia. 'Because you're going to take us to Earth. That is, if you want it to remain "just a scratch".'

Fitz boggled. 'I can't take you to Earth,' he said. 'Surely

Daddy can buy you a spaceship if you're that desperate. Hey, you could probably build one yourselves, you seem to have quite a way with a screwdriver.'

Asia shook her head. 'That's not what we mean. We want you to take us to the real Earth.'

'To ancient Rome,' added Africa.

'To twentieth-century London!' sighed Antarctica.

'Well, I definitely can't do that,' Fitz said.

Asia held up the Walkman he'd been listening to in his dressing room earlier. 'Oh yes you can. You travel in time and space in a machine called the TARDIS. It can go anywhere. It can take us to Earth.'

'Oh great,' said Fitz. 'So that –' he indicated the Walkman – 'isn't actually a listening-to-music device, it's a read-Fitz's-mind device? Typical. Just typical. But if you've read my mind, you'll know that I can't control the TARDIS.'

'Don't believe you,' said Asia. 'We saw you arrive, in your mind.'

'You obviously didn't look close enough! Yeah, all right, I travel in the TARDIS. But I can't pilot it. Only the Doctor can.'

'But we don't have the Doctor,' Africa drawled. 'We have you. You have to do what we say.'

Fitz hit his forehead in exasperation. 'I'm not saying I won't: I'm saying I can't. Which bit don't you understand?'

'Are you really telling the truth, Fitz Fortune?' Antarctica asked.

'Yes! Yes, I am! I mean, apart from the inability to pilot a time machine, what other reason could I have for refusing to take you three lovely girls back to my home planet?'

'Mmm,' said Antarctica.

'I could find out if he's telling the truth,' breathed Africa.

'I *am* telling the truth!' yelled Fitz.

Asia took Africa's arm, steering her away from Fitz. 'There is another way to find out,' she said. 'Go and fetch the machine.' Africa smiled and left the cell.

The machine? Nothing good could possibly be called 'the machine'. 'What machine?' Fitz asked.

'This is very important to us,' said Asia. 'We have to find out if you're telling the truth. You lost the death match, you see. The only reason you're still alive is because we want you to take us to Earth. We have to find out if you can or not. If you're lying to us, we ought to kill you.'

Hang on. If he was lying to them about not being able to take them to Earth they were going to kill him? Not very logical. He pointed this out.

'Hmm,' said Asia. 'I see what you mean. Well then, if you're telling the truth we'll kill you.'

'What?'

'Oh, Asia!' cried Antarctica. 'Let's just find out the truth. We can decide whether or not we're going to kill Fitz Fortune afterwards.'

Asia looked indulgently at her sister. 'All right. Let's let the machine do its work.'

The machine. Still didn't sound good.

And this must be it. The door opened, and Africa pushed in a large contraption on wheels. It looked a bit like something that might be found by an intensive-care bed. Lots of switches and dials and little coloured lights. Harlequin patterns flickered over the stone walls.

'We call it our Memory Machine,' Antarctica told Fitz. 'We can take deep memory and personality prints with it, not like the surface scans from the portable machine.' Africa was flicking switches, and the thing was humming into ominous life. 'You just have to relax.' Africa was now plugging in small headphones – worryingly featuring metallic spikes that looked like they'd stick right in your earholes.

'It may not work on me,' he said, trying to be casual. 'There might be… complications.'

'Oh, because of your being artificial?' said Asia. 'Don't worry, it'll be fine.'

Fitz yelped. 'You know?'

'Yup. Sorry, is it supposed to be a secret?'

'I thought you said you'd only taken a surface scan thingy?'

'Yes, we did. And that knowledge was the closest to the surface of all. When we made a copy of you –'

'You made a copy of me?'

'It was all it could think of. Bit disappointing, really.'

'You made a copy of me?'

'Well, yes. Didn't want your friends finding the real you, now, did we?'

'I wanted to keep you!' put in Antarctica, cheerfully.

'Let's just hope that the Doctor hasn't left in his TARDIS already with your double. That would be unfortunate.'

'Unfortunate…' echoed Africa, coming over and running a finger down his cheek. Fitz instinctively shrugged her off, which was possibly not the best way to treat a homicidal lunatic, however much shorter than him she was. She hissed, and stepped back to the machine. Oops. Possibly a terminal 'oops'.

'The Doctor's cleverer than that,' said Fitz. 'He'd spot it was a fake. He'll still be looking for me.'

'Like he did before?' asked Asia, and Fitz's stomach did a flip-flop as he realised just how much they knew even without this deep-memory thing. 'This copy – does it have my –' how to phrase this? – 'inhibitions?'

Antarctica giggled. Asia gave her a look. 'Do you mean will it tell the Doctor how he abandoned the real Fitz, then killed him and then destroyed his own planet?'

'Um… well, that's what I was basically getting at, yes.'

'Don't know. Sorry. Anyway, put those on.' Asia was gesturing at the spiky headphones that Africa was holding out. 'Take them, or we kill you now.'

Fitz opened his mouth to start trying to reason with them again, but decided it was pointless. Logic didn't seem to mean much to them. Wordlessly, he took the headphones.

Surprisingly, they didn't hurt. The metal bits filled up his ears and were a bit uncomfortable, but there was no pain. So they were probably not devised by Africa. They blocked most of the sound from outside, and when Asia flipped a switch a low hum began, which drowned out the rest. He could see the trips' mouths moving, but couldn't tell what they were saying. More switches were flipped, and the hum grew louder. Unbidden, images crowded into Fitz's head. Things he'd been thinking of only recently, like his childhood trip to the zoo, and going off with Sam and the Doctor, and, well, and Gallifrey and all that stuff. Things he'd done lately, like waiting in London for the Doctor, and all that stuff in Belgium with Anji and Dave. The triplets seemed to be getting a bit agitated, mouths opening and closing swiftly, but he was so caught up in his past that he didn't care what was happening out there... Back a bit, to Compassion, and then a brief trip through all the girls he'd loved and lost (or abandoned) – Filippa, Maddy, Kerstin, Arielle... God, there had been a few, anyone would think he had commitment issues – and before that, to his early travels with the Doctor, and, yes, what he knew about the TARDIS and how to use it but how it was only the Doctor that knew how to use it really and now probably even he didn't. And then he had to go through his mum dying again, and then he was looking after her when she was ill, and the first time he'd – well, something good to relive at last – and his first girlfriend, and looking after his mum after his dad died, and then the kids at school were celebrating the death of a stinking old Kraut, and then his dad died, and then his dad was ill, and then Fitz was a kid and didn't understand the things that were being shouted at him in the street.

Faster and faster. Spending entire days as Dick Barton, Special Agent. Mum and him being spat on in an air-raid shelter when they found out their surname. His fifth-birthday party, where there were Spam sandwiches and his mum wasn't going to let that nasty Hitler spoil little Fitzie's day. Buckets and spades and the incredible smell of salty sea air. Riding on a bus. Being carried everywhere. Mummy. Daddy. Food. Sleep. Mummy, Daddy, food, sleep. Cry. Mummy. Cry. Warm and cosy and didn't want to move ever and...

'*Aaaaargh!*' Fitz yelled, as Asia took the headphones off him. 'I was being born! Oh my god, I was being born!'

Asia was frowning. 'He's overloaded the machine.'

'Oh no, poor machine,' gasped Fitz.

But they were ignoring him. 'Look at this,' Asia said to her sisters, showing them something Fitz couldn't see.

'They're all on the surface,' said Africa.

'Sort of like bubbles,' said Antarctica. 'Ew!'

'What?' said Fitz. 'Tell me what!'

Asia condescended to answer him. 'You have to dig deep, normally. There are barriers – things you don't want to remember, things that happened long ago, things you didn't understand. Your barriers are gone, if they were ever there. When you were given your memories, you were given them all. Every single thing that'd ever happened to you – to Fitz – brand spanking new in your head. They're just bubbling up to the surface.'

'Well, I hope you haven't burst any!' said Fitz, freaked out again.

'Might have. Sorry.'

'What!'

'Probably not, though. The copied stuff's probably all right. It's the new stuff that's a bit unstable. Your old memories aren't fading into the background like they should, so there's not really that much room for anything else. Ooooh!'

'What? What?'

'One of your memories just popped out of existence, all by itself! Cool! I've never seen that happen before.'

Fitz was not calm. 'Oh, I'm so glad my brain is entertaining you. Are you telling me my memories are just disappearing? This is my mind you're talking about! My life! Could you not be quite so casual about it?'

Asia just shrugged.

Africa looked up from where she'd been examining the machine. 'It's all right, he hasn't damaged it.'

'Oh, hurrah! Long live the machine! Everything's OK, then!'

Antarctica frowned at him. 'The machine's very important, Fitz Fortune,' she said, moving over to it and beginning to spin dials.

'More important than my brain? No,' as she opened her mouth, 'don't answer that. But at least you know I'm telling the truth now, right?'

'Yes,' said Asia. 'So you're going to have to take us to the Doctor, and tell him to take us to Earth.'

'He won't listen to me.'

'I think he will.'

'Supposing I refuse. Are you going to kill me?' After the last few minutes/hours/days, Fitz was able to say

194

that quite calmly because, really, he didn't have any distress left.

'Yes,' said Africa.

'No,' said Asia at the same time. 'Not necessarily,' she continued, shaking her head at her sister. 'But we think you'll want to help us. When you see what we can do for you in return.'

Fitz looked enquiringly at her, hoping they weren't going to suggest something that might make him explore bits of his mind where he didn't want to go, because after all they were only thirteen.

'We've read your mind, Fitz,' she went on. 'And we can make people. Antarctica?'

'All ready!' said the third trip. 'Put these on, Fitz Fortune.' She held out the headphones again.

'No way.'

'Please?' said Asia, surprising him by sounding genuine.

'And these,' said Antarctica, holding out a pair of large goggles.

'Why?' Fitz asked.

'Just put them on.'

Once again, Fitz capitulated. He didn't really feel he had much choice. But as he put the goggles on…

'Woah!' he cried, putting out his hands to steady himself as the floor seemed to rush out to meet him. He felt someone grab his arm. 'It's OK, Fitz Fortune!' he heard dimly, on the other side of the headphones. 'It's just virtual reality. This is what we could give you if you do as we say…'

*

Anji, Xernic and Hanstrum had reached the theatre. Anji glanced at one of the FITZ FORTUNE! posters, amused to see a velvet-suited Fitz apparently winking at her. But there were no signs of life.

They went to the dressing room where the replicant had been. There was no sign of Fitz.

'He could be anywhere by now,' said Xernic, unenthusiastically.

'He'll be wherever the girls are,' said Hanstrum. 'We find them, we find your friend.'

'But we don't know where to look!' wailed Xernic.

Anji was determined to remain calm. She certainly wasn't going to let this Hanstrum see that she was worried. 'We use this as our starting point,' she said. 'We'll explore the theatre – look for clues.'

They looked into the other dressing rooms, those marked ELVIS. Nothing. Anji found a door into the main auditorium, but there was nothing there except scattered popcorn and ice-cream wrappers.

It was Xernic who found the door to the basement. It was behind a curtain backstage, and had a NO UNAUTHORISED ENTRY notice on it. He called the others over. Anji, who would once have never dreamed of disobeying a sign, pushed the door open. And then she heard it.

'There's something moving down there!' she hissed, letting the door swing shut again.

'And is that not what we're looking for?' questioned Hanstrum.

Anji wanted to slap him.

'I was only telling you,' she huffed. 'And now I'm

going down there.'

'Would you like me to go first?' asked Xernic nervously.

Anji, who desperately would have liked that, said, 'No, thank you,' defiantly, and opened the door again. She crept down the stairs, treading carefully to stop her heels clicking on the bare steps. Xernic and Hanstrum followed.

There was the noise again, a sort of shuffling. She hoped to goodness it wasn't rats. It was coming from behind a door – a door that was obviously lockable but that was standing ajar. So whatever was making the sounds wasn't a prisoner, then... but what was that horrific smell?

Holding her breath, Anji pushed the door open, shrieked, and jumped back into Xernic's arms. As she huddled there, embarrassed, Hanstrum went past and into the room.

'Oh dear,' he said. 'Not very pleasant, is it?'

Anji composed herself, and extricated herself from Xernic, who was just standing there bemused. With another deep breath – which she instantly regretted, because of the smell – she followed Hanstrum into the room.

'There's nothing to worry about. They're all long dead,' said Hanstrum, condescendingly.

Anji took in the bones hanging from the walls, the rotting flesh on the floor, and shivered. 'None of these could be Fitz, could they?' she asked.

'Not unless he was already massively decomposing when you saw him yesterday,' Hanstrum said. Anji kicked herself. She knew that.

'But what was making the noises?' Xernic said. Anji took a step backwards as the scuffling came again. Her eyes darted around the cell. It was coming from a pile of clothes in the corner. Please not rats!

Xernic nervously crept forward and whisked aside a purple velvet coat. Anji almost shrieked again when she saw what was under it, but decided to laugh instead. Curled up on a silver lamé shirt was a tiny crocodile, a pink ribbon around its neck.

'Ah,' said Hanstrum. 'Princess Leia.'

Pardon?' spluttered Anji.

'Princess Leia. She belongs to Antarctica.'

'So we're probably close,' said Xernic. 'Unless she's abandoned it.'

Hanstrum shook his head. 'No, she loves that thing.'

'It's ticking,' said Anji.

'Well, it is a crocodile,' said Xernic. 'It's got an alarm clock inside it. All Earth crocodiles have. Didn't you know that?'

'No, I didn't,' said Anji, giving him a look. She picked up the velvet coat that Xernic had dropped to one side. 'The poster-Fitz was wearing a jacket like this,' she said. 'Do you think it could be his?'

'Possible,' said Hanstrum.

'Well, are there such things as tracker crocodiles?' Anji asked. 'Could we get, er, Princess Leia here to sniff Fitz's coat and hunt him out?'

'It seems unlikely,' said Hanstrum with a sneer.

'But it's worth a try,' said Xernic, encouragingly. 'Or maybe she'll be able to find Antarctica, if she's her pet.'

'It *is* worth a try,' agreed Anji. 'So we'll try it.' She scooped up the little ticking creature, taking care to point the teeth-end away from her – although surprisingly, it didn't seem to be aggressive at all. It seemed quite happy to be sitting in her arms. But once they'd left the room and were at the top of the stairs, the reptile began to squirm, trying to get down. Anji hurriedly dropped it on to the floor and it began to scamper forward, inasmuch as its tiny legs could scamper.

'I think it's working!' Anji cried. They followed the animal as it hurried through the backstage area, and went behind another curtain. They found themselves in a dark corridor, which the crocodile continued to run down.

Hanstrum was ridiculing the whole situation. 'She's probably just seizing the chance for some exercise,' he said. 'We'll find ourselves in a swimming pool or something.' Anji and Xernic ignored him.

There was a door at the end of the corridor; Princess Leia obviously was keen to go through, so Anji opened it.

She found herself in a strange parody of a boxing arena. There was an actual ring in the centre, roped off, and seats round the outside. Princess Leia had trotted over near to the boxing ring, and was examining the floor. Anji went over to see what she was sniffing at. 'Blood!' she said.

Xernic had climbed up to look inside the ring, and called, 'There's lots more here. A huge pool of it. Do you think it's Fitz's?'

'No!' said Anji. It wasn't going to be Fitz's. She wasn't going to lose anyone else, even someone she barely knew and didn't like that much. 'Anyway, now we know what Princess Leia was tracking. She wasn't homing in on anyone after all, she just smelled the blood.' She didn't look at Hanstrum as she said that, she didn't want to see the 'I told you so' expression she was sure he'd be wearing.

'It looks like the body's been dragged away,' Hanstrum said, adding, 'whoever it was.' There was a clear trail on the floor, from the ring where Xernic was, via the traces Princess Leia was smelling, all the way out through a door on the other side of the room.

'Then that's where we'll go,' said Anji. She bent down and called to Princess Leia, but it seemed that having found the source of the smells, the little crocodile wasn't very keen on budging, so in the end they left her there and set off following the blood trail on their own.

'I'm the President of this world,' Hoover was saying to the Doctor. 'I can't just... wander off on my own.'

'Then bring some guards with you. Do whatever you like. Only don't try to stop me, because I am going to find Anji, because I believe she is out there with a murderer. And considering everything else she's been through in the last few days, I think she deserves to be rescued.' The Doctor was striding through the palace corridors, ignoring the startled guards who jumped to attention as their ruler passed by.

Hoover's voice was pleading, desperate. 'I can't... just...'

The Doctor stopped suddenly, and Hoover almost walked into him. The Doctor spun on his heel and stared the President in the eyes. The intensity of his gaze made Hoover take a step back. 'You want me to make it all go away, don't you? You want me to tell you what to do, take away the responsibility; to solve everything, make it better. Well, I can't. If you want to make it up to the triplets for imprisoning them for over half their lives for a crime they didn't commit, then you're going to have to make that decision yourself. You can come with me now, and maybe save a few lives in the process, or you can sit on your golden throne and worry about whether it's the best course of action. Only decide now, because I am leaving.'

Hoover tried to draw himself up to the Doctor's height. 'I am the President, Doctor, and you are an escaped criminal! I could stop you leaving with a snap of my fingers!'

'No,' said the Doctor, 'you couldn't.'

Hoover looked at the Doctor's face, and involuntarily took another step backwards.

In the end, they took two guards with them. Hoover was clearly disconcerted about leaving his palace with no ceremony, and the looks of astonishment on the faces of everyone they passed on their way out showed how infrequently he left at all. The four of them took a ground-car, the Doctor insisting on driving. 'What a lovely machine!' he cried, delighted, as they climbed in. 'I bet she handles like a dream!'

He kept up a cheerful but one-sided conversation

all the way to the main entrance. Occasionally Hoover tried to ask him about Gregor Mendel, or this alleged murderer they were going to apprehend. The Doctor just looked pityingly at him, and began to talk about the best method of growing roses, or his theories on possible ways to escape the gravitational pull of a black hole.

The Doctor parked the ground-car with a screech of brakes, and swept into the reception area. Hoover and the guards had to almost jog to keep up.

'Do you know where we're going?' Hoover panted. 'Do you know how big this place is?'

'I have a fair idea,' said the Doctor, whipping the guidebook from his pocket. 'The question is, how to get there quickly? They do have several hours' head start on us, after all. Come along, come along.' He carried on through the control centre. 'I do think it's ridiculous that you can't get a ground-car into it anywhere.'

'It's not authentic, Doctor,' Hoover explained. 'What would they do if a visitor saw a ground-car driving through ancient Rome?'

'Oh, let's think,' said the Doctor. 'What normally happens to visitors to this place? Do they get to go home with a packet of holiday snaps and lots of stories to tell the grandchildren, or do they get killed by your daughters? Hmm. I would imagine that seeing an anachronistic vehicle would be the least of anyone's worries.'

'But that wasn't anticipated in the building specifications,' Hoover mumbled. 'None of this was anticipated,' he added, virtually to himself.

'Well, never mind that now,' said the Doctor. 'Perhaps we can hitch a lift on a dinosaur!' Hoover looked alarmed. 'It's all right,' the Doctor reassured him, 'that was a joke. All the dinosaurs are out of action. But there was something else I spotted, not that far away from here. I think getting a ride is still a distinct possibility...'

Anji, Xernic and Hanstrum had gone along several long corridors, down a flight of stairs, and then through a huge wooden door into another corridor. Anji was guessing they were underground, and had passed from one zone to another, because this was clearly mock-medieval. The walls were made of stone, and the electric lights had given way to flaming torches stuck in brackets. She kept a close eye out for rats.

Suddenly Xernic clutched at Anji's arm. She stopped, and looked at him enquiringly. 'I thought I heard a voice,' he said. He pointed along the passage. 'Down there.'

Anji listened hard. 'I'm not sure,' she said. 'There might be something.'

They crept carefully along, all ears pricked.

FITZ.

Fitz was in a room with a redheaded girl – a remnant of a long-ago adventure. He'd loved her, for a while. And she was the only woman that he'd ever loved for whom the 'while' kept being extended. True love is where you haven't seen the other person for an eternity, but just know they're still feeling the same way. Possibly.

Or was it just a case of 'absence makes the heart grow fonder'? No, probably not. Fitz was an 'out of sight, out of mind' guy, really. Except in this case. Her name was Filippa. Ha! He remembered her name – it must be love.

'Hello, Fitz,' she said.

'You're not real,' he replied.

'As real as you,' she said.

'I'm not real, either. I've just found out.'

'You mean I fell for a fake Fitz?'

"Fraid so, babe.'

'You must have a very low opinion of me, then. To think I would be taken in so easily.' She gave him a pretend-hurt look.

'Um…' Witty comeback or heartfelt denial? By the time he'd considered it, it was too late for either.

'I fell in love with you, Fitz. We weren't in a real situation, but you were real. You fell in love with a girl from her memories alone, and she with you. I was Essence of Filippa, and you were Essence of Fitz.'

'By Calvin Klein,' said Fitz, unable to help himself.

She carried on, brown eyes staring deep into his, and he wondered if she could see herself in them. 'I couldn't have loved you if you weren't real, and you couldn't have loved me. You did love me, so you *were* real. Have we cleared that up?'

'Yes, Filippa,' said Fitz meekly.

'Good. Now, you're meant to be deciding if you want to have a construct of me to join you. That bargain thing with the triplets, remember? Of course, this construct would look like me, have my personality as you remember it – though I notice already that my speech patterns have degenerated into a cross between my own and yours – and would also, to a certain extent, have my memories – what you know of them. But – and this is the crucial difference – it wouldn't have Essence of Filippa.'

'By –' began Fitz.

'I ignored that the first time,' said Filippa, 'because it wasn't funny even then. OK?'

'Yes,' agreed Fitz. He really loved this woman. 'So, two artificial constructs together – you don't think it would work, then?'

She sighed. 'Don't be silly. You know perfectly well it wouldn't. You'd be aware the whole time that I was out there somewhere else. And will you stop saying you're an artificial construct? You are no more so than Compassion was, and you treated her as a person. Well, in your own inimitable way, you did, anyway. To put it bluntly, you're bloody real, Fitz. And I've just shown how much I mean it, because in your memories of me, I never swear. Now just go and live your life, you idiot, and stop wallowing in self-pity because of something that happened in the past that you can't change. If it helps, wonder if anyone who feels that amount of self-pity could possibly be a fake Fitz. See?'

'But will I ever see you again?' asked Fitz, torn between relief and trauma.

'Well, I don't know, do I? I'm not a fortune teller, I'm an aspect of your mind. Do you think you'll ever see me again?'

Fitz considered this for a moment. 'I think I probably

will. I'd like to. But I'm not going to destroy what we had by building impossible dreams on it.'

'Good answer,' said Filippa, smiling. She moved closer, and kissed him. Much to Fitz's surprise, he felt it. 'Now, go on. Back to the Doctor.'

'Couldn't we just –'

'No. Go!' But she was grinning as she said it.

'Fitz! Are you OK?' cried Anji, bursting through the door.

'I am now,' said Fitz.

CHAPTER NINE
NIGHTS AT THE ROUND TABLE

The cell was getting very crowded now. Fitz, the triplets, three new arrivals, a robot and a corpse, as well as the quite chunky Memory Machine.

The kid that Anji had dragged along – Xernic – was obviously terrified of the triplets. Fitz would have found the idea of a grown lad being given the heebie-jeebies by three adolescent blondes hilarious, if he wasn't terrified of them too. He might also, under other circumstances, have found Anji's marching up and demanding his release vastly amusing, as she was actually several inches shorter than the girls. It must be a bummer to be short. Maybe that was why Anji shouted so much.

The other person with them, however, inspired much less laughter. He was as blond as the triplets, but much taller than they. And he had an arrogant look in his eye that Fitz recognised from all the power-hungry dictators he'd met. This man wanted to be in charge.

'Hanstrum!' Antarctica cried as the man entered the cell, and flung herself on him in a giant hug, which he coldly returned.

The others were less enthusiastic. 'Have you come to stop us playing?' pouted Africa.

'I've come to get you out of here,' he replied.

Antarctica extricated herself from him. 'Oh no!'

'We're not coming!' yelled Africa.

'Why do you want to take us away?' Asia asked.

The man seemed slightly taken aback. 'You can't possibly stay here. The whole system's been fused. What would you do?'

'We'd have fun!' said Asia. 'That's what we always do. We can't have fun locked up in the palace. We want to stay here.'

'Maybe they're worried they'd be put on trial for murder if you take them back,' Fitz suggested.

'Oh no,' said Hanstrum. 'We know that any deaths that may have taken place must have been accidental.'

Fitz opened his mouth to strongly deny this, sharply aware of the corpse of Elvis only a few feet away, but thought better of it. Hanstrum looked like a man who knew it wasn't the truth, and didn't care. And even if not, Antarctica's giggles gave the game away more than Fitz's words ever could.

'The President will no doubt agree,' Hanstrum continued.

'But we don't want to go back!' cried Antarctica.

Hanstrum was glancing around himself distastefully. 'We can't talk in here,' he said. 'Could we go somewhere a little more –' he gestured at the body – 'aesthetically pleasing?'

Asia shrugged, and gestured to the open door. 'We're near the banqueting hall,' she said. 'We can go there.'

'But we're not dressed for it!' Antarctica complained, until she was shushed by Asia.

*

Presumably the hall was also part of the Medieval Zone. There was a big central table (round), and massive candelabras lighting the room, but possibly someone should have told the designers that tapestries usually went on the walls and rushes on the floor, not the other way round.

Hanstrum placed himself at what, as soon as he sat down, became the head of the table, even though a round table logically provided no such thing. He was facing the door, where a golden robot stood guard. Asia sat directly opposite him, Africa on her left-hand side and Antarctica to her right. Fitz, Anji and Xernic huddled in a corner of the hall.

'I want you to come home with me,' Hanstrum said.

'Father will be cross,' said Antarctica.

'He'll lock us up again,' said Africa.

'Do you love your father?' Hanstrum asked.

The girls exchanged puzzled glances.

'No,' said Asia, finally.

'He locks us up!' said Africa.

'We loved Mother, though,' added Antarctica. 'I don't know why we killed her.'

'But you did,' said Hanstrum, smoothly. 'You killed someone you loved. So surely it would be much easier for you to kill someone who you *didn't* love – someone who locks you up…'

The triplets looked at each other again. 'You want us to kill Father?' Asia asked. 'Won't people be cross?'

'Not if they don't know about it. Not if you replace him with an android…'

'Hmm,' said Asia, seemingly considering the idea.

Then, 'No. Don't think so.'

Hanstrum pushed back his chair angrily. 'Why not?' he shouted. 'You could rule, then! Isn't that what you want?'

'No,' Asia told him. 'What we want is to go to Earth. Real, proper, old Earth. The Doctor is going to take us there in his time machine.'

Anji shot an alarmed look at Fitz, who tried to shoot one back that said, 'Don't worry, he won't, only we might have to play along with it for now to get out alive.' He hoped she got all that.

Antarctica and Africa stood up and pushed back their chairs.

'Where are you going?' Hanstrum demanded. 'I haven't finished!' They ignored him, and walked over to the door, patting the golden robot on the way out as though it were a pet dog.

Asia smiled thinly at Hanstrum. 'My sisters are going to get changed,' she said. 'They are uncomfortable being dressed inappropriately for their surroundings. My sisters...' The smile changed to one of amusement. 'My sisters are ruled by their instincts. I wonder if you can understand that.'

'What I understand,' Hanstrum glowered, 'is that you prefer to carry on with your insignificant little games rather than play the one great game – power!' He leaned forward, gazing at her imploringly. 'Can't you see it? Hoover stands down. The throne would be yours – all yours! You wouldn't have to hide away here in secret: the whole planet would be your play area!'

'Ask him what's in it for him,' Anji muttered. Rather

too loudly, as it turned out, as Hanstrum shot her a chilling glance. Fitz gave her a nudge in the ribs. Hadn't she worked out by now that you didn't wind up any of these loonies? God, he'd just survived a death match, for goodness' sake; he didn't want to end up in a wooden overcoat 'cos of some Asian chick's big mouth. He glanced sideways at Anji. Even if it was quite a nice mouth.

'What's in it for you, Mr Hanstrum?' asked Asia, brightly.

Hanstrum glared at Anji again, but answered, 'You are young,' he said. 'The people, alas, would not accept you as rulers until you reach the age of maturity. Your father, therefore, would have to appoint a presidential regent to rule in your stead.'

'Huh,' said Asia. 'You just want to be in charge. You're not doing this for us.'

'You're wrong,' said Hanstrum. 'I want you on the throne. That would make me happy. But until that is possible...'

'This is all wrong!' Xernic hissed to Anji and Fitz. 'This isn't what ANJI stands for!'

'Pardon?' said Fitz.

'I've made such an impression on this world that they've named a terrorist organisation after me,' Anji told him.

'You don't seem to understand,' Asia was saying. 'We used to want to be president, long ago, when we thought it would mean people doing what we said.'

'It does!' interrupted Hanstrum.

'But,' she continued, 'that was when we were young

and locked up and didn't know any better. Now we know what it's like to have real fun with real people, and we want lots of it. And we want to go to the real Earth, instead of some silly fake Earth or a stupid world that tries to be like Earth but doesn't have a clue.'

'But you can't!' said Hanstrum. 'The succession…'

'You're not going to stop us doing what we want because of some silly succession,' said Asia. 'We won't let you. We don't care about this planet. We only care about Earth.'

The door creaked open. Fitz assumed it was Africa or Antarctica coming back, and kept his eyes on Asia and Hanstrum. Mistake.

There was a chink of metal.

Asia suddenly screamed. Full-hands-to-the-head-feet-apart job. Fitz turned to see a massive knight in full plate mail standing over him, broadsword held threateningly in one hand. He yelped, and began to scuttle away, unfortunately falling backwards over Anji and Xernic as they tried to move in different directions. But… and this was the weird thing he observed as he half raised his head… Asia was running now but she wasn't running *away* from the knight, she was running *to* him…

And as Fitz sat up, he saw Asia reach the knight. She clung to his arm. 'Oh, Sir Lancelet!' she cried. 'This evil man was trying to keep me prisoner!' She pointed at Hanstrum, who was getting to his feet and looking thoroughly bewildered. 'I am so scared of him, please take him away and lock him up or kill him or something.'

212

The knight strode forward towards Hanstrum. He spoke, his voice deep and musical. 'So, you threaten these ladies, varlet?' he said.

'Get away from me!' yelled Hanstrum angrily. 'Do you know who you're talking to, android? I am the President's chief technician!'

The knight laughed humourlessly. 'Do not try to fool me with your sorcerous words, cur.'

'I thought none of the androids were working!' Anji hissed at Fitz.

'They weren't!' he whispered back. How did she expect him to know what was going on? 'Africa and Antarctica must have fixed him somehow.' Fitz jumped as another knight appeared in the doorway. 'And him,' he added. 'Oh... and them.'

Three more knights came into the room.

'We know their own robots were on separate circuits,' Xernic murmured. 'Maybe they've fitted these up, too.'

'Then why haven't they done that before?' said Fitz. 'I'm sure they would have if they could.'

'Maybe they didn't have any more of the circuits,' suggested Anji.

'So where exactly have they got them from now?'

'Perhaps...' That was Xernic. 'Perhaps they've cannibalised their working robots.'

As one, they turned to look at the golden humanoid in the doorway.

'It's not moving,' whispered Anji.

'Not making a sound,' said Xernic.

'Run for it!' yelled Fitz, and the three of them were

on their feet and through the door in a split second.

They heard Asia's shouts from behind them: 'Get them! Kill them! They're sorcerers too!' And then the clank of metal footsteps running after them as the knights started in pursuit.

'They won't be able to run fast in that armour,' panted Anji. 'We've just got to keep outdistancing them until we find a way out!'

'And your plan for that is… ?' asked Fitz, who was wondering if taking the escape initiative had been such a wise move after all.

'Just keep running!'

'Here we are!' beamed the Doctor, gesturing behind him with a flourish. Not that he needed to point anyone in the right direction: Hoover and the two guards were already staring open-mouthed at the bright-red double-decker bus that the Doctor was standing beside.

'You expect us to travel in that… relic?' Hoover said, incredulously.

'Yes!' said the Doctor, jumping on board and giving two sharp tugs to a bell pull. 'All aboard. Any more fares, please, any more fares?' He leaned forward and addressed one of the guards confidentially. 'I've always wanted to do this.'

With some trepidation, Hoover and the guards climbed on board. 'Room for three upstairs!' called the Doctor, adding, 'You'll get a better view from up there.'

'No, thank you,' said the President, perching gingerly on a side seat, 'we're fine down here.'

'Fair enough,' the Doctor grinned, sliding himself

into the driver's seat. He rubbed his hands together happily. 'Suddenly the day seems so much brighter!' he said.

Anji, Fitz and Xernic were outpacing the knights, but Anji was breathing heavily now and knew she couldn't keep going for much longer – even with the benefit of Elastoplast – whereas the androids, of course, would be able to keep running indefinitely. And presumably their feet would be pain-free as well. Not fair. She wondered if her life was going to be one long string of running away from things until she got back to Earth. At this rate, she'd have had enough practice to enter in the 2004 Olympics. She was also writing up a mental list of The Rules: no high heels, carry spare clothes (or at least a ball of string), always make sure of an escape route. Possibly also, if she wanted to be plagiaristic, 'Trust No One'. Well, almost no one. What she wouldn't give to see the Doctor right now.

They'd turned the wrong way out of the round-table room and couldn't retrace the route to the Twentieth-Century London Zone, and although Xernic had suggested hiding behind a curtain, waiting for the guards to pass and doubling back, no such curtain had presented itself. Now they'd gone up a long flight of stairs, and Anji was fairly sure they were on ground level rather than beneath it. Surely there had to be another exit – it would be ridiculous to expect the general EarthWorld tourists to enter a medieval castle by way of the back stage of a theatre. Though quite why they'd want to come here she didn't know; all it seemed to consist of was dull stone corridors. And Anji kept catching her heels in the casually scattered tapestries.

Suddenly Xernic cried, 'Light!'

'Sorry,' said Fitz, patting his pockets, 'I dropped it earlier.' Idiot.

Xernic shook his head, looking a bit puzzled. 'No, look over there. That's not torchlight, is it?'

And indeed, at the end junction of the corridor, there was a tiny pale patch on the floor that might – just might – be made by natural daylight. 'There might be a window! We can climb out!' said Xernic, eyes shining. The idea gave them the impetus for a burst of speed, and they dashed down the passage.

It *was* daylight, and it *was* a window. Unfortunately, it was not one that any of them could climb through, even Anji, unless she lost a considerable amount of weight, and probably several limbs. Anji peered out of the narrow slot, and was dismayed to see a large expanse of water directly below them. 'We're surrounded by a moat!' she said. 'Even if we find a window we can squeeze through –'

Fitz interrupted her. 'Well, there must be a door somewhere. People have to come in and out. There'll be, you know, a drawbridge kind of thing.'

She nodded. He was right. They just had to find it. 'At least we're at the outside wall,' she said. 'Theoretically, all we have to do is follow it around, and we'll come to the way out eventually.'

'And just hope we don't meet the guards coming the other way,' said Fitz cheerfully.

'Well, would you like to stay here and wait for them

to catch up with us instead?' she asked, calmly and not showing her frustration with him in any way.

'No,' he said. 'In fact, I suggest we start moving again right now. I think I can hear them coming.'

'Fine!' she agreed. And then a loud '*Grrrr!*' as her heel caught again and tore a large chunk out of the tapestry. 'What sort of idiots built this place?' she said, running off again.

'Don't blame them for your impractical gear,' said the irritating Fitz who, she decided to point out, was wearing nothing but a pair of shiny boxers under his coat.

And they were both so busy arguing as they ran, that neither of them noticed as Xernic caught his foot in the torn tapestry and crashed to the floor. Just as the knights rounded the corner.

The Doctor was currently singing about summer holidays and doing things you've always wanted to. Hoover wasn't an appreciative audience. All *he'd* ever wanted was to rule wisely and to prove worthy of the honour bestowed upon him by Earth. And he'd lost his wife, and his children, and soon he'd lose his whole planet. And who was this Doctor to make him feel so guilty about it all?

But then... who was he, to continue ignoring the guilt he deserved?

They followed the corridor along. There were more of the slit windows on the outer side, and no more torches; but the slits let in so little light that they almost missed the wooden door – in fact, they *would* have missed it if Fitz hadn't been trailing his fingers along the wall. He suddenly let out a short cry and stopped dead. Anji came over to look. She tried the door – but it wouldn't open. Fitz tried too. No luck. And the knights' pounding footsteps were getting nearer and nearer.

'We'll have to leave it!' Anji cried.

'No!' said Fitz. 'Maybe we can break it down.'

Anji looked at the solid wood. 'No chance.' She looked closer. 'There's a keyhole,' she said.

'Well, what good's that! I haven't had a chance to send off for my picklocks yet!'

'We can look through it,' she said, and bent to do so. There were only cracks of light, faintly illuminating a bit of iron grid here, a chain there. 'I think the drawbridge is up,' she said. 'We'll have to lower it when we get through.'

'If we get through!' said Fitz.

Anji tried to calm down and think logically. Drawbridges – as far as she knew, and assuming this future version played by the rules – could be raised and lowered only from this side of the moat. Which meant that the door had been locked from this side, too. So, unless the keyholder was still in the gap between this door and the drawbridge – which seemed unlikely – the key was somewhere on their side of the door. Assuming one of the triplets hadn't nipped up to lock them in – which was possible – then one of the castle's 'inhabitants'may have locked the door – after the attraction closed for the night? – out of habit, just like she double-locked her front door before bed and hung the key on a hook next to it…

She began to feel her way around the door frame. Just a chance, but… yes! Her fingers grasped a hook, and on it hung a large key. She grabbed the cold metal, and jammed it into the keyhole, struggling to turn it as the knights rounded the corner and began to move inexorably towards them, as fast as their armour would let them.

It wouldn't turn! 'Xernic! Fitz!' she cried in desperation, and other hands grabbed hers, adding more weight to the key. With a screech of metal, it clicked round. They dived through the door, and slammed it behind them. Then Fitz hurriedly opened it again, retrieved the key, shut the door and locked it from their side. There was a metal thunk, which Anji presumed was an android knight thumping the door in electronic frustration.

They looked around them. They were in a small – well, call it a gatehouse, although it was like no part of any tourist-friendly castle Anji had visited back on Earth. In front of them was an iron portcullis, and on the other side of that a slab of wood with chains hanging down – presumably the drawbridge. And on the other side of the drawbridge, presumably the moat.

'We'll never get through this lot in time!' said Anji 'We'll have to keep running. Find our way to the exit we used before somehow.'

'Are you joking?' cried Fitz, rattling the portcullis. 'There's a horde of killer knights gaining on us with every step. Our best bet is to hold them off in here for now. We'll have to get this metal thing up somehow.'

Anji glanced round to find some sort of leverage to pull up the portcullis. There was nothing. What there was… was a push-button control panel. Damn.

'I don't suppose you have a sonic screwdriver?' she said to Fitz.

'No,' he said shortly.

'Xernic, you wouldn't happen to know the code, would you?'

Silence.

'Xernic?' Anji looked right round. 'Fitz! We've lost Xernic!'

'Yes, I know!' said Fitz. 'He wasn't with us out in the corridor.'

Anji stared. 'And you didn't think to mention it?'

'Well, I rather assumed that you'd noticed it too! It's not my fault! He's your little camp-follower.'

'And what's that supposed to mean?'

Fitz gazed at the ceiling. 'Oh nothing, nothing. Come on, we've got to move this gate.'

'We've got to go back for Xernic!'

Fitz seemed irritatingly unconcerned. 'Well, we can't. Let's concentrate on getting us out of here right now. He'll probably find his way out the way you came.'

'But he's only a kid! What if the knights have caught him?'

Fitz sighed, and spoke to her as if she were only a kid too. Patronising git. 'Once we're out of here, we can get backup and go and look for him. If the knights have caught him he's either dead or locked up, so we either can't help or will do better when we've found the Doctor. If not, he'll probably find his own way out.

There are knights right outside the door, so if we try to go back we'll definitely be killed or captured, neither of which is going to help him.' Anji wanted to hit him. She probably would have, if he hadn't been completely right. Wasn't she supposed to be the logical one? Logic didn't seem nearly as attractive when other people used it.

'There's only ten buttons,' said Fitz. 'Perhaps we could work out the code.'

Anji's turn to be patronising. 'If it were only a two-digit code, there'd still be ten to the power two possible combinations. That's one hundred variations,' she added, because someone who thought they could easily crack an unknown numerical combination probably wouldn't understand such technical terms. 'If it's a three-digit code, that's another ten to the power three – that's one thousand – combinations. And the amount of possible combinations increases exponentially with the number of digits in the sequence. For all we know it could be a… a seventeen-digit code.'

'You could have just said no,' said Fitz. 'What's your suggestion, then?'

Anji looked at the control panel. Behind the wooden door, she could hear sounds – sounds like knights shouting and brandishing swords. She thought of all those possible mathematical combinations. Then she took off her left shoe, and smashed the heel right into the panel.

'What on Earth did you do that for?' Fitz yelled.

But his complaints were drowned out by the screeching of the portcullis as it slid upwards – and the creaking of the lowering drawbridge.

'You could have fused the whole thing! We could have been stuck here!' Fitz seemed to be saying above the noise.

'Could have – but didn't,' replied Anji, pitching her voice above the shrieking metal. 'I knew it was a good idea to wear high-heeled shoes.' She tried to yank her shoe out, but it was jammed fast. Something thumped hard on the wooden door and she knew she didn't have time to extricate it. 'Damn! Come on! Quick!'

She ducked down to crawl under the portcullis, still grinding its way upwards. Fitz followed, with slightly more difficulty, as he had twelve inches more body to manoeuvre. He yelped, and Anji turned back. 'What is it? Are you all right?'

'I caught my coat on a spike!'

'Is that all?'

'It's brand new! It must be a cursed coat. This world doesn't like it!'

There were more noises from the other side of the wooden door. It sounded like the knights were charging it. But the drawbridge was still rasping its way down. Anji looked at the moat – it was about twenty metres across, and she really didn't fancy swimming it. Besides, having met the triplets, she was rather worried that the occasional bubble bursting on the surface might be from a shark, or a shoal of piranhas.

'Come on,' she called to Fitz, who was still extricating himself from the bottom of the portcullis – and was in danger of being carried up with it if he didn't get a move on. She began to crawl up the drawbridge, which was now at a forty-five-degree angle. It wasn't easy, but she figured the further away from the knights she was, the better.

Fitz, finally free, began to climb after her. 'Is this such a good idea?' he said.

Anji had reached the end of the bridge, and was beginning to wonder that herself. She was flat on her stomach, holding the edge of the wood with a death grip as the bridge continued to jolt its way downward. It was down to about thirty degrees, creaking and clanking and...

And then there was silence. Both the portcullis and the drawbridge had stopped moving. Fitz and Anji were suspended in midair.

And the silence was broken by a tremendous crash as the wooden door fell and the knights poured into the gatehouse.

Fitz clambered up to Anji's side. 'The bank's only about ten feet in front of us,' he said, peering over the front edge of the drawbridge.

'Yes, but we're ten metres in the air!' she countered. 'We can't get a run up at this angle – we'd break every bone in our body!'

'They'll break them for us if we don't at least try!' yelled Fitz, gesturing behind them. Anji turned to look. The knights had reached the portcullis, but luckily their heavy plate armour was proving an obstacle in navigating the only half-lifted grille.

'Can you swim?' she asked Fitz.

'No!'

A knight was partway through the barrier.

'Well, now's the time to learn. We stay here, they catch us. We're going to dive off the side. You watch me, and then copy what I do. When you hit the water, don't panic, and move your arms up and down. I'll help you to the bank.'

Fitz's eyes were wide open in horror. 'But…'

Anji decided she'd better not mention her shark/piranha theory.

The knight had made it under the portcullis, and was beginning to struggle up the sloping drawbridge towards them.

'No time to argue!' she called, kicking off her remaining shoe and standing up and praying for balance. She tossed her bag as hard as she could towards the shore, hoping that at least a few things in it would survive. 'Just remember not to panic!' she said. And taking an enormous breath, she dived off the side of the bridge.

She'd never dived from such a height before. In, fact, it had been a long time since she'd dived at all. But for those few brief downward moments she remembered it all, the thrill of the air rushing past her and the glory of uncontrollable flight. Then she hit the water with a crash, and was in another world. Sounds were distorted underwater. She was aware of nothing but the rushing of the moat in her ears, and a dull brown haze in front of her, which showed nothing but the bubbles escaping from her mouth (no sign of hostile life, thank goodness). She was reluctant to break the surface again, to find herself once more in the noisy, dangerous world waiting up there.

As she surfaced, a streak of black flashed past into the water in front of her. An air-pocket-filled coat kept the body afloat for a second, while arms and legs thrashed around it in a seemingly random order. Anji swam a couple of strokes across, and managed to persuade Fitz to roll over on to his back. 'I told you not to panic!' she said.

'I know, but it's a bit hard not to when you're drowning!' he spluttered.

'You're not drowning,' she told him. 'Just keep calm and we're going to reach the bank.' She hooked an arm around him, and began to slowly swim forward, dragging Fitz with her. He was thankfully sensible enough to stop thrashing about as she did so.

They'd landed only about four metres from the bank, but it felt like four miles. Anji did – had done – aerobics two lunchtimes a week, so she was not unfit, but she was not exceptionally strong, and Fitz was much bigger than she was. But they made it in the end, and Fitz clung tight to the bank while she scrambled out.

Once on land, Anji took a few moments to get her breath. She glanced up at the drawbridge, scarcely able to believe she'd been up there just a minute before. And that wasn't the only surprising thing. 'Oh no!' she gasped.

'What?' asked Fitz, beginning to haul himself up.

'The knight – it's reached the end of the drawbridge! It's going to jump! It can't – it's an android!'

'Well, it doesn't know that,' said Fitz. 'It thinks it's human. Anyway, what's the problem? With that amount of armour on it'll just sink.'

'Fitz!' cried Anji, grabbing his arms and desperately trying to help him up, 'have you ever dropped a toaster in the bath?'

He gave her a puzzled look. 'No.'

'Well, that's one reason why you're still alive today! Come on!'

The knight was on the edge of the bridge. He was going to jump. He was jumping...

And Anji summoned every last drop of her strength, took Fitz's coat in both hands, and pulled as hard as she could. Fitz rolled on to the bank as the android hit the water. A blue flare danced momentarily across the surface, and Fitz and Anji lay wide-eyed and gasping in each other's arms.

'Oh wow,' he said, after a while. 'I could have been Kentucky Fried Fitz. Thank you.'

She felt a bit embarrassed. 'That's OK,' she said. 'I think we're safe now. The other knights won't follow after that. So unless they get the drawbridge working again...'

Fitz nodded his agreement. They both began to get to their feet, clothes and hair dripping all over the place. Anji picked up her bag, but couldn't face looking inside to see the damage. 'We should try to find Xernic now,' she said, trying to wring out her blazer without taking it off and showing Fitz her bra.

He shook his head. 'We have to find the Doctor first. That's the most important thing.'

Anji sighed. 'I don't know if I can walk all the way back like this – soaking wet and no shoes...'

But Fitz wasn't looking at her. He was gazing over

her shoulder as if all his dreams had come true at once. Anji spun round to see what he was looking at.

'We could walk…' said Fitz. 'Or we could just hitch a ride on that bus…'

Anji wanted to cheer. A huge red double-decker bus was trundling over the grass towards them – it was one of the old type, open-topped and with that entrance at the back where people jumped on in movies. And leaning out of the driver's window, making cheerful 'Hello! Come and get on the bus!' gestures while presumably steering one-handedly, was none other than the Doctor himself.

'I think the Doctor's been taking lessons from an old friend,' Fitz grinned. Anji looked quizzical. 'Oh, we used to know a… bus driver,' he said. 'But I bet the Doctor's forgotten her. Come on, let's get on board.' And they jogged to meet the bus as fast as their sodden clothes would allow.

The Doctor had stopped the bus and given both Fitz and Anji a huge hug, seemingly oblivious to their wet and muddy state. Anji was shivering now, but it somehow warmed her inside to see just how pleased the Doctor was to see them again. He helped Anji to take her blazer off – somehow it didn't matter that the Doctor was seeing her like that, he seemed to count in her head as another girl – and gave her his velvet coat to replace it. She huddled inside the soft green fabric, pulling it as tight around herself as she could. He'd then looked around to try to find something new for Fitz to wear, but Fitz said he'd decided now that his coat was lucky and he'd like to keep it on for now, thank you, however wet it was.

'We'll go back to the main centre and find some dry clothes for both of you,' the Doctor said.

'But we have to go back in there!' said Anji, gesturing at the castle outside the window. 'Xernic's still in there.'

'And my daughters,' said a man's voice. 'Are they in there too?'

'Who are you?' Anji asked, turning to see a dark-haired, dark-eyed man in a seriously tacky gold-coloured jumpsuit. 'Oh no, don't tell me you're the President of New Jupiter?'

'I am,' the man said, frowning.

'Well, I can only assume you've never read the works of Dr Benjamin Spock,' said Anji, adding, in case Fitz was about to say anything, 'and no, that's not the guy from *Star Trek* – or indeed, anything else on responsible parenting. Did you know that your children are in there terrorising people?'

'Anji Anji Anji,' said the Doctor, interrupting, 'I don't think this is the time or place. Mr Hoover is terribly sorry his daughters keep killing people, and he's going to try to do something about it. Now,' he continued, giving Anji a look that made her swallow the biting put-down she was about to come out with, 'I still think we should go back to the main centre. You can tell us what's been going on, and we can work out a plan of campaign. Agreed?'

'Agreed,' said Anji, resigned. She pressed herself as far as she could go into the corner of a bus seat, trying to conserve warmth, and settled back for a bumpy ride.

*

Back at the main centre, the Doctor had sent the President and his guards off to look for clean clothes for Anji and Fitz. Anji noted with interest how the President seemed to meekly obey the Doctor. She saw the guards exchanging looks as well.

Then the Doctor sat his companions down and listened to their stories.

It was a while before Hoover and the guards returned, but that was just as well because Fitz and Anji had a lot to tell. The Doctor occasionally interrupted to ask for more details, or to say a sympathetic word or two, but more or less let them get on with it. When they could think of nothing more to add, he just nodded his head and sat there in silence, obviously pondering it all. Anji was keeping her fingers crossed for a miracle solution. She really, really wanted to leave.

Hoover and the guards dumped armfuls of clothes in front of them. 'Costumes for those androids,' one of the guards said, vaguely indicating the direction from which they'd come. Anji shuffled over to the pile, still shivering. She was not particularly amused at what she found. Fitz held up a leopard-print bikini in a suggestive way, but she ignored him. Not only were there no twentieth-century-type clothes in the heap, very little of what there was seemed to be made for someone of her petite stature. In the end she opted for a medieval gown of crimson velvet, with dropped waist and huge sleeves that almost covered her hands. There was a pair of soft moccasins that just about fitted her, too – they wouldn't stand up to much hard wear, but, boy, would she appreciate them. From now on, she was never, ever going to venture out of the TARDIS in anything but trainers. She peeled the soggy, muddy plasters off her feet and applied clean dressings, then slipped the shoes on. Bliss. Sheer bliss. And then she realised that she'd been thinking in terms of future TARDIS trips, not just going straight home. Which worried her a bit. Something to consider more thoroughly later...?

When she'd finished changing she joined the others again, and found Fitz had also gone for a medieval theme, complete with doublet and hose. He was still holding on tight to his lucky coat, though. Reminded by that, Anji returned the Doctor's own coat. He thanked her with a smile.

'Now, the problem is,' the Doctor said, 'that we're not going to be able to get anywhere near the triplets if they're guarded by Sir Lancelot –'

'Lancelet,' corrected Hoover.

'Sir Lancelet and all the knights of the round table – all those who didn't decide to try their luck at swimming, that is. But we need to get in there, to rescue Xernic –' he nodded to Anji – 'and to apprehend Hanstrum before he takes over the planet, and so the President here can attempt to make amends with his children. I fear the last may be a task too far –' he glanced sadly at Hoover – 'but that doesn't stop us trying.'

'Can't you just disable all the androids again somehow?' Anji asked.

The Doctor shook his head. 'If you're right and they've transferred the independent circuits to the knights, then it wouldn't work – even if I could knock up a replacement for the boys' zapping device.'

'What about the sonic screwdriver?' asked Fitz.

The Doctor shook his head again. 'I could perhaps knock them out one at a time – but not all at once, and not at a distance. I could possibly disorientate them slightly... but no, this calls for more subtle means.'

One of the President's guards offered his gun. 'Oh yes, very subtle,' said the Doctor. 'Thank you, but no. There's no guarantee that would harm them, and I am not a fan of gunplay. Play... play...' he looked at Fitz and Anji. 'You two have just given me an idea! We play their own game against them...'

'Murder in the Dark?' asked Fitz.

'Oh no,' said the Doctor. 'Charades...' He spun to face Anji. 'How well do you know the legends of King Arthur?'

She frowned. 'Not very well. I've seen a few films... He pulled the sword from the stone and became king, and then there was something about the Holy Grail...'

'Fitz?'

Fitz nodded. 'Yeah, I'm quite hot on the stuff, actually. Gawain and the Green Knight, Camelot, Morgan le Fey, and, well, Avalon obviously, though that's not... What are you laughing at?'

Hoover was barely concealing a smirk. 'I fear you don't know as much as you think,' he said. 'I have studied the story of Mort and Arthur, and you are, I'm afraid, woefully inaccurate.'

'Oh yeah?' said Fitz, looking as if he were about to hit him.

The Doctor calmed him down. 'Now, now, Fitz,

I think we should hear what he has to say. When in Rome, you know…'

'People get savaged by lions,' Fitz muttered. Anji wondered if there were bits of his story they had yet to hear.

Hoover had wandered off, and was looking round the gift-shop section of the reception area. 'Here it is,' he said, holding up a small disc, 'the most recent edition of *Mort and Arthur*. The definitive work on the subject.' He fed the disk into a nearby computer terminal, and indicated that Fitz should come and look.

'But… but this is ridiculous!' Fitz spluttered. 'Listen to this bit: "And Arthur knew that to be king, he must pull the stone sword out of the lake. In the lake he met with the lady, who lived there with a marlin and a lancelet" – what are they when they're at home?'

'The marlin is a large Earth sea fish,' said the Doctor. 'And the lancelet is a fishlike marine animal, also from Earth.'

'Sounds a bit fishy,' said Fitz, continuing. 'And this bit: "The magical marlin transformed himself and his friend the lancelet into humans, so they could protect the King from the evil Mort."' He looked up from the screen. 'This is just rubbish! It bears no relation to reality!'

'And what exactly makes you think the stories you know bear any resemblance to the Arthurian reality?' said the Doctor.

'Well,' began Fitz, but the Doctor carried on.

'This is important,' he said, 'because these are the legends that have filtered through to today, and so that's how "Lancelet" and the others will be programmed. Now, read on, Fitz, please.'

'Well, "Arthur was married to Guinevere" – it's spelt Gwinnyveer, but at least the name's the same... "and she betrayed him with the human lancelet, who had fought Arthur on the bridge over the lake and become his chief knight... They went on a quest for the Holy Grel, a tentacled monster that would reveal to them good holy facts and bad holy facts" – this is ridiculous! – "and the King had three evil sisters, Morgan, Leigh and Fay" – I don't believe this!'

'Three sisters, hmm?' said the Doctor, interested. 'How very, very convenient. But the big question is: how many of these characters are already represented by androids. Any ideas?'

Everyone shook their head. 'The guidebook?' Anji suggested.

'Good idea!' The Doctor pulled the book out of his pocket, and flicked through the pages. Anji couldn't believe he read that fast – but apparently he did.

'"Medieval banquets with Arthur and the knights of the round table." You didn't see an Arthur android, did you, though? No? I'm not surprised – the girls would have only reprogrammed the androids they could easily control, and you can't order a king around. He's probably safely tucked away in his box, or whatever. Now, let's see... Lancelet, Haywain – hmm, I think I've seen his portrait by Constable – Gallyhad, Purposeful – isn't he one of the seven dwarves? – Beddyveer... good, no mention of Guinevere at all. Right, Anji –' the Doctor turned to her, and he was looking very serious – 'I'm going to ask you to do something that's going to be very difficult for you, but I would ask you to think carefully about it, because it could be our best chance.'

Anji half smiled. 'I think I can guess. You know, people have often told me I bear a startling resemblance to Vanessa Redgrave.'

Fitz gaped at her.

Anji was going to direct them to the entrance through the Alhambra theatre. The Doctor had tried to persuade Hoover and the guards to remain in the centre, but they'd insisted on coming too. The Doctor had told them they had to stay in the bus, though.

'Now, you know what you're doing?' the Doctor asked Anji, anxiously.

She nodded. 'I'll be fine.'

He handed her his sonic screwdriver. 'And you remember how to work this?'

'Bamboozlement frequency 47, twist and point.'

'And you've got the communicator?'

She patted a pocket.

He grinned. 'Attagirl!'

'Well… wish me luck!'

'Good luck,' said the Doctor, echoed by Fitz. 'And remember, we'll be right behind you.'

There were frozen android rats along the passageway. The flickering torchlight had made them look alive, at first. Anji kicked one. It made her feel a bit better.

Deep breath. Don't think of this as walking into a

life-or-death situation. Think of it more as… amateur dramatics.

Pretending to be someone else. It was what Dave had done for a living – not a very good living, admittedly, but… She'd never got the hang of it, though. She needed all her energy and concentration to make a success of being herself.

But now she had to do this. Darling, she thought, offering up words as if he could hear, it's not cheating on your memory when he's an android and I'm only pretending. Is it?

Deep breath. Ready to take the stage. She stood up straight, and opened the door. There was a knight in the corridor beyond.

'Halt!' he cried, raising his sword and moving towards her.

'Frequency47twistandpoint!' gabbled Anji, waving the sonic screwdriver at him. The knight stopped, frowned and shook his head.

'Knight! How dare you speak to your queen like that! It is I, Gwinnyveer! Now take me to Sir Lancelot. Let. Take me to Sir Lancelet.'

The knight shook his head bemusedly again. Anji lowered the sonic screwdriver and put it in her kirtle pocket. 'Knight! Did you hear me?'

The knight fell to one knee. 'Please forgive me, My Lady! I know not why I spoke so.'

'We-e-ll…' said Anji – then decided not to push her luck. 'You're forgiven,' she said. 'So… ?'

'I shall take you to Sir Lancelet this instant, My Lady!' the knight declared, jumping to his feet.

So Anji followed him down the stone corridor.

It turned out that Lancelet was still in the round-table room, with the triplets. There was no sign of Hanstrum or Xernic. One of the girls – the one in the blue dress – leapt to her feet when she saw Anji. 'What are you doing?' she screeched at Anji's accompanying knight. 'You were supposed to have killed her!'

As the knight looked puzzled, Lancelet jumped to his feet and unsheathed his sword. 'Never fear, My Ladies, I shall rid you of this sorceress!'

Anji crossed her fingers, and pulled out the sonic screwdriver again. This time she was more careful. This was the big one, the one that counted. 'Frequency 47... twist and... point!'

Sir Lancelet staggered backwards. 'I... I...'

'My love,' said Anji, trying not to think about what she was saying – because she didn't mean it, but it was still difficult – 'it is I, Gwinnyveer. I have come to rescue you from the dread enchantment placed upon you by these enchantresses, Morgan, Leigh and Fay.'

'Don't listen to her!' yelled blue-dress. 'She's not Gwinnyveer! There isn't a Gwinnyveer! We never made one! *She's* the enchantress!'

But Lancelet was looking at Anji. 'Gwinnyveer? My love?' He sheathed his sword and scooped Anji up in his arms.

'Stopitthekingmightseeus!' hissed Anji, desperately. She couldn't bear to be embraced by another man, even if he was made of plastic. Luckily there was a fictional justification for that.

'The King is away, My Lady.' He smiled at her

encouragingly. Anji wondered if that was in his programming. According to the Doctor's guidebook there was a King Arthur android around here, it was just that the triplets probably hadn't resurrected him, so Sir Knight here had to be trying to pull a fast one. Adulterous androids – now there was a thing. She briefly wondered if, for example, her kettle had a bit on the side with her toaster when the percolator was switched off, something like that. She'd never look at her appliances the same way again. If, of course, she ever got to see them again full stop.

The blue-robed triplet had come over and was pulling on Lancelet's arm. 'She's enchanted you! Can't you see it? She's cast a spell on you! She's evil! What are you doing?' This last was squeaked at Anji, who was waving the sonic screwdriver at Lancelet again.

'They're the evil ones!' Anji insisted. 'They're Morgan, Leigh and Fay! Lancelet – darling!' she added with difficulty, taking his other arm herself. 'You have to believe me!'

'I would never doubt you, sweet lady of my heart,' he declared, and called out, 'Knights! To me!'

The girl in the blue dress seemed to have realised she wasn't winning. She let go of Lancelet's arm – but he grabbed hers. 'Where do you think you're going, sorceress?' he said, menacingly.

The other triplets – one in green and one in orange – had obviously sized up the situation too. They were almost at the door when a horde of knights arrived. 'Stop them!' roared Lancelet, and the knights, in some confusion, did so.

Lancelet turned to address them all. Anji waved the sonic screwdriver at them, just in case. 'My brothers,' he declared, 'we have been under the most terrible enchantment from these evil sorceresses, Morgan, Leigh and Fay. But thanks to our good lady Gwinnyveer –' he gestured at Anji, and the knights cheered – 'we have been freed from their spell! Take them to the deepest dungeon and lock them up, till the King returns and can decide upon their fate!'

Screaming their protests – mainly dwelling upon what they were going to do to Anji later – the triplets were dragged away.

'Now, My Lady, we are alone...' began Lancelet.

'No, we're not!' squeaked Anji She pressed a button on her communicator. 'Er, Marlin! Sir Fitz! You can come in now!'

'Marlin is here?' said Lancelet, sounding astonished. 'I knew not that he was expected. And who is "Sir Fitz"?'

'An old and dear friend of mine, and a very loyal knight,' said the Doctor, striding into the room. He held out a hand. 'Lancelet! Wonderful to see you.'

Lancelet held out his hand, looking confused. 'Marlin...?'

'Yes, Lancelet, it's me.' He turned to Anji. 'My lady Gwinnyveer,' he said, bending low over her hand. For some reason, Anji felt herself blushing. 'Now,' said the Doctor, straightening up, 'I understand you have the traitor Sir Mort here, Lancelet.'

'We do?' said Lancelet.

'Oh yes,' said Anji. 'Tall, blond, pompous guy? Poncy green robes?'

'Oh, indeed, I remember the knave,' said Lancelet. Anji could almost have felt sorry for him, seeing the puzzled look on his face – but he wasn't really feeling anything, she knew. No more than her toaster or her kettle or her percolator could feel anything. 'We locked him up some hours since. I had not an idea in the world that he was the dastardly Mort!'

'The sorceresses' spell confused you,' said Anji, soothingly. 'But you did the right thing in locking him up.'

'He wasn't the only person you locked up, though, was he?' said the Doctor. 'There was another – a young lad?'

'Indeed,' said Lancelet, 'there was such a lad.'

'Is he all right?' cried Anji. 'You didn't kill him or anything?'

The knight shook his head, and Anji gave a sigh of relief. 'No, My Lady. The sorceresses –' he shuddered – 'had ordered he and the other criminals –' he gave Anji a puzzled look then, and she hastily flashed him an encouraging smile – 'to be killed. But the boy was unarmed, and had fallen. It would not have been chivalrous to kill him thus. He was therefore placed in the dungeons.'

The Doctor nodded. 'I see, I see. Well, the thing is, that young lad was... was...'

'Was my squire,' completed Fitz, jumping in. 'My squire, young Xernic. Your locking him up was all part of that spell thing. So if you could just let him go...'

'Assuredly, good Sir Fitz,' agreed Lancelet, nodding his head in a curt bow. 'I will send a knight to release him this very instant.' He went to the doorway and called out: 'Beddyveer!'

The Doctor gave Fitz a hurried thumbs-up. 'Good thinking, Fitz. And Anji… well done.'

'Yeah,' Fitz said, grinning. 'Looks like you did all right.'

And then Lancelet was back with them, and they had to talk of courtly subjects again.

The first thing Xernic did when he was led in was to rush over to Anji and hug her. 'Thank you!' he said. 'Thank you so much!'

Anji automatically gave him a quick hug back, and then pushed him away as Lancelet was giving them a very suspicious look. 'It is wonderful to see you too, Squire Xernic,' she said, shooting him an apologetic look. 'Your master, Sir Fitz, here –' she indicated Fitz, in case Xernic had forgotten who he was – 'has been most concerned. However, thanks to the magicks of the good Marlin –' and here she pointed at the Doctor – 'the enchantments of the three evil sisters Morgan, Leigh and Fay have been broken, and they and the traitorous Sir Mort –' she raised her eyebrows, hoping he was getting all this – 'have been locked in the dungeons by my most loyal knights.'

Xernic mouthed a silent 'Oh!' and raised his eyebrows in return. He seemed to be trying to tell her something – ask her something? Had she got a bit of mud on her face or something? Oh!

'Yes, I, your *Queen*, *Gwinnyveer*, tell you these things.'

He smiled and nodded. 'Thank you, Your Majesty.'

Anji turned to Lancelet. 'Now, I must ask you to leave us, good Sir Knight. The D- Marlin and I have important matters to discuss with Sir Fitz.'

Lancelet frowned. 'My Lady?'

Anji put her hands on her hips. 'Who's Queen?' she asked.

'Actually,' said the Doctor, interrupting, 'if I might just ask a favour of Sir Lancelet…'

'Oh yes,' said Anji, relieved that he was taking charge, 'of course you may.'

'Lancelet, would you round up all the knights and assemble them here in, say, five minutes?'

Lancelet was still frowning, but gave the Doctor a short bow. 'As you wish,' he said, and left.

Anji collapsed into a chair. 'I did it!' she said. 'I don't believe I did it! Can we go home now, please?'

The Doctor sat down on the next chair and put an arm around her. 'I am so proud of you, Anji,' he said. 'So very proud. I know it can't have been easy.'

Anji thought back to Lancelet's arms around her, and shuddered. 'No,' she said. 'It wasn't.'

To: cybertron@xprof.net
From: anji kapoor@MWFutures.co.uk
Date: 15/2/01 10:07
Subject: Faithfulness

Dear Dave,

Did you know, I was never once unfaithful to you. I never even drunkenly kissed another man

241

at the office Christmas party (and believe me, I had offers. Some guys can only deal with their power issues in the office by trying to gain power elsewhere. Or I suppose they might have just fancied me. Whatever). Anyway, the point is, I resisted all temptation. Although to tell you the truth, it wasn't that much of a temptation, not usually. You see, I'd found you. And although we might have had our problems… but no. That's not what we're talking about right now.

There's that theory that you can only have a successful relationship with someone you perceive as being on 'the same level' as you. So, if you're rich and ugly you can go out with someone poor but beautiful, but if you're poor and ugly you don't stand a chance unless they are too. That sort of thing.

A friend of mine once said, 'You're too good for him.' But that's not true. If anything, it was the other way around. Oh, you used to wind me up sometimes – well, a lot – and occasionally I got peed off that I couldn't afford to take risks with my job, because I had to be the main breadwinner for both of us. Seema – my friend – called you my 'kept man'. I just laughed. At least I kept hold of you. You see, you had qualities I didn't, like patience, and the ability to laugh at yourself. I never had that, I've always cared too much what other people think. I'm ashamed now that I let our few problems – tiny, tiny problems – creep into my mind.

I wonder if you were ever unfaithful to me? In thought, word or deed. Thought, possibly, but I really don't think either of the other two. I'll never know now, but I think not. I think you really loved me, and I didn't deserve it. Didn't deserve you. Because… Oh, this is too difficult.

I still love you

Anji xxx

Send now/send later: send later

Sir Lancelet and the knights were sitting around the round table, along with the Doctor, Anji and Xernic. Fitz had been sent off to fetch the President and his guards.

'Thank you all for coming,' the Doctor said, for all the world as if he was chairing a local council meeting. 'As you may have heard on the grapevine, you have all been under an enchantment from the evil sorceresses Morgan, Leigh and Fay. Thanks to the gallant Sir Lancelet they are now under lock and key, along with the treacherous knight, Sir Mort, and with my powerful magicks – and the help of Queen Gwinnyveer – the enchantment has been lifted. Brave Sir Fitz, the, er, Knight of the Archway, has gone to fetch your King from the place where he was trapped by his wicked sisters. I should warn you that there may still be some residual traces of the spell they cast on him, making his countenance seem strange to you if you happen to bump into him. Now, is there anything I've forgotten, My Lady?' he said, turning to Anji.

'Not at all, Marlin,' she smiled. 'I think that explains everything perfectly adequately.'

The Doctor smiled back, and turned to the knights again. 'The King will, of course, wish to interview all the prisoners himself, but myself and Sir Fitz will be adequate protection. You are free to leave us now. Thank you.'

He stood up, signalling that the meeting was at an end. The knights stood up, too, and all left the room – except Lancelet.

'You may go now, good Sir Knight,' said the Doctor.

'With the deepest respect, oh Marlin,' said Lancelet, obviously not meaning it at all, 'I do not take my orders from you: I take them only from my liege. I will await his instructions.'

'I assure you, I speak with his authority!' insisted the Doctor.

Lancelet shook his head. 'I do not doubt your word. Yet I would hear it from the King himself.'

The Doctor looked flustered. 'Sir Lancelet...'

Anji rose to her feet. 'Sir Lancelet,' she echoed. He turned to her. 'I would not presume to give you an order, Sir Knight, but instead I ask you to grant me this request: that you will leave me to greet my husband alone.'

Lancelet stared at her – a hurt-puppy-dog look that

he was trying not to show. These things seemed so human! Finally he nodded. He moved over to Anji and took her hand. 'As My Lady requests,' he said, kissing it. He nodded again. 'Marlin… Squire Xernic.' He turned back to Anji and looked her straight in the eye. There was pain there, she knew it! Then with no more words he left the room.

'Phew!' Anji sank down on a chair.

'Well done, Anji!' said the Doctor. 'Very quick thinking. We can hardly get on with what we have to do with a load of knights looking over our shoulders!'

'The thing is,' said Anji, slowly, 'I'd swear he was really feeling things. He looked so hurt. How can something that's not a person react like that?'

'He's not real, Anji,' said the Doctor. 'The positronic brain is a wonderful thing. A simulation of life.'

'So…' said Anji, thinking about this, 'there's no way of telling if a person is real or not?'

'Well, there are hints, suggestions – the amount they blink, that sort of thing.'

'But you can't tell from their reactions, the way they act?'

'At this level of sophistication, not usually, no. Especially if they think they're alive. They can't tell any differently.'

'But surely that means –'

But just then Fitz arrived with the President.

The triplets had been locked up in the same cell they'd put Fitz in. They didn't seem that bothered. They'd lit candles all round, and sat up Elvis's corpse in a corner with its finger up its nose. Asia was wearing the headphones from the Memory Machine, and the other two girls were gathered round it watching its screen and eating sweets. They didn't even glance up as the Doctor and Fitz looked through the door grille.

The Doctor gestured at Hoover and his guards to stay outside, and unlocked the door. He walked in. 'Hello,' he said.

Asia looked up. 'Hello. You're the Doctor,' she said. She gestured at the Memory Machine. 'We've watched some of your adventures.'

Fitz, standing in the doorway, tried desperately to catch her eye, and give her a pleading 'Don't tell him anything!' look.

'That's right, I'm the Doctor. We've actually had quite a long chat together, you and I, but you wouldn't remember because you were electronic at the time.'

She thought about that for a second. 'You met some of our androids?'

'The ones back at the palace. Your substitutes. They were very good. You must be very clever at making things.'

'Don't speak to us as if we were a child,' she said, pouting at him.

'I'm sorry,' he said. 'The thing is... I've brought your father to see you.'

The other two looked up now, frowning. 'Father never comes to see us,' said Africa.

'He doesn't care about us,' sighed Antarctica. 'Not since Mother died.'

Fitz tried half-heartedly to stop the President entering

the room, but he pushed past. There were tears in his eyes. 'I'm sorry,' Hoover said, kneeling down beside the triplets. 'I'm so, so sorry.'

They looked at him as if he were a curious insect. 'Are you?' said Asia.

'Yes! Yes, I am!'

'Prove it.'

He looked up at her, questioning. 'How?'

Africa and Antarctica made a grand sweeping gesture. 'The marvellous Memory Machine!'

'It will show us how you feel,' said Asia. 'What you thought about us killing Mother.'

The President looked up at the Doctor. 'I have been shown…' he said hesitantly, 'I have been shown that… that you may not have killed your mother after all.'

There was a silence. Asia finally broke it. 'We… didn't kill Mother?'

'No.'

Antarctica gave a cry of delight. 'I knew I loved Mother!' she said.

Africa was scowling, but looking slightly disconcerted. 'But I like killing,' she said. 'I thought killing was what we did.'

Hoover spoke to the Doctor. 'I'd like Hanstrum to be here for this,' he said. 'I know he's betrayed me now, but if he understands this too – well, it might change things.'

The Doctor gave Hoover a peculiar look, a sort of 'You really don't get it, do you?' But he didn't stop the guards going to find Hanstrum.

Asia slipped off the headphones and handed them

to Hoover. 'Put these on,' she instructed. He did so. Fitz had the feeling that the President's willpower and sanity were swinging back and forth. Mostly back.

'It won't hurt much,' Antarctica said.

'It doesn't hurt at all,' said Fitz, trying to be reassuring. He glared at Antarctica.

Asia was adjusting the controls. 'Are you sitting comfortably?' she asked her sisters, who nodded eagerly. The machine began to hum.

At that moment, the two guards brought in Hanstrum. He was looking wretched, as if he'd been in the cells a month rather than an hour or so.

'What's going on?' he asked hoarsely.

'The triplets are reading their father's memories and emotions,' the Doctor said. 'They're discovering that he doesn't think they killed their mother after all.'

Hanstrum took a step back. 'He doesn't?'

'No, he doesn't. But he hasn't worked out what really happened yet. I don't expect he ever will – his mind's not equipped to figure out treachery. He always goes for the easiest answer.'

Hanstrum was looking worriedly at the President. Hoover had taken off the headphones now, and the three girls were surrounding him. Africa offered him the bag of sweets, and he took a toffee, thanking her.

'You really don't think we did it,' said Asia, wonderingly.

'You want us to forgive you,' said Africa.

'And you think that even if we *had* done it, you shouldn't have blamed us but tried to help us,' said Asia.

'But now you're going a bit mad,' added Antarctica.

Hoover nodded to all of it. 'We can go back to the palace now,' he said. 'Try to be a family. Make up for lost time.'

'Send out a mass apology to everyone they've murdered,' murmured Fitz.

But the triplets were shaking their heads. 'We're not going back to the palace,' said Asia.

'We don't want to stay on stupid old New Jupiter,' Antarctica added. 'We're going to Earth in the TARDIS with the Doctor and Fitz Fortune.'

The Doctor laughed. 'I'm sorry, that's just not possible.'

'Fitz Fortune promised!'

'I did not!' said Fitz.

'We offered you your heart's desire!'

'Yeah, and I said no!'

'What's your heart's desire, Fitz?' enquired the Doctor, interestedly.

'Oh, nothing important,' said Fitz. 'The point is, I didn't agree to anything of the sort. There wouldn't be much point. You've obviously forgotten how to control the TARDIS anyway.'

The Doctor shot an awkward look at Anji, but she wasn't paying attention. 'You can give anyone their heart's desire with that?' she was asking Asia.

'With the right data we can do anything,' the girl said.

The Doctor jumped forward and grabbed Anji by the shoulders. 'Don't be tempted!' he said. 'Oh yes, they could make you a copy of Dave, but you'd always know

249

he wasn't the real thing, and in the end it'd make the pain much, much worse.'

Anji turned to him, blank-faced. 'I wasn't thinking of Dave,' she said. 'I was thinking of you.'

'You want a copy of the Doctor?' asked Fitz, incredulous. Surely one was quite enough for anyone!

She shook her head dismissively, turning back to Asia. 'If you can copy someone's memories – well, how deep can you go?'

'Depends,' said Asia. 'We can take surface prints from anyone.'

'Easy peasy,' put in Antarctica.

'What they're thinking about at the time, what's happened recently, anything that's near the top. No problem. Deep stuff – well, you have to probe about a bit. And it's much easier for people to resist that, so they've got to agree, really. Like we did. All our androids were deep copies.'

'What about things the person's forgotten because of some kind of amnesia. Could you still access those?'

Fitz had a horrid feeling he knew where she was going with this.

'Oh, yes. The memories and knowledge should still be there. If they're blocked, you can knock your way through and get them; if there's been some sort of brain damage you might have to build a new pathway, that's all. We tried it with some of Africa's pets. It works.'

Anji turned to the Doctor, her eyes shining. 'You could do it, Doctor!' she cried. 'Access your memories! Find out how to use the TARDIS!'

'He doesn't need to!' Everyone jumped as Fitz yelled out. He looked a bit sheepish. 'Ha-ha, I mean, he's not forgotten much. He's hundreds of years old, remember, bound to forget a few things...'

'Really, Fitz, I thought you'd be pleased! The Doctor can't remember how to work the TARDIS, didn't have a clue what his sonic screwdriver did, and you told me earlier he couldn't remember if his former best friend was a man or a woman!'

Fitz was struggling now. 'He'll remember! Anything he needs to remember, he will. He's worked out the sonic screwdriver now! For goodness' sake, do you really want to let these mad kids loose in the Doctor's brain?' He turned to the Doctor, silent through all this. 'Tell her, Doctor. Tell her you don't need it!'

But the Doctor was leaning forward, examining the machine. 'You know,' he said, 'it might just work. I'd be able to get you home, then, Anji.'

She shrugged. 'That's not the reason I suggested it, you know.'

'I know,' he said. He was far too bloody understanding. *Tell him that is why you suggested it and then I can say you're selfish and make the Doctor ignore you,* Fitz mentally beamed at her. It didn't work.

'Let's do it!' said the Doctor.

'And then you'll take us to Earth?' said Asia, businesslike.

'Yes yes yes,' said the Doctor. Fitz knew he was lying, and was slightly surprised. Still, lying to homicidal children probably didn't count in the big tally of bad things to do.

'Can we do it straightaway?' asked Antarctica. 'Now?'

'Why not?' The Doctor grinned. 'Just explain to me exactly what you're going to do.'

'If the memories are in there but you can't get to them, we need to find the closed areas, download a copy, and then sort them out – unravel them, you know. Then we copy them back in over the blocked areas and they're fully accessible. It's a perfectly simple operation – if you're geniuses, like us.'

'Vee are geniufef,' agreed Africa, slightly muffled by a sherbert lemon.

'Download the memories – into this machine?'

'Nope.'

'So where, then?' said the Doctor patiently.

'The machine's just the tool. We can record things with it, but to actually do things with what we get, we need a clean slate to work on. We usually use each other's brains.'

Fitz thought of numerous comments, but decided he'd better not say any of them. He contented himself with a warning. 'Do you really think it'd be a good idea to stick the secrets of time travel into these girls' heads, Doctor?'

The Doctor frowned. 'Good point, Fitz. We'd better use you instead. You don't mind, do you?'

'No! I mean, yes! Yes, I mind!'

'Fitz…' The Doctor looked disappointed.

It was all Fitz could do not to shout out, 'I'm doing this for you, you stupid git! I'd do anything to help you, but this isn't going to help!'

'I just don't think it's a good idea, Doctor,' he said.

'I'll do it,' said Anji.

Fitz wanted to hit her. 'I don't think *that's* so good an idea, either,' he said.

'Why not?'

'I just don't think *any* of this is a good idea! Do you really want these loony girls poking around inside your head?'

'If it helps the Doctor get his memory back, then yes, yes I do.'

'Fitz!' The Doctor was smiling at him now. 'I appreciate your concern, I really do, but I've looked at this machine and I don't think there's a risk. It's an extremely sophisticated instrument. And the girls will be doing their very best to make it work – won't you, girls? – because they know that unless this succeeds they're never going to Earth.' And Fitz realised that, however hard the Doctor had been trying to hide his frustration at his loss of memory, it was there all right. The Doctor wanted this more than anything else in the universe, and Fitz wasn't going to be able to stop him. Even if he told the Doctor there were things he'd be better off not remembering – and how would he do that anyway? – the Doctor would say it's always better to know. He could hear him now. 'Ignorance is never bliss, Fitz. It's better to *know*.'

And while he was still considering what to do for the best, the Doctor and Anji were being hooked up to the machine by chief mad girl Asia.

Oh, God. He wasn't any good at this sort of thing. Look after number one; he could do that. Not this, this, this *altruism*. This need for fast-thinking decisions;

working out what was best for other people. He just couldn't do it.

And, as with the man in the Roman arena earlier, while Fitz was worrying over the moral dilemma it was already too late and things had happened.

CHAPTER TEN
BEING OTHER PEOPLE

Woooooooooh! I feel sick!

DON'T WORRY, ANJI. SOME DISORIENTATION'S ONLY TO BE EXPECTED.

I wasn't expecting it to be like this. It's like – oh, the bit where you get off a roller coaster and you don't know which way's up and which way's down. Where am I?

WE'RE IN THE MACHINE. AN OPEN CHANNEL. A MEETING OF MINDS.

So it's all right? It's working?

I THINK IT IS. YOU WON'T FEEL ANYTHING. AS LONG AS OUR MINDS ARE RELAXED, THEY CAN COME AND GO AS THEY PLEASE, WHILE WE'RE IN HERE. COME ON, LET'S EXPLORE!

Aargh! I touched something. I felt… something. For a moment there, I was… Fitz! Oh, *ugh!*

THIS THING'S BOUND TO BE CHOCK-FULL OF MEMORY PRINTS. ONES THEY'VE TAKEN IN THE PAST. FITZ'S IS BOUND TO BE NEAR THE TOP, AS THE MOST RECENT. I DON'T THINK IT WOULD BE VERY POLITE TO EXAMINE HIS MIND, THOUGH.

Don't worry, I had no intention of doing so! It's a very uncomfortable place to be, I'm sure. Oh, I touched something el- Doctor?

DOCTOR WHO

YES?

Your body is so beautiful. I am going to run my hands over your smooth pale skin, softly, so softly, so you shiver at my every touch. Your body will be mine and I will hurt it, beautifully, you will feel every caress of pain. I will hurt you and hurt you, and when you think there is no pain left I will hurt you again. I will take you far away, to pain you could never dream of. And then you will bleed for me, a trickle, a torrent, a stream, until the last drop of your life falls to the floor and I can taste it. And I will, finally, feel whole and fulfilled, through you. I will – *aaaaargh!*

IT'S ALL RIGHT, IT'S ALL RIGHT. SHHH. YOU'RE OUT OF THERE NOW. ANJI, HUSH, DON'T WORRY, YOU'RE SAFE.

But... but it was awful. Feeling like that. How could you live if you felt like that? She felt so... hollow. So incomplete.

WHO WAS IT?

One of the triplets. Africa, I think. But – she didn't think of herself as one of the triplets. She thought of herself – oh, I don't know how to describe it – as *part* of the triplets. As if they were a single entity, not three separate girls. She was only part of a person, the part with the basest desires. Oh...

HUSH. IT MAY BE A GOOD THING TO COME INTO CONTACT WITH SUCH A MIND. IT REASSURES YOU THAT YOU'RE NOTHING LIKE THAT!

Hmm... I'll try to think of it like that! But –

DON'T *THINK* ABOUT IT. COME ON. LET'S GO DEEPER IN.

*

256

Asia looked up at her sisters. 'It's working,' she said. 'I'm copying the memories across now.'

OH!

What is it?

I KNOCKED AGAINST SOMETHING. IT'S SOLID, WON'T LET ME IN.

Someone's memory?

I THINK SO.

Leave it, then.

NO, THIS IS INTERESTING. I THINK — YES, I'M SURE I KNOW WHAT THIS IS. IT'S A DELETED FILE.

But it's still there?

DELETING SOMETHING DOESN'T NECESSARILY DESTROY THE ACTUAL DATA, JUST THE LINKS TO IT. IT COULD BE HIDDEN DEEP INSIDE STILL, WITH NO ONE KNOWING IT'S THERE. THE TRIPLETS HAVE GOT RID OF THIS, NOT REALISING IT'S STILL EXTANT AT THE BOTTOM OF THEIR MACHINE. I WONDER WHOSE MEMORY IT IS.

Doctor, you said it's not polite...

AREN'T YOU CURIOUS? I AM. JUST A QUICK LOOK, SEE WHOSE IT IS AND THEN OUT AGAIN. AH! THAT'S DONE IT. I'M... JOHN — I KNOW YOU WANT TO HAVE CHILDREN. SO DO I, OF COURSE, MY DARLING. AND WE WILL, I PROMISE YOU WE WILL. YOU WOULDN'T REALLY PUT ME ASIDE, WOULD YOU, JOHN MY LOVE? I PROMISE YOU, I WILL BEAR YOUR CHILDREN.

Asia gasped. 'Mother?'

The other two ran over to it. 'What is it? What's happened?'

'They've found Mother in there. Mother's memories.'

'But… they can't have!'

'Why not?' asked Fitz.

'We never kept them,' said Antarctica. 'We never kept any of our early experiments. We didn't really know how to access the data then, we were too young.'

'The Doctor says they're down there!' Asia insisted. '*All* our deleted files could be down there! All our early experiments. Do you realise what this could mean?' She was shouting now. 'There might be enough of Mother's mind in there to restore her!'

In the clutches of a guard, unnoticed, Hanstrum shivered.

Doctor!

HMM, INTERESTING. YOU KNOW WHO THIS IS?

I think I can guess. The President's wife. The one in the coma.

YES… FASCINATING, ISN'T IT? I'M GOING BACK IN. I WANT TO SEE HOW CLEAR THE PRINT IS. HEY, HERE'S ANOTIIER ONE. I WONDER WHOSE THIS IS. COME AND HAVE A LOOK WITH ME.

Oh, all right, I'll look. It'd better not be another psycho, though. Oh! Elizabethan. Elizabethan, don't do this to me…

'You copied your mother's memories?'

Asia smiled indulgently. 'Of course we did, Father. We had to practise on someone. Mother and Hanstrum let us copy their voice prints for our experiments, but we decided to take their memories too. Our techniques were very crude, though… Didn't really know what we were doing. Deleted most of the stuff because we didn't know what to do with it. We've matured a lot since then.'

'Hey! What d'you think you're –' Fitz had launched himself at Hanstrum before his conscious mind had really realised there was anything going on. His mind seemed to be watching it all in slow motion.

It went something like this.

Asia was talking to her father. Everyone was listening.

Hanstrum was listening the most intently of all. He grabbed a gun from one of the guards.

Fitz dived at him, knocking him back, but –

Hanstrum shot at the machine.

The machine exploded.

The Doctor and Anji, strapped to either side, fell back silently.

Asia screamed.

She was thrown back, back across the room, and her scream died as the explosion did. As she did.

Africa and Antarctica began to scream, and didn't stop.

Fitz ran to the Doctor first. He was vaguely aware of the guard grabbing Hanstrum and the gun dropping to the floor, and of frantic shouts to shut off the power. But all he cared about was the Doctor. After everything, everything the Doctor had been through, he couldn't die on this insignificant planet for no reason, through some stupid guy shooting at some stupid machine.

But there was a pulse. A double pulse. And he was breathing OK.

Satisfied, he moved on to Anji. Xernic was kneeling beside her, and Fitz saw that he was crying. But he looked up and said, 'It's all right. She's alive.'

Africa and Antarctica were still screaming. It was clear they didn't have to check for a pulse to know that the two of them were alone now. Fitz tried to imagine what it must be like to have a part of you ripped away like that, but he couldn't. But then he remembered how the triplets had killed a lot of people, himself almost included, and didn't feel sorry for them at all.

The screams were dying down now into a hysterical, breathless sobbing. They'd lost their mind, hadn't they, almost literally? Asia had done the thinking for them – all they had left now were their instincts. The guard had opened the door, was leading Hanstrum out. The murderer escaping. That's what it looked like.

That's what it'd look like to them.

And Fitz was shouting 'Look out!' almost before he saw one of the girls beginning to move. She was moving – which one was it? – moving towards the door, towards Hanstrum – towards the gun on the floor. She scooped it up. 'You killed me!' she screamed, and shot. Acting by instinct. And there was a gasp, and a thud, and another body on the floor.

The girl – and Fitz realised with a start that it was Antarctica – dropped the gun, and moved back to her sister. Together they knelt beside Asia's body, wailing and tearing at their hair.

That's all they've got left now, Fitz thought. They're not human beings any more. That's the last defining action of their lives. And it's all over, Hanstrum's plotting and scheming and the triplets' murdering and everything. Years and years of stuff, over in a few seconds.

Fitz was amazed to find that he was shivering.

Xernic dragged Fitz back to reality. 'Anji!' he was calling. 'She's waking up!' She was fluttering her eyelids, little moans coming from her mouth.

Fitz looked at her and then went over to check on the Doctor. Suddenly two huge bright blue eyes were staring at him. 'Doctor! Thank goodness you're all right.'

The Doctor was frowning. He began to push himself up, not speaking. Anji was getting up too. She was staring at the Doctor. He was staring back. They were both completely ignoring Fitz, Xernic and everything else. They moved closer to each other. And to Fitz's incredulous horror, the Doctor and Anji began to kiss.

Chapter Eleven

DEAR TARDIS...

The Doctor and Anji moved apart, eyes still locked. 'Don't be angry,' said the Doctor. 'It's what I have to do. It's right, you know it's right.'

Anji turned away. 'You'll lose everything,' she said. 'And so will I.'

'Um, Doctor? Anji?' said Fitz. They ignored him.

'I can leave your name out of it. I'll just tell him they're not his,' said the Doctor, confusing Fitz no end.

'And you think he won't work it out? Who else had access to you in your confinement? Me! Only me!' Anji was shouting now. 'For Earth's sake, Elizabethan, you can't do this to me!'

The President was watching, eyes wide. Fitz saw him mouth 'Elizabethan?'

'The girls can't be allowed to take over, Guy. They're unstable. They mustn't rule.'

'Then have more children. A male.'

'I can't risk it! Look what happened with the girls – that can't happen again!'

Fitz saw the President mouth 'Guy?' and turn to look at Hanstrum's body. Elizabethan and Guy? Fitz thought. The President's wife and Hanstrum? Had their spirits taken over Anji and the Doctor somehow?

'So you're just going to tell your darling husband

that you've been lying to him all these years?' shouted Anji. 'That to stop him throwing you out on the streets you had another man's children?'

The Doctor's eyes blazed. 'I was never unfaithful to him!'

Anji snorted. 'It wasn't a question of faith. If you'd let things happen the normal way instead of being so bloody pure then our children might have been normal.'

The Doctor slapped her. Fitz's mouth dropped right open. That was the Doctor, and that was Anji, but they weren't, and the Doctor had just... hit her?

'How dare you!' the Doctor cried. 'We needed an heir –John will understand that I was doing it for him for the people!'

'You were doing it for yourself,' sneered Anji. 'President's wife: most important woman on the planet. You just couldn't bear the thought of being put aside for someone else; letting someone else have the glory. There! Can you take the truth? Or are you going to hit me again? Go on, hit me again.' She offered the Doctor the other cheek.

He was quiet now. 'I'm going to tell John,' he said softly. 'I'll try to keep your name out of it, but New Jupiter must come first. Our daughters must never see power.' He turned away.

Anji reached down and picked up a lump of metal – part of the Memory Machine's casing. 'My daughters will succeed...' she muttered, and raised the metal above her head...

'No!' Fitz realised what she was intending just in

time, and dived forward. He grabbed the metal rod from behind, and pulled it down, Anji with it. He pushed her to the floor and sat on her. 'Help me!' he cried, as she struggled beneath him. Xernic came over and held down her arms, shushing and cooing. Behind them, the Doctor stood still, staring at the door.

The President was frowning, seemingly unaware of what was going on. 'Elizabethan…' he was saying. 'Guy? Not my children…'

'Stay down, Anji!' Fitz yelled. 'Whatever it is, we'll sort it. Does anyone here know how to do an exorcism?'

Xernic caught his eye 'I think it was the Memory Machine,' he said. 'You heard the princess say they'd found all these old memories inside, their mother and that. I think the Doctor and Anji were inside those memories when the machine exploded, and they sort of… stuck. For a bit. I think it should fade, though. I expect they just should have come out of it slowly, that's all.'

'You'd better be right,' said Fitz, grimly.

But Anji was indeed stopping struggling, and in a few moments her eyes closed again. Fitz and Xernic got off her, and turned to look at the Doctor. 'So he should be all right now too?' Fitz said.

'I *think* so,' said Xernic. 'But – well, I think he thinks he's dead now.'

'What?'

'What they were doing – that really happened, I think. That was the President's wife, and Mr Hanstrum. He killed her, the princesses didn't. And that must be why he shot the machine, when he found out those old memories could be inside. He didn't want to be found out after all these years of safety. So the President's wife – well, she's not a part of it any any more. She's not in the memory, except dead. So the Doctor's not got a part to play. These must be Mr Hanstrum's memories, what he remembered doing.'

Anji's eyelids were flickering open again. 'Hold her arms again, just in case,' Fitz murmured to Xernic. 'Anji? Anji, can you hear me?'

She let out a shuddering breath. 'Yes…'

'You're not going to try to kill the Doctor again, are you?'

Her eyes flew open at that. 'Fitz? What on Earth are you talking about?' Then a pause and, 'Ow! My cheek hurts. What's going on?'

Fitz grinned, relieved. 'It's you again. Phew.' And to Xernic: 'You can let go of her now.' Though Fitz did notice, as he turned back to the Doctor, that Xernic looked a bit reluctant to relinquish his hold.

The Doctor was still standing there, unmoving. Fitz went over to him, and waved a hand in front of the Doctor's face. The Doctor didn't respond. Fitz leaned his ear close to the Doctor's face. The Doctor didn't seem to be breathing. 'He thinks he's dead!' Fitz yelled. 'He really thinks he's dead! Help!'

Anji scrambled up off the floor, looking confused but reasonably composed. As she ran over to join Fitz, Xernic was still holding on to her arm.

She put her hand to the Doctor's neck. 'No pulse. Quick, help me lay him down.'

The Doctor was standing solidly upright. With the

desperation of the situation, Fitz gestured Anji around behind the Doctor, and then pushed. The Doctor fell backwards, still rigid, like a cartoon character hit by a frying pan. Anji caught him, and lowered him to the ground, and began doing efficient-looking things like tilting his head back and what appeared to be sticking her fingers down his throat. 'Checking his airway's clear,' she said in response to Fitz's worried sounds. She leaned in to the Doctor and breathed into his mouth a couple of times, pinching his nose closed as she did so. 'Now, you start chest compressions.'

Fitz looked blank.

'Fitz! Oh, no time, no time!' Anji moved down to the Doctor's side, and began to do what were presumably 'chest compressions'. 'You travel through the universe fighting monsters and don't even know basic first aid?' Anji cried.

'No!' Fitz yelled back, guilt making him defensive. 'Look, I've saved more lives than you have. And you do know he's got two hearts, don't you? You could be hitting the wrong bits!'

Anji stopped her rhythmic presses and moved back to the Doctor's mouth. 'No time to argue,' she said, bending over him.

She breathed into the Doctor's mouth. Suddenly his eyes flew open, and he coughed. Anji sat back quickly. Not quickly enough. The Doctor grabbed her, and planted a huge kiss on her lips.

'Thank you!' he cried. 'You saved my life!'

No, she didn't, thought an inner mean bit of Fitz. You just turned your body off for a bit. You can do that.

You just probably don't know it.

Anji was detaching the Doctor's arms and standing up. Fitz noticed her surreptitiously wiping her mouth, and was quietly pleased.

The Doctor jumped up, too. 'Where am I?' he said. 'No no, don't tell me... yes! I remember!'

Fitz's stomach did a leap. Surely... *surely* there hadn't been time for the triplets to sort everything out.

'We're on New Jupiter!' concluded the Doctor. Fitz breathed easily again. The rest of the room suddenly came back into focus. Antarctica and Africa were still weeping over their sister's body; they'd not looked away once throughout the drama. The President was staring forward with glazed eyes. The Doctor was looking at all this too. 'Oh no no no no!' he cried, bounding over to where Asia lay, Fitz and Anji following. The Doctor examined the slender corpse, lying peacefully and looking for all the world like a sleeping angel. 'I'm sorry,' Fitz heard him whisper under his breath, but the other two triplets ignored him.

Then the Doctor went over to Hoover. Fitz and Anji hung awkwardly back. The Doctor sat down beside the haunted man. 'She loved you, you know,' he said. 'It wasn't true, what Hanstrum said. She knew how desperately you wanted children, how important it was to you. And you see... she knew you could never have them.'

That caught the man's attention. He turned a puzzled face to the Doctor.

'She was a geneticist. She carried out tests... Oh, I know you didn't know about that. She didn't want to worry you. She didn't want you to know. She loved you so much.' The Doctor turned away then, and Fitz saw a strange look in his eyes. Not like the Doctor. Was he still feeling what Elizabethan had felt? Then the look passed, and the Doctor continued: 'Her course of action was… possibly not the most sensible or rational. But perhaps being locked up for so many years didn't help her to think straight.' The Doctor looked more like himself, with that. The judgemental Doctor. Condescending to the forces of oppression. 'She knew that Hanstrum wanted her – the only man allowed to see her.'

'My wife… my best friend…' muttered the President.

'No!' Fitz jumped slightly at the force in the Doctor's voice. 'He wanted her, *but she remained faithful!* That's how much she loved you, and you insult her by believing her to have betrayed you. He was all over her – it would have been so easy. But she wouldn't do it. Have you heard of in vitro fertilisation? Well, that's what she did, and it hurt her. Hurt her a lot. And because she didn't really know what she was doing, she managed to split her one child into three, and goodness knows how she damaged them. She was stupid and irresponsible, but she was doing it all for you. Do you think she deserved that?'

'And then she died,' said Anji, stepping forward. 'I remember that bit. Hanstrum had power over her, and he didn't want to give that up. Oh, and he wanted his children on the throne, as well. But she was going to throw it all away, and he would have been ruined. So he killed her.'

'And you locked up those three children for the rest

of their lives,' said the Doctor. 'And now one of them is dead. Lots of people are dead.'

Fitz winced slightly. Hoover was crying now, and whatever the man had done, Fitz wanted the Doctor to stop this. Stop kicking him while he was down. Stop rubbing it in. It wasn't as if the guy had done any of it on purpose.

Suddenly Hoover looked up, gazing right into the Doctor's eyes. 'She's in you,' he said. 'You can make it all right again. Bring her back. I can ask her… to forgive me.'

'That's all you seem to do,' said the Doctor. 'But it wouldn't be her. There were broad sweeps of her personality in there, a few memories, but not enough.'

'It would be enough!' cried Hoover. 'I want her back! Please, I need her! Give me back my wife! Give the children back their mother!'

The Doctor looked over to where Antarctica and Africa were still keening over the body of their sister. Fitz thought they looked more animal than human.

'She won't be the same,' said the Doctor. 'But I'll try. Not for you, for them. They need someone to love them. They're still children.'

The Doctor was staring at the girls so hard that Fitz was worried. 'Doctor, they've killed people!'

'I know,' he said, turning now to Fitz and freezing him with a flash of those ice-blue eyes. 'Do you want them to kill more? It's not all their fault!'

As the Doctor turned away, he said something else under his breath. Fitz couldn't make out what it was, but it started with 'M'.

The Doctor knelt down beside the trips' Memory Machine. 'It's burnt out, isn't it?' asked Fitz. 'Can you fix it?' He was hoping the answer was no.

'No,' said the Doctor. Phew. 'But I know an old girl who can.' Bum. 'That is, I think that if I link this up to the TARDIS, she'll be able to fill in the missing connections for me. I think she'll know what to do.'

Fitz was on the verge of saying, Well, she did it for me. He caught himself just in time. Keeping secrets was difficult.

Before they left, Fitz had asked the Doctor to wait for five minutes, and, after checking something with Anji, had made his way to the boxing ring. There he found Princess Leia happily sniffing around the puddles of blood. Elvis's blood. Fitz scooped up the creature and took it back. He thought it might help Antarctica to have her pet around. He wasn't sure why he cared. But, somehow, he did.

They took the bus back to the EarthWorld reception. The Doctor let Fitz drive, which turned out to be a mistake, as he managed to plough straight into a stationary triceratops while distracted by a frozen female android in a miniskirt. They had to walk the rest of the way. The Doctor carried Antarctica in his arms, and Hoover carried Africa. Anji was carrying Princess Leia. Fitz had to push the trolley with the Memory Machine on it.

They couldn't all fit in the ground-car, so the Doctor, Fitz, Anji and Xernic were going to wait behind in the reception centre while Hoover and the guards took the girls back to the palace, and brought back Elizabethan. Fitz took back Princess Leia from Anji, and handed the crocodile over to Antarctica. The girl said nothing, but hugged the little reptile tight to her chest. Fitz was still spooked that this bothered him. He stood and watched as the girls were put in the back of the ground-car. He thought he could still hear a faint ticking from Princess Leia, even after the car door had been shut; even after they were driven away.

The four who remained stood silently for a moment. No one had anything to say.

'So, you're a terrorist?' said Fitz after a while, to break the silence.

'I don't think I am any more,' replied Xernic. 'I wasn't really one in the first place, anyway. The others are probably... well, I don't know what they'll be doing now. I don't expect I'll see them again.'

Fitz couldn't think of a way of carrying on that conversation. He turned to Anji, and was startled to see that she was crying. 'Anji!' he said, alarmed.

'Distract me!' she cried. 'I don't have any distractions any more! Please!'

The Doctor dived at a gift display, grabbed a snowstorm of the Eiffel Tower and a can of Coca-Cola, and took an apple out of his pocket. He began to juggle them, higher and higher. Closer and closer to the ceiling – and then they vanished. Fitz shook his head. The Doctor sure was clever.

Anji was almost smiling, though the tears still shone

on her cheeks. The Doctor put an arm round her. 'We'll be back in the TARDIS soon,' he said. 'Then I'll take you home.'

Fitz noted that it was Xernic who looked upset at that news. Then there was a sound from outside.

'I think they're back,' Fitz said, and they wandered out to meet them.

The President had returned alone, save for the inanimate form of what was presumably his wife, a blonde-haired woman lying across the back seat.

Not long afterwards, their little procession set off for the TARDIS. Anji had asked Hoover how the girls were, and he hadn't answered. She asked the Doctor whether they'd be all right if someone got an android of Asia back on line. The Doctor had said no, they wouldn't be all right. Because they really did think of themselves as three parts of the same person, and now the links were gone for good. No android could replace that. And as Asia had been the controlling triplet – the brain, if you like – then they weren't going to be able to function properly ever again. If there was someone to love them and look after them, perhaps they might cope. And once again Fitz felt a touch of grief, and wondered why.

They had made it uneventfully to the Prehistoric Zone, and now the Doctor's party was tramping across the plain towards the TARDIS. Every now and again they passed a stationary robot – a dinosaur, a horse, a medieval peasant. Fitz caught a glance of what might be a frozen triplet behind a rock, and shivered. He didn't look closely, and didn't point her out to anyone else. Hoover was doing this weird manic sleepwalking thing. He didn't seem to know quite where he was or what was going on, he just kept calling out that they were going to find Elizabethan, and he was going to ask her forgiveness. Which was made even more strange because Xernic and Anji were carrying the limp body of the President's wife between them. Fitz was absolutely certain by now that the kid fancied Anji. She didn't seem to have twigged, though. And then there was Fitz, coming in last, trying to keep one eye on the Doctor striding ahead of them all, while not losing control of the Memory Machine that he was wheeling in front of him.

They reached the TARDIS at last – well, Fitz finally stumbled up with his trolley about thirty seconds after the Doctor had already opened the door and breezed in. This meant Fitz missed all the usual reactions of strangers entering the TARDIS for the first time – or perhaps there hadn't been any: Hoover was too spaced out and Xernic had probably heard all about it from Anji.

The Doctor had opened up a panel on the TARDIS console, and wires were spilling out. He grabbed the trolley from Fitz and began attaching the wires to bits sticking out of the Memory Machine. Fitz was convinced that he didn't have a clue what he was doing.

Anji and Xernic were laying Elizabethan down on the scarlet plush sofa that sat on the left-hand side of the console room, between the entrances to what the Doctor had named the filing alcove and the reference room, though Fitz didn't like to ask what it might be referring to. He still had a lot to get used to in this new-look TARDIS…

Anji said, 'Doctor…?'

He looked up from his spaghetti wiring. 'Yes?'

'If you get the machine working again, we could continue what the girls were doing, couldn't we? Give you your memory back.'

He seemed to be considering it. 'Possibly, possibly. It depends. Did they do the initial work? Is there a copy of my memories in your head?'

'I don't know,' said Anji.

'I don't think so,' Fitz put in. 'I'm pretty sure there wasn't time. In fact, I'm certain.' This was not going to happen.

But the kid, Xernic, had to butt in. 'The princess said she was copying the memories across. And then they were talking for a bit before – you know. I think it could have happened.'

'I don't think so!' shouted Fitz, possibly a bit too forcefully.

The Doctor shot him a concerned look. 'Well, let's not worry about it now. Plenty of time to sort it out once I've done this. Even if they haven't copied my memories into Anji's mind, I'm sure I can work something out with this marvellous machine.' He patted it fondly.

While he'd been talking, the Doctor had finished lashing up the machine to the console. He tried to run a lead across to Elizabethan but it wouldn't quite reach, so Anji and Xernic had to drag the sofa a bit closer in order for the Doctor to be able to attach connections to the android-woman's head. Then he knelt down next to the nightmare contraption and plugged himself into the controller's section – where Asia had died. He flashed a smile at Fitz and Anji. 'Here goes!' he called. And that was it, with no ceremony he'd flicked a switch and a look of fierce concentration took hold of his face.

Fitz couldn't drag his eyes from the Doctor. What if this was the last time he saw the Doctor he knew? His mind had been almost destroyed once by what he'd done. What would happen this time? And he couldn't tell the Doctor that it was a really bad idea to have his memories restored, because he'd have to explain why and that would be just as bad. No, if the Doctor was going to remember, he had to do it naturally. In his own time. So it wasn't another sudden, Doctor-destroying shock.

Everyone was busy, fussing about what was going on. No one noticed Fitz slip through the big wooden doors on the far side of the room.

He wandered down the corridors, not quite sure where to go. The console room was the obvious place, the heart of the TARDIS, but that was no good at the moment, being full of people as it was. In the end, he decided on the library. It seemed a very Doctorish sort of place.

With Compassion he'd just sort of talked and she'd heard him. He'd never tried to speak to this TARDIS before. But the Doctor referred to it – her – as a person. It was worth a go. He still felt a bit silly, though.

He stood in the middle of the library, clutching a

copy of *The Tale of Peter Rabbit* for emotional support. He spoke quietly.

'Um… I don't know if you can hear me. But if you can, I expect you probably… well, care about him, like I do. And you mustn't let him use that machine. Please. Um, that's all. Thank you.' Then he went back to the console room.

He took a deep breath in the calm of the corridor before stepping back into the chaos.

It seemed he'd missed most of the action. The Doctor and Elizabethan were still hooked up to the Memory Machine – and the TARDIS console. But the Doctor's eyes were flickering open, and he was sitting up. Fitz spared a glance for the President's wife, and saw that her lips were opening soundlessly. Words were forming, but he couldn't tell what she was trying to say. Her husband was kneeling by her side, mumbling incomprehensible sounds of encouragement. He was holding her hand so tightly that her fingertips had turned bright red.

Back to the Doctor, whose eyes were open now. 'It worked, didn't it?' he said, smiling. 'I could feel it working. Well done, old girl.' He reached an arm up over his shoulder to pat the central console.

The console spat sparks at him. The Doctor yelped and leapt up, clearly astonished.

'Something's going wrong!' cried Anji – and something certainly was: an electric-blue current streaked down the wires towards the Doctor and Elizabethan. The Doctor yanked the connectors from his head, and dived towards the unconscious woman, but Anji had got there first and grabbed a handful of wires. With a scream she was thrown backwards, hitting her head and lying still. Xernic was by her side in a second.

Fitz was rooted to the spot. 'I didn't mean you to hurt anyone,' he whispered. 'I wanted to stop people being hurt.'

The Doctor was with Elizabethan now, detaching wires from the spasming body. The last one gone, she lay still. And the Memory Machine exploded.

Fitz managed to move this time, throwing himself towards the Doctor, trying to get between the Doctor and the explosion... which wasn't happening.

There was an *un*explosion, just as Fitz landed on top of the Doctor.

The Doctor beamed at him. 'The TARDIS! She's contained it! The clever old thing.' Then he glanced ruefully at the imploded shell of the machine. 'Doesn't look like I'll be able to use that again, though.'

'Oh,' said Fitz, unable to bring himself to offer any insincere sympathy.

There was a groan from the other side of the room as Anji sat up. Fitz noted that she automatically shrugged off Xernic's helping hand, and saw the hurt-puppy-dog look in the boy's eyes. It could be hard, being a teenager.

'I'm all right,' she called across to Fitz and the Doctor, 'don't worry about me.' Fitz thought her tone was unnecessarily sarcastic, and was reminded for one horrible moment of Compassion. He really hoped that Anji was going to be a more amenable travelling companion than the TARDIS bitch queen from hell. Would it hurt the Doctor too much to pick up someone who was sweet and amenable and had good taste in men (i.e. fancied Fitz) once in a while? Surely not.

And Anji wasn't the only person to wake up. On the sofa, Elizabethan was stirring. Her eyes opened, wide dark-brown eyes full of pain and confusion. She looked dazed, and whispered, 'John?'

The President threw himself on her, hugging her so tight that Fitz hoped she had reinforced ribs. Of course, she probably had.

The Doctor was talking, as much to himself as to Fitz. 'Of course, an electrical shock was just what she needed to jump-start all the circuits, get everything working in harmony again. Why didn't I think of that?'

You might have done, given time, thought Fitz. But we didn't have time. He shot a glance at the TARDIS console. 'Guess you knew what you were doing after all,' he breathed, and gave it a surreptitious pat.

Now the Doctor was examining Elizabethan, but speaking to Hoover. 'She should be fine now,' he was saying. 'She shouldn't need physical rest, but she will need time to reassimilate everything. After all, as far as she's concerned it's about seven years ago.'

Hoover drew the Doctor to one side as they both stood up. 'But what about... about...'

'She only remembers up until the last time the triplets took a memory print, and even that will be vague. Which means she does not remember her death. That's a good thing, at the moment. Eventually, you will have to tell her. But the most important thing now is to reunite her with her daughters. And choose your chief technician more carefully next time.'

Fitz half expected the Doctor to recommend Xernic for the post. It would, after all, tie things up nicely. But he didn't. Fitz hoped Hoover might think of it for himself. He was pretty sure that he, Fitz, would have got over his teenage unrequited loves a lot quicker if someone had given him a planet to run.

'Now,' said the Doctor briskly, addressing the room, 'is everyone fine?'

Everyone said they were. Perhaps they didn't want to hurt his feelings.

'We shouldn't trespass on your kindness any longer, Doctor,' said Hoover, helping up the still dazed Elizabethan.

'Oh, that's fine, that's fine,' said the Doctor, who was now examining the console. 'You've obviously got a lot of catching up to do. And an opening ceremony to cancel, I assume. I would offer to give you a lift back, but I think you'll be safer walking.'

But Elizabethan had sunk back on to the sofa. 'My legs!' she croaked in a long unpractised voice.

'Oh dear,' said the Doctor. 'Of course, there will be a lot of muscle wastage.'

'We'll have to help them back,' Anji said.

'But it's miles!' Fitz cried automatically. Then he felt a bit ashamed. 'Couldn't she be wheeled on that trolley?' He put out a hand to indicate the trolley on which the machine's remains sat, then snatched it back with a cry. The metal was red-hot. 'OK, maybe not,' he said.

'I'll help carry her,' said Xernic unenthusiastically,

looking at Anji as he said it.

But the Doctor's eyes were shining again. 'No, Fitz is right. I have a better idea.' He suddenly dashed from the console room, and everyone else looked at Fitz.

'What did I say?' he asked. 'I didn't say anything!'

It wasn't surprising that Fitz couldn't work out the Doctor's plan. When the inner doors opened again, a grinning Doctor was pushing a great big black motorbike – complete with sidecar – into the room. 'Spotted this earlier,' he said. 'I assume it's mine to give away, unless anyone knows differently?' He looked at Fitz, who shrugged. He wished he'd known there was a bike in the TARDIS before: he could have had some fun. But maybe it hadn't been there, back then.

Anji was frowning. 'I hope you've got some crash helmets for that thing,' she said.

The Doctor kept grinning. 'Oh, I'm sure I have. I'm very safety-conscious.' Fitz stifled a snort of laughter. The Doctor closed his eyes and spun round in a circle with his arm outstretched. When he stopped, he strode over to the roundel his finger was pointing at, and to Fitz's surprise, clicked it open to reveal a storage space.

Inside were two crash helmets. One was grass-green, with a white-and-yellow daisy painted on it. The Doctor took that one out and handed it to Hoover. The other was shiny black with a mirrored visor. He gave that to Elizabethan, and then helped Hoover to lift her into the sidecar. 'There only seem to be two,' he called across to Xernic. 'Sorry.'

'That's all right,' said the boy, not sounding all right at all. 'I'll walk.'

Fitz, trying to help, flipped the switch to open the main doors. For some reason, he half expected them to be in another world already, even though the TARDIS hadn't moved, but the same barren prehistoric plain was outside. They wheeled out the bike, everyone trying to help a bit, the Doctor helping Hoover to carry Elizabethan while giving him instructions on what bit of the bike did what, and how to stay upright. Fitz wondered how much of it the President was actually taking in, because he seemed unable to take his eyes off his wife. But after she had been laid in the sidecar, he climbed on to the saddle as the Doctor indicated, and an instant later the bike was roaring into life. Fitz thought he made out a 'thank you!' over the noise of the engine, and Elizabethan seemed to be trying to raise her arm in farewell – and then the President and his wife were zooming across the rocky ground, and soon they were just a faint dark blob on the horizon.

'Well, that's everything sorted,' said the Doctor. 'Come on Fitz, Anji, time we were off.'

Sorted? Well, perhaps. The President's right-hand man was dead, along with a young girl (albeit a homicidal one), and a lot of other people as well. The planet's main social and economic hope (as Fitz understood it) was now useless, and the woman who had been running it was among the dead, anyway (although she'd been homicidal, too. Perhaps it was something in the water…). Oh, and Anji had probably broken someone's heart without realising it. All of this they'd 'sorted'.

But he decided not to mention it to the Doctor. He

just gave Xernic, the poor kid, a 'so long' wave, and went back into the TARDIS. Behind him, he heard the Doctor say goodbye, and then he followed Fitz inside. On the scanner, they saw Anji give the boy a hug and a peck on the cheek. Xernic seemed to be about to say something – but then he didn't. Anji came back inside too, and the Doctor switched off the scanner. The picture shrank down to a white dot, just as it did on the TVs of Fitz's time that the scanner resembled. Then even the dot disappeared.

A green-sleeved arm stuck out of the door and waved for a moment, before vanishing back inside. A few seconds later the whole police box disappeared. Xernic stood watching the empty space for a few moments. He unzipped the top of his jumpsuit, and folded it back. He unpinned the small badge reading ANJI, and zipped up his top again. He looked at the badge for a while, then fastened it to the front of his jumpsuit. Then he sat down in the middle of the grey featureless plain, hugging his knees to him, staring sightlessly ahead. After a while, he got up and began walking back to the city.

Almost the instant she was back inside the TARDIS, Anji had rushed off. To her adopted room, Fitz reckoned. Probably best to leave her alone for a bit.

Now it was just Fitz and the Doctor again. Less than a week since they'd stood together like this in Compassion's control room, the Doctor leaping from control panel to control panel, Fitz looking on as always. But the Doctor... he'd lived several human lifetimes since then. He still seemed to be the week-ago Doctor, though, in all the ways that mattered. And it was Fitz's job to make sure he stayed that way.

He took a deep breath. 'Doctor…' he said, 'um, you remember when we went to… to Gallifrey…?'

He could sense the Doctor's mind working 6/8 time. 'We go to so many places, Fitz,' he said.

'But Gallifrey – we could maybe take Anji there? For a holiday?'

'Oh yes, someday, perhaps. Lovely place for a holiday. Very –' the Doctor was trying to think of a word that could cover all options, not show that he had no idea, Fitz *knew* that – 'very… tranquil.'

'Yes, Doctor. Fair enough, just thought I'd mention it.'

Yes, the Doctor was himself again, and that was good. He wasn't the wreck he'd been after the destruction of his home planet, Gallifrey, and that was good, too. He didn't know Fitz was a fake, or that he'd killed the real one, and that was *very* good. But… how fragile was this new-old Doctor? Knowing all these things had all but destroyed his mind in the first place; was he any more fitted to cope with the knowledge now? And knowing that he had to protect the Doctor above all things – however horrified the Doctor would be if he found out Fitz was protecting him – Fitz decided he would have to sacrifice any dreams of going back to Filippa, any hopes of Anji's of getting home, any hope of comfort from the Doctor for his unreal state, in order to keep this Doctor whole.

Giving things up for the Doctor felt good. He – well, the real Fitz, anyway, but it *felt* like it had happened to him – had gone with his mum to see a play of Oscar Wilde's. Am dram – support the local community and they might begin to like us. There was a lot of keeping secrets for the good of others in that, and the young Fitz had been rather dissatisfied with the ending, because all the secrets were kept and the characters went on, he assumed, to live happily ever after. He'd wanted to see the big dramatic scenes where all the secrets were discovered, and his mum had said he was missing the point. Now, the mature Fitz could see the point: could understand that Oscar Wilde had had the right idea all along. If keeping a secret could make someone else happy, then hey, secrets were a good thing. There might be some weird sense of closure if everything came out in the open, some soap-opera resolution, but happy endings were infinitely preferable.

The Doctor had looked after Fitz – had thought he was looking after Fitz – for years now. Fitz might not be the real Fitz any more, but that was irrelevant. He had a purpose in life now. He was going to look after the Doctor. Whatever it took.

To: <u>cybertron@xprof.net</u>
From: <u>anji kapoor@MWFutures.co.uk</u>
Date: 15/2/01 15:14
Subject: Your Death

Dear Dave

I wish I hadn't been thinking of leaving you. It makes things so much worse – for me, that is, thinking selfishly, but then, when haven't I been? I miss you terribly, but I have so many guilt feelings where the grief should be. It wasn't as if it was something I'd consciously decided – I wasn't planning on walking out or anything, there had just been feelings of 'is this all there is?' and wondering if I might be better off somewhere else, with someone else. But I wasn't going to do anything about it. Not really. Now, although I am utterly miserable, I feel I have no right to be – you weren't my whole world, you were just a habit. And you can miss a habit, but you shouldn't mourn it. And then I think: no. No, that's not how I felt about you. I did – do – love you. Just because it wasn't a fairy tale any more doesn't mean it wasn't love. I am allowed to grieve. And just because I was brought up not to feel sorry for myself doesn't mean I never have anything to be sorry for myself about. Does that make sense? Probably not. I'm not exactly in the mood to be particularly lucid. Earlier today I… experienced what it was like to kill your lover. When things get bad, I can think: well, at least I didn't do that. But of course, maybe it would be better if I had, because then I'd have been the one in control; it would have been my fault and I wouldn't have to *bear* it like this.

Though I do keep thinking that I should have tried harder to save you, or stayed and died with you; though I know that the first was impossible and the second illogical.

Ha! Me and logic! BEING LOGICAL DOESN'T MAKE IT RIGHT! Repeat till you've learned it.

I wish I believed in reincarnation. It's one of those things that you're brought up with, and although once you have outside experiences your rational mind dismisses such theories as illogical, you still have it hanging in the very back of your mind. I wonder what you'd come back as. You were a good person. What's a step up from a man? (XY chromosome that is, none of this 'mankind' stuff, women are definitely a step down officially.) Perhaps you'd come back as an alien. You'd probably like that.

Distractions, distractions. Because there's something else I have to confess. Something else that's awful. Really, really awful, not pretend oh-no-I'm-such-a-bitch. I wouldn't tell you this if you were alive. Your death has given me power over others, and this horrible, deeply hidden bit of me secretly likes the drama. I hate knowing I have that in myself. It's not happened much: a few times Fitz has caught himself saying something about relationships, and stopped, because it might upset me. Someone said something about my boyfriend, something like that, and I quite calmly said he'd been killed recently. Their expression! I'm using your death to get attention. It's quite the most loathsome thing I've ever done. The only person that doesn't happen with is the Doctor. He seems to understand everything; to know exactly the right things to say. I think, with the Doctor's help, I may be able to grieve properly.

That's not to say you have to worry. I don't fancy him. He's the sort of man I might have said 'He's gorgeous!' about to tease you, if he'd been on TV, but you'd know I didn't mean anything by it. And, you know, of all the bad things I might be, I'm not rebound woman. And anyway – amazing eyes, gorgeous smile, but several thousand years older than me. That was one of the fun things we had – OK, so you went to Sunday school, not temple, and drama school, not university, but we both remembered Spangles and Space Hoppers and The Adventure Game on telly, and did GCSEs and bought albums by ABBA and Nik Kershaw, and the first Bond either of us saw on the big screen was Timothy Dalton, and we could argue about whether he was better or worse than Sean Connery. Shared experiences. How am I going to relate to people with whom I don't have those little cultural touchstones? People for whom things like e-mail and Professor X aren't everyday currency. You remember how, to start with, I had to keep explaining to you what I meant when I said ordinary things like bhangra or chakra. Well, England 2001 has suddenly become the biggest in-joke in the universe.

I'm talking about me again. I think it's because as

soon as I start thinking of you, I have to either hate myself or cry. I love you, Dave. I really, really love you.

All my love
Anji xxxxx

Send now/send later: send now

Unable to send: fatal error

Anji reached the door to her room and went in, shutting it behind her. She sat down on what was now her bed, and kicked off her shoes. But she wasn't really there.

The door opened, and Dave came in.

He'd been in all day, of course, and Anji'd been in the office till seven, but he hadn't got them any tea. 'Been too busy,' he'd said, although she knew that that meant sitting in front of the TV and occasionally flicking through the HELP WANTED ads. But he'd taken off her shoes and rubbed her feet, ignoring the smell, and kissed her legs all the way up to the hem of her skirt. Then he'd grinned and offered to pop out for pizza.

He put the pizza down on the table in front of her. Then produced a can of fizz out of each coat pocket, and let her choose which one she wanted. And he'd got a portion of coleslaw too, even though she was the only one who liked it.

They snuggled in front of the telly, teasing out strands of mozzarella from each other's pizza slices. Dave picked the olives off of his half and left them in the box lid. They kissed, but didn't hug because their hands were greasy. And then Dave ran her a bath with as many bubbles as in the TV commercials, and lit scented candles around the bathroom, and afterwards kissed her from head to toe and took her to bed. They were both laughing.

The door opened and Dave came in.

He'd been for an audition and they'd given him the part on the spot. Only a weekend's work, but he opened a bottle of champagne to celebrate. They'd drunk it in about ten minutes flat, and she hadn't stopped giggling for two hours. They'd played strip scrabble, even though neither of them could work out what the rules for that should be. Anji'd still won. When the programme had come on TV she'd videoed it and watched his two-and-a-half minutes eight times in a row while he was out. She'd never told him that.

The door opened and Dave came in. Same time every night, and the same routine. Old-married couple stuff. Spontaneity would be good. But there were bits of her that'd miss the routine if it went.

The door opened and Dave...

The door opened and...

The door opened...

The door didn't open.

The door was never going to open again.

And once she started crying, she was never going to stop.

The door opened, and the Doctor came in. He held out a hand, and helped her to her feet. Still holding her hand, he led her out of the room. 'There's something I found earlier,' he said. 'I think you should see it.'

They went down lots of corridors; Anji knew she'd never find her way back on her own. Finally the Doctor turned off into a room.

If it could be called a room. It was amazing.

It was just like being in the countryside. There was lush green grass instead of a floor, and blue skies where there should be a ceiling. The whole place exuded an aura of tranquillity and Anji breathed in deeply. The air smelled so fresh. She almost smiled.

The Doctor led her further in, and they sat down on a flowery slope under a tree, placing themselves carefully so as not to crush any daisies. Neither of them said anything for quite a while. Then Anji began to cry: a few sobs at first and then she was wailing her heart out. The Doctor put his arms round her and held her close. Eventually, the tears subsided. Embarrassed, Anji pulled away, looking anywhere but at the Doctor. It was then she noticed the chrysalides.

They were everywhere. By each daisy, on each twig. There must be thousands of them. 'What are these?' she asked the Doctor, without turning round. 'What will they become?'

'I don't know,' he said softly. 'But it's new life. Isn't it wonderful?'

Anji took a deep breath. Then she laid her head back on the Doctor's chest, and cried again.

Next in the Doctor Who 50th Anniversary Collection:

ONLY HUMAN
GARETH ROBERTS
ISBN 978 1 849 90519 0

The Doctor Who 50th Anniversary Collection
Eleven classic adventures
Eleven brilliant writers
One incredible Doctor

Reports of a time disturbance lead the Ninth Doctor to modern-day London, where he discovers a Neanderthal Man – twenty-eight thousand years after his race became extinct. A trip back to the dawn of humanity only deepens the mystery: who are these strange humans from the far future now living in the distant past? The Doctor must learn the truth about the Osterberg experiment before history is changed for ever.

An adventure featuring the Ninth Doctor, as played by Christopher Eccleston, and his companions Rose Tyler and Captain Jack Harkness.

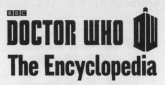

DOCTOR WHO
The Encyclopedia

Gary Russell

Available for iPad
An unforgettable tour of space and time!

The ultimate series companion and episode guide, covering seven thrilling years of *Doctor Who*. Download everything that has happened, un-happened and happened again in the worlds of the Ninth, Tenth and Eleventh Doctors.

◊

Explore and search over three thousand entries by episode, character, place or object and see the connections that link them together

◊

Open interactive 'portals' for the Doctor, Amy, Rory, River and other major characters

◊

Build an A-Z of your favourites, explore galleries of imagery, and preview and buy must-have episodes